MW00577222

The Poison Dart

GERI L. DREILING

Copyright © 2024 Geri L. Dreiling

All rights reserved. The characters and events portrayed in this book are fictitious. Any similarity to real persons, living or dead, is coincidental and not intended by the author.

No part of this book may be reproduced, or stored in a retrieval system, or transmitted in any form or by any means, electronic, mechanical, photocopying, recording, or otherwise, without express written permission of the publisher.

ISBN:13: 978-1-7350303-3-3

"No man is an island,
Entire of itself.
Each is a piece of the continent,
A part of the main.
If a clod be washed away by the sea,
Europe is the less.
As well as if a promontory were.
As well as if a manor of thine own
Or of thine friend's were.
Each man's death diminishes me,
For I am involved in mankind.
Therefore, send not to know
For whom the bell tolls,
It tolls for thee."

For Whom the Bell Tolls, John Donne

"Never say goodbye because goodbye means
going away and going away means forgetting."

Peter Pan, J.M. Barrie

1 REUNION

Dismounting from the white Arabian horse he'd named Frost, Arthur Morgan walked through the ragtag camp filled with people on the run from the law; men, women, and, yes, even one kid. Each had their own reason for living outside proper society. Some had been wrongfully persecuted; others had been persecutors themselves. But somehow, they'd found one another and banded together to survive in the post–Civil War Wild West.

"Mornin' Arthur," said a woman with her dark hair in a messy bun, her light eyes briefly meeting Arthur's.

"Mornin' Abigail," he replied. With his three-quarter-length burgundy shotgun coat, two rifles strapped crisscross over his back, two revolvers on his hip, and a tan Panama hat on his head, Arthur Morgan was a *Red Dead Redemption Two* video game character whom Caleb

Webb had outfitted according to his own tastes and preferences.

And while some players chose to have Arthur Morgan act out their most violent fantasies during side missions, such as robbing helpless strangers, stealing horses, or burning homes just for the hell of it, Caleb gravitated toward more honorable pursuits, helping damsels in distress and righting the wrongs inflicted on innocent folks, even as his morally ambiguous video game character edged ever closer to what, Caleb guessed, would be a violent or tragic end.

At twenty-five, Caleb had reflected more than once on the pattern of his in-game choices. So-called "good" kids might use the games as a place to live out their dark fantasies, the chance to destroy pixels organized in the shape of a human and break laws they'd never dream of transgressing in real life. But not so for Caleb. In real life, he'd been branded the bad twin.

Video games gave him a chance to play against type.

Caleb's smartphone vibrated on the elegant dark wood coffee table his mother had selected. The furniture, indeed the condo itself, belonged to the real estate company his parents owned. The family company had built the upscale high-rise in Clayton, an affluent inner St. Louis suburb. The residence his parents had chosen for him boasted floor-to-ceiling windows, dark hardwood floors, trendy gray walls with wood trim painted a clean white, and milky quartz countertops.

Everything an upper-middle-class member could desire.

The condo also had dramatic French doors leading out to a balcony, big enough to host dinner parties for four while gazing at the downtown Clayton skyline. But instead of entertaining, Caleb preferred to sit outside by himself. Using his tenth-floor perch like a luxury box seat, he watched the work theater play out below. Lawyers in suits carrying briefcases scurried to the St. Louis County Courthouse. White-collar drones clad in business casual and tennis shoes poured out of office buildings at lunchtime, squeezing in a few more steps that would be recorded on their Fitbits and iWatches. Wasted effort toward meaningless goals. Their lives would end like Arthur Morgan's—in death. And there wasn't a damn thing that ten thousand steps could do to change that fact.

Caleb paused the video game, picked up his phone,

and swiped an app to let his guests into the building. He rubbed his nose and ran his hand through his thin blond hair, too thin for a twenty-five-year-old. His tresses had finally gotten some shine back during the last sixty days in rehab, but his hair was nowhere near as thick as Connor's. There was a time when he was in high school that girls loved to play with Caleb's hair. But those girls had been warned away from Caleb by their parents. Stuck-up bitches. So much for the allure of bad boys.

Caleb rose from the sofa, opened the front door a crack so his buddies could enter, and then resumed his game.

Alex Underwood, a thin young man with hollow eyes, his brown hair shaved close to his head, entered the condo first and spotted Caleb on the couch. "O Captain, my Captain!" Alex called out.

Caleb looked up from his game and smiled broadly. He'd missed his buds.

A young woman with long black hair, smudged eyeliner, and a gaunt face followed closely behind. "Dude! Happy New Year's Eve, man! So glad to have you home," Mackynzie Holloway said as she sank down on the couch next to him. "You still playin' *Red Dead*?"

Caleb grinned as he glanced briefly at his childhood friend. "Whassup, Mace? What can I say? I missed Arthur."

Mackynzie was Macie to almost everyone. She'd been close to Caleb and his twin brother, Connor, since they were seven, the three of them having grown up in the same upscale neighborhood in the outer St. Louis suburb of Chesterfield. Calling themselves the three amigos, they'd go swimming in Macie's backyard pool, or she'd come over to the twins' house and they'd play *Zelda*, *Madden*, and *The Knights of the Old Republic*. When Connor picked on Caleb, Macie was the one who'd put her hands on her hips and call Connor a pencil dick. It was an insult none of them fully understood at the time—other than the one saying it would get mightily punished if their parents heard.

"You got maced!" Caleb would gloat when Macie put Connor in his place.

The nickname stuck. But only Caleb was allowed to call her Mace. Anyone else using the name would get slugged in the shoulder by Macie. Or worse, she'd use her clever tongue to administer a humiliating retort.

While she was a whiz at delivering verbal blows, Macie

5

had always been a sucker for sensitivity. And she didn't like bullies. When they were kids, Connor tormented his brother by turning Mr. Turtle, named after a character on one of their favorite television shows, on his back. Caleb's face would transform from friendly to furious in a split second. He'd punch his brother, then turn the pet over gently while checking to ensure no lasting trauma. Macie was drawn to Caleb's sweetness.

Caleb, on the other hand, had been attracted to Macie's feistiness. Moxie was the word Caleb's mom used to describe Macie in the long-ago days when his mom liked the girl.

Macie took a rubber band out of her purse and pulled her long black hair into a loose ponytail.

"You got your nose pierced while I was gone," Caleb said, briefly taking his eyes away from the screen.

"Yeah," Macie said with a smile. "Drivin' my parents fuckin' cray-zee."

"You still working for your dad?" Caleb asked. After all, a lot could change in two months. And with his phone confiscated the first thirty days, then monitored closely the second thirty, he knew he was out of the loop. Macie had been one of the people he'd been forbidden to contact.

Alex chimed in. "Shit, yeah, she's still working at her old man's accounting firm."

"Still suck?" Caleb asked.

"What do you think?" Macie grimaced.

"That's messed up. You've got a chemistry degree, for fuck's sake. You should be at Monsanto or some shit. Or whatever they're calling Monsanto now."

"Bayer," Macie said. "And you know what happened last time I worked for a company with chemicals. My parents got me out of that trafficking BS, but they said there's no way the cops would cut me a break again."

"You two are puppets," Alex said. "Rich kids dancing while your parents yank the strings."

Caleb rolled his eyes. "Yeah, I know the only reason I'm living here is so my parents can keep an eye on me. It gives them one more thing to threaten me with, too. Step out of line? You get thrown out on your ass." His parents had anointed him with the title of onsite manager. But it had come without the responsibilities. They all understood that what he was really getting paid for was to stay out of trouble.

"You should be your own man," Alex said.

Macie snorted. "Right. And sleep on our uncle's couch like you do?"

"Yeah, yeah." Alex waved his hand in the air. "That's just temporary."

Macie laughed. "Hey, it's me you're talking to. I'm the one who ordered sandwiches from you earlier today."

"At least when I do H, I don't do it to escape my parents," Alex said.

"So we gonna chase the dragon or what?" Caleb asked.

"You know it," Alex replied. "I'm ready for a toot."

Macie rubbed her arm. "Caleb, you just got outta rehab. I don't know if it's a good idea."

"Shit. I just served my sixty-day sentence. It's New Year's Eve. Let's celebrate our reunion," Caleb said as he turned off his game. "I got some really good stuff. From a friend."

Alex laughed. "Yeah, from a friend. Listen, I ain't no mooch. I got a job. I brought my own."

Macie sighed. "I got some Narcan. I kinda figured you'd want to party, even though it is a terrible idea to do it when you've been clean for a while."

"I love terrible ideas," Caleb said as he got off the couch and walked over to the teak Danish mid-century modern desk in the corner of the living room. It was the only piece of furniture, besides an original oil painting, that he'd picked out for himself. He found it in a window of an antique shop while hanging out on Cherokee Street in the city. It was love at first sight, even if the legs were a bit beat up. His mom hated it. Doesn't go with the decor, she'd insisted.

That made Caleb love it even more.

Sliding open one of the drawers, he pulled out a small box containing his personal syringe.

"I woulda thought your parents had trashed your contraband," Macie said.

"I hid it so good they couldn't find it. Opened up one of those expensive throw pillows my mom bought. Along the seam. Took out a bunch of stuffing and then shoved this inside. Put the stuffing back in and sewed it back up. No one noticed."

"You sew?" Alex asked.

"Just barely," Caleb said. "One of those summer camps that our parents stuck us in as kids had a needle-and-thread art class. Remember that, Mace?"

Macie smiled. "Yeah. I remember you and Connor getting in trouble when you stitched dirty words into the cloth we'd been given to work with."

Caleb laughed. "Good times."

Macie rubbed her arm again, then reached for a well-loved hockey stick in the corner of the room. She traced the handle with her finger.

"What?" Caleb asked.

"I don't think shootin' up is such a good idea, Caleb. You've been off the stuff too long."

"Good ol' Mace. I could always count on you to look out for me," he said. "Alex, whaddya think?"

Alex exhaled. "I think you're a grown man. And if you OD, we'll just give you a puff up your nose. What could go wrong?"

Caleb smiled. "Yeah. And I just got some outstanding shit."

"Do you know the source?" Macie asked. "I mean, there's a lot of fent going around. That stuff will kill ya."

"You sound like my mom. Don't worry. Perfectly safe. Trusted source," Caleb answered as he grabbed a baggie with brown powder and gave it a shake. Macie walked over to the spot where Alex had left a shopping bag. "Give me one of those beers. I'm gonna just sit this one out." Macie opened the bottle, set it down on the coffee table without taking a sip, and walked over to the French doors leading out to the balcony. She had to keep her wits about her. And it was too hard to watch everyone else shoot up without giving in to the urge to join them.

Caleb sat back down with his kit. "Oh yeah, my parents took my lighter," Caleb said.

"Your grandpa's lighter? The gold one?" Macie asked.

"Yep."

"That sucks."

Alex stood up and rummaged around in his front pocket. "Here."

Just seeing the lighter made Caleb's body tingle. He'd been dreaming of this moment for sixty days. Even when he was sitting in group, claiming he was done, he knew it wasn't true. He'd say whatever he had to just to get out. There were times that, yes, when his parents came, he felt bad. His mom would cry. His dad would remain the aloof motherfucker he always was. But his mom. That was different. Sometimes he thought he should change for her. But his mom was just no match for heroin.

Caleb put the brown powder in the spoon from his kit. He opened the vial of distilled water. If you were going to get high, you might as well do it with style. Caleb gently moved the flame under the heroin. Slowly, evenly, he applied the heat's gentle kisses to the drug, melting it with his slow caress.

Caleb pulled out a syringe. He put the needle in, pulled the plunger up, then flicked the side of the syringe to force the air bubbles up. Caleb removed the rubber tube tied around his upper arm and pushed the needle into his arm. Since he hadn't shot up for two months, the purple vein in his arm had ample time to heal.

Liquid peace, Caleb thought as his body welcomed its old friend.

Caleb slumped back on the couch, briefly taking in Macie as she stood on his balcony. Her back was to them, but he could tell she was jittery by how she rubbed her hands against her thighs.

"Good ol' Mace," Caleb mumbled. His head, too heavy for his neck, lolled back onto the couch.

Alex picked up the spoon, ready to repeat the process with his stash. His attention focused on prepping his dose. It wasn't until he'd shot up that he looked over at his motionless friend.

"Hey, Macie," Alex called out, "Caleb's noddin'."

Macie turned around and walked back into the living

room. Just in case.

She noticed Caleb's lips turning blue. His head was back, gurgling noises coming from his throat.

Macie pushed Caleb's shoulder. "Caleb," she said firmly. "Cut it out. This isn't funny."

Caleb didn't move.

Macie pushed harder. "Caleb!"

She opened his eyelids. His pupils were no bigger than the needle mark left in his arm.

"Shit!" Macie said. "Alex, I think Caleb OD'd."

Alex, his voice slurring, said, "Well, that's why we got the Narcan."

Macie grabbed her purse and rummaged through it. She took out the package of nasal spray and tore it open. She took the cap off and shoved the nozzle up his nose until her fingers touched the bottom of Caleb's right nostril.

"You gotta really push that plunger," Alex mumbled.

Macie pushed hard. The foil seal broke with the pressure. The full dose emptied into his nose. Macie held her breath. It should just be a couple of moments, and Caleb would pop out of his coma.

Caleb didn't move.

Macie shook Caleb's shoulders. "Caleb!"

She grabbed the empty Narcan spray and put it up his left nostril, trying to get more out of the already-spent antidote.

"You got another one?" Alex mumbled. "Sometimes it takes more than one."

"I've only got the one," Macie said. "Call an ambulance!"

"Man, we can't be here," Alex slurred.

"I'm not leaving!" Macie said.

2 HISTORY LESSONS

Debbie Bradley pushed her dark-blue-rimmed glasses up on the bridge of her nose with her forefinger. The writer for *River City* magazine had recently also started hosting her own podcast. She smoothed her chestnut brown hair, neatly pulled back in a long ponytail, then picked up the headphones on the desk in front of her. Carefully, she placed them on her head. Then she smiled at her podcast guest, Jack Flannery.

A retired police officer still called captain by everyone who knew him, Cap'n Jack looked more like an aging rock star than a cop. Wavy, shoulder-length silver hair, a grizzled beard, and a relaxed way of speaking marked him as a storyteller, not a police officer. He'd been a rookie during the St. Louis mob wars of the 1980s. His nephew, Detective Daniel Flannery, had suggested Debbie talk to the man who'd become something of an amateur crime historian and local raconteur in his retirement.

The recommendation had been hard won. Detective Flannery hadn't been Debbie's biggest fan when they first met. It had taken time, one brush with death, and what Debbie suspected was the detective's crush on her clueless mother to turn him into an ally, albeit a reluctant one.

The twenty-eight-year-old host leaned toward the microphone. "Welcome to *Crime Beat*, a *River City* podcast. This week, we're looking back at St. Louis and the mafia war in the nineteen eighties. My guest is retired St. Louis Metropolitan Police Department Captain Jack Flannery. Welcome, Cap'n Jack."

"Mornin', Debbie. Thanks for having me," he replied.

"So let's start with the mayhem that broke out after Anthony Giordano—Tony G.—died of cancer," Debbie said.

"Sure," Jack replied, his husky voice carrying the mark of the Camels he once, but no longer, smoked. "What you've gotta remember, back in the seventies and early eighties, St. Louis was controlled by three organized crime families. One was headed by the mafia, another by a Syrian-Lebanese syndicate with roots in St. Louis, and the third crime family was out of Illinois with ties to Chicago. All three groups were embedded into several of the unions here in town. To keep the peace, the three cooperated, but Tony G. was at the top of 'em all. In late August of nineteen eighty, everything falls apart after Tony G. up and dies. I mean, it wasn't too long before all hell broke loose."

"Why was that?" Debbie probed.

"You see, everyone thought that Horseshoe Jimmy…"

"You're referring to James A. Michaels Senior, right?" Debbie interjected.

"Yep, by nineteen eighty, he was a dapper granddad, thick white hair and a cleft chin, who had spent his life as part of the Syrian-Lebanese syndicate. He'd gotten his start in organized crime as part of the Cuckoos, a south side gang from the times of Prohibition. By twenty-five, he was already in prison after holding up a railroad office in East Saint Louis. And there's a great photo of him from nineteen fifty-nine just before he tried to slug a photographer."

"I know the one you're talking about," Debbie said. "It appears in the story I wrote for this month's issue about the mob war. That picture was taken at police headquarters after he was nabbed in a liquor raid."

"Yep, good photo," Jack said. "Anyway, by early eighty, Horseshoe Jimmy was the one everyone thought would take Tony G.'s place. But a fella named Paulie Leisure had other ideas."

Debbie chimed in. "Paulie was a mob enforcer who belonged to the Syrian clan, right?"

"Yeah, he'd once been Tony G.'s bodyguard," Jack clarified.

"So Tony G. dies in August," Debbie said. "What happened a few weeks later, on September seventeenth?"

"Whew," Jack said, shaking his head. "Well, the old man, Horseshoe Jimmy, meets his grandson, Jimmy Beans, er Jimmy Michaels, for lunch."

Debbie interjected for the listeners, "They meet at St. Raymond's, the Maronite church just south of downtown that hosts a Lebanese lunch every Wednesday?"

"That's right," Jack said, nodding. "For many Lebanese and Syrian immigrants who moved to St. Louis over the past century, St. Raymond's is their spiritual

18

home."

Debbie smiled and added, "I remember my parents making pilgrimages to the Wednesday lunches at St. Raymond's."

Beth Hughes and Cary Bradley had met in law school, married, then started their own personal injury practice together: Bradley & Hughes. When Debbie told her mother she was working on the St. Louis mob war story, Beth recalled how she would join her husband for lunch at St. Raymond's. His eyes would widen just before he'd lean over and whisper the name of so-and-so sitting nearby. "Your dad," Beth said, her eyes lighting up, a smile spreading across her face, "he just loved reading all that mafia stuff. I guess I know where you get it." And just as quickly, the twinkle in her mom's eyes disappeared. Cary died of a heart attack while Debbie was still in high school. Now, even though more than ten years had passed, Beth's stories about her partner in life and the law were three parts joy and one part sadness.

Jack's voice brought Debbie back to the interview. "The Wednesday lunch at St. Raymond's. Didn't matter if you were a politician, a reporter, or part of the mob. That was where deals were made, alliances were forged, story ideas were birthed, and plots were hatched. Even today, you can grab a meat pie, grape leaf roll, and tabouli salad at a great price at St. Raymond's. For me, parsley is a spice, not a dish. But after a few beers," Jack paused, "geez, I sound like a commercial, don't I?"

Debbie laughed even as she checked the clock on the wall. "Okay, what about September seventeenth, nineteen eighty?"

"Right," Jack replied. "Horseshoe Jimmy parks his seventy-nine Chrysler Cordoba in the church lot. And while he was having lunch with his grandson, some of Paulie's crew planted a bomb under the car. The bomb had a remote detonator attached to it."

Debbie replied, "But they had trouble setting it off, didn't they?"

"Yeah, so when Horseshoe Jimmy leaves lunch, the three clowns follow the Cordoba in a van. At first, one of 'em suggests letting the bomb rip just outside the church. But that would look bad. Real bad. So, once the Cordoba was a few blocks from St. Raymond's, the guys in the van tried detonating the bomb. No luck."

"Any clues why it didn't go off?" Debbie asked.

"Some have speculated that perhaps they weren't close

enough," Jack answered. "Who knows. They were a bunch of clowns. Horseshoe Jimmy gets on Interstate 55, heading to his home in South County. The Leisure crew finally catches up on the highway near the Reavis Barracks Road exit, and they give it one more try. This time: Boom! Orange flames and black smoke shoot up into the air. Oil from the Cordoba rains back down. Horseshoe Jimmy is blown in two—literally two pieces, severed at the waist. I kid you not; part of his body slammed into a passing car. Helluva scene." Jack paused and shook his head. "Helluva scene. I arrived soon after the blast. Damnedest thing I ever saw. Still the craziest thing I've ever seen. And I've seen a lot. Luckily, all of the other cars on the road were able to avoid crashing into Jimmy's car—or one another."

"And this triggered more waves of violence, right?"

"You bet. Jimmy Beans blows parts of Paulie's legs off less than a year later. Paulie had been at his ma's house. He gets in his car to leave, and then the bomb goes off. The back-and-forth strikes went on for a few more years."

Debbie added, "In the meantime, Tony G.'s underboss and successor, John Vitale, was also serving as an FBI informant."

"Yeah, Johnny was a snitch, feeding the feds all sorts of info. He died of a heart attack in eighty-two, but a lot of the dirt he shared ultimately helped wipe out the crime syndicates."

"Now we've covered a lot of names, a lot of last names that today are quite familiar in St. Louis. Business leaders, lawyers, and politicians share some of the same last names. It wouldn't be fair to paint them with the crimes of those folks, would it?"

Jack shook his head. "Weeds and wheat, weeds and wheat."

"That phrase comes from a Bible story, correct?" Debbie asked.

"When I was a boy, my good Catholic mom, God rest her soul, made me go to Sunday school. She hoped to save me; 'twas a futile effort, but anyway, I remember being taught the parable about the farmer who plants wheat. The farmer doesn't know that one of his enemies sabotages his field and scatters weed seeds. Long story short, when the wheat starts to grow, surprise, the weeds also pop up out of the ground. But rather than pull up the weeds, the farmer tells his workers to let them grow together. And when harvest comes, they'll separate the weeds and the wheat." Jack paused. "And so they do. They separate the weeds from the wheat and burn the sh..., er, crap out of those weeds."

"Interesting," Debbie said, waiting for her guest to connect the dots.

Jack continued, "I guess you could say that every family, every community, most of the individuals are the wheat, a few are the weeds. It isn't fair to generalize."

"That is certainly one way to look at it," Debbie said. "And a lot more charitable than we've become used to nowadays; the urge to scapegoat whole groups of people, entire religions, or those who aren't part of our own flawed tribe is so strong."

"To quote the old ladies from back in the day when my own blessed mother forced me to church, 'Amen.'"

"So, getting back to our topic, the criminal organizations were busted up. And everyone lives happily ever after?"

"Yeah, right. The dog barks. The caravan moves on," Jack said, shaking his head. "No. No. Not at all."

"What do you mean?"

"Look, you get rid of one group of bad guys, but all

you're doing is clearing space for the next set of rat bast—'er, whatever you wanna call 'em: mobsters, gangsters, narcos, the syndicate. They're all the same. And so long as there's a demand for the sh…er…crap they're peddling, they'll always survive. Doesn't matter whether it is drugs, prostitution, or money laundering. Despite its brutishness, organized crime still runs on the twin pillars of charm and threats. There's the promise of easy money, a few well-placed donations, or much-needed favors granted. Suddenly, the sneaky SOBs are part of the community. Mark my words, Debbie Bradley, the weeds always find a way to grow back."

"How was the interview?" Sam Hitchens asked when Debbie entered the office of *River City*'s editor. The angle of his computer screen gave her a glimpse of the draft he was editing, splashed with yellow highlights and comments floating in the margin.

"Please tell me that's not one of mine," she said.

"Naw. Freelance piece. I'm already done with yours."

Debbie glanced at the McDonald's wrappers in her editor's trash. "Sausage biscuit with cheese and hash browns again this morning?"

Sam frowned. "Eating crap makes editing crap easier."

"Okay. I can see you're in a good mood today," Debbie answered.

Sam was a daily news veteran whose passion for truth was rivaled only by his deep disappointment in humankind. He'd been lured to *River City* by its owner, Chris Radcliffe, a tech titan who'd made a billion or two off social media. Sam hadn't been an easy convert to the magazine format or for answering to a tech billionaire. But Chris Radcliffe was a persistent man. To be sure, the fat salary was tempting. And being a tiny sliver of a tech empire meant he had a bit more job security than with a daily. Just maybe, by making the switch, Sam could finish his career as a journalist rather than as a phony PR flack.

But what had sealed the deal was the publisher's promise that, as editor, Sam would be free to "comfort the afflicted and afflict the comfortable." So long as it was done shrewdly.

"Readers don't like to be on the receiving end of a sermon," Chris argued. It was a stance that Sam agreed with. As a journalist and an editor, he'd discovered that heavy-handed pieces tend to turn readers off rather than convince them to tune in.

They'd struck a deal. The magazine would retain the generous coverage of society news, spa treatments, and rah-rah hometown fare readers loved. And it would add hard-hitting articles, the sort of pieces that might prick readers' consciences. The magazine could help rid the once-great industrial city of the stench of corruption that seemed to cling to it like that sour smell on T-shirts that had been left in the washing machine too long.

After he was hired, Sam set out to convince Debbie Bradley to join the staff. Sam had been a guest lecturer for a year at Mizzou, and Debbie had been one of his students. They'd kept in touch over the years. When Sam reached out, she was working as a reporter in Washington, D.C. He promised her a platform for exploring injustice, with the advantage of knowing that deep pockets covered her back.

"Like covering peas with mashed potatoes and gravy. Mixing shredded carrots into cherry Jell-O," Sam had said to Debbie when he was trying to explain the publisher's approach.

The timing of the offer also mattered. Debbie's engagement was falling apart, and her mom had been diagnosed with breast cancer. The proposal gave her an elegant escape from her relationship problems while maintaining the guise of sacrificing for her mother. Of course, her mother saw through the whole thing. But that was a different matter.

Debbie had planned for the gig to be temporary. A layover. Just long enough for her mom to recover and for Debbie to sort out her life. Like all of her plans, this one didn't work out either.

She didn't plan on stumbling across a deep web of corruption. It was a story that launched the magazine's profile onto the national stage, earning the gratitude of her editor and the publisher.

"CBG, Glad you're safe. Amazing work. TY. CR." It was a note from Chris Radcliffe, scribbled on an otherwise blank five-by-seven note card, taken from the stack Debbie kept on her desk that she used to scrawl her daily to-do lists.

CBG: Crime Beat Girl. It was the original name Sam had given Debbie's column. One she hated. But after turning down an offer to return to her old job in the nation's capital, Debbie demanded her editor drop "girl." She was a grown woman, after all. She'd also negotiated a raise, but in return, Chris, through Sam, insisted that podcasting be added to her list of duties. With no fanfare or prior announcement, the reporter arrived at work on a Monday to discover that a windowless inner conference room had been converted into a sound-conditioned studio.

"So you've edited my latest piece on the mayoral race. What did you think of it? I mean, maybe it wasn't as exciting as the look back at the mob wars, but I thought it was solid."

Sam swiveled his chair so that it faced Debbie directly. "I think we need to have a talk about the mayoral race."

"What's the problem?"

Sam's placed his elbows on his desk and clasped his hands together. "Now that Darlinda Owens is running for mayor, I think you need to figure out which hat you're wearing. Are you a reporter, or are you her publicist?"

Debbie crossed her arms. "What do you mean?"

"Look, I know you have a history with Darlinda," Sam said, referring to the candidate's work as the executive director of Teen Alliance.

"So what does that mean? I shouldn't report on her?"

"I didn't say that," Sam said. "On the one hand,

having a good relationship with a candidate, and if she gets elected, well, anyway, that's a first-rate connection and good for our magazine. But you've got to be fair. We've got readers who support her opponent. We have readers who haven't made up their minds. If you want to help them, you'll remove your thumb from the scale while writing a story."

"C'mon, we both know she's what this city needs," Debbie replied. "She understands the challenges faced by some of our most disadvantaged citizens. As a fundraiser and community leader, she knows how to work with corporate execs and suburban folks. She's smart. She's tough. She's got empathy. And as a Black female, she's the role model we need in this town."

"See, that's what I mean. You could go write her campaign commercials. Either you let her make her own case—and you report on it—or you let me assign someone else to cover her," Sam said. "And one last thing. What if you find out something negative about her? Will you hide it, or will you report it?"

Debbie sighed. "That would be awful. But my duty is to the truth. To the readers. Not Darlinda."

Debbie didn't mention that Darlinda had already

hinted that if she won the mayoral race, she was hoping Debbie would join the administration as her spokesperson. She hadn't said it in so many words, but there were clues. But until she came out and actually offered her something, it was still just a hunch. A hunch, Debbie thought, that wasn't worth disclosing yet. But Sam was no dummy.

"Take a look at my edits. Think it over some. And let me know if you really think you're up to the task. In the meantime, I've got a story tip for you. But it has connections to the upper crust in town. You gotta go about this smart. No Debbie-in-a-china-shop approach."

Debbie grimaced. "C'mon, I'm not that aggressive."

Sam raised his eyebrows. "Really?"

"Assertive doesn't mean aggressive," Debbie argued.

"Look, you get the job done. I like that. You're persistent. But I'm warning you that this will require more stealth and charm."

"Hey, I went to an all-girls high school. I've got plenty of charm," Debbie said.

Sam frowned. "I have a hunch that an all-girls school filled with overachievers made you more combative, not less. Anyway, we both know that heroin has been ripping through the middle- and upper-class ranks here in St. Louis; teens and young adults are hardest hit."

Debbie nodded. "Yeah. The little sister of one of my high school friends died last year from an overdose."

"Well, the garbage has gotten worse. Deadlier. It's getting mixed with fentanyl. That stuff is so lethal that it can kill an elephant. And now it is killing kids. While we don't know for sure if heroin, fentanyl, or both played a role in the demise of a guy named Caleb Webb, it is strongly suspected."

"The twin? Connor and Caleb Webb?" Debbie asked.

"You know 'em?"

"No, not personally. They were a few years behind me. But I know the family owns a real estate company. The Webb boys went to one of the boys' schools in town. So Caleb is...?"

"Dead," Sam said. "Overdose. I got the tip from Chris Radcliffe. He thinks we should look into the toll heroin and fent are taking on our town. But he's not sure about talking to the Webbs. It would be a great coup for the magazine if you could get them to sit down. Our readers would want to know what they have to say. But piss them off, and you'll make a lot of our readers mad. That means canceled subscriptions, disinvites to all those charity balls."

"I thought you didn't like the charity balls."

"I don't. But our readers do. So I need you to take the temperature of the family. And you can't even think the name Chris Radcliffe when you're around them. He doesn't want to be associated with the tip right now."

"You know I'm good at keeping secrets and sources under wraps."

"That's why I'm feeding the tip to you. But it will force you to be smarter, quieter, less zealous."

"I can do that. Easy."

"Radcliffe wasn't so sure when I told him I planned on giving you the story," Sam said as he turned away from her and back to his edits. As she got up to leave, he added, "Don't disappoint me."

Beth Hughes sat at the kitchen table, her black ink pen scratching loudly across a yellow legal pad. The lawyer's laptop had been pushed away, but the screen's blue light illuminated the fifty-four-year-old's blond bobbed hair tucked behind her ears.

Debbie knew that concentrated look. When she was a toddler, Debbie would watch *The Lion King* or *The Wizard of Oz* on the couch. At the same time, her mom crammed in just a bit more work from a makeshift desk fashioned out of a folding table while sitting on the sofa next to her daughter.

"Hey," Debbie said as she entered the kitchen her mom had recently remodeled. Light gray quartz countertops replaced the old green Formica. A milk-color farmhouse sink in place of the old stained, stainless steel one. And cheap white cabinets had been exchanged for dark gray painted ones. But Beth had refused to purge her beloved oversized wooden table to make way for an island. She was far too attached to it. Too many joys and dramas of Beth's life had played out around it. Getting rid of it would mean getting rid of a piece of her.

The table had belonged to Beth's grandparents. As a little girl, Beth had shared many family meals and afternoon visits with them at the table. When her grandparents transitioned to an assisted living center, Beth was married and pregnant with her only child. The table found a new home with Cary and Beth, the center of happy family breakfasts when Debbie was a child. Beth had spent countless mornings drinking coffee with her husband and evenings leaning over Debbie's shoulder, helping with homework questions. The table had been where Beth and Debbie cried together after coming home from the hospital, knowing Cary wouldn't ever pull a chair out again to join them.

It wasn't just a piece of furniture, just like her house, a three-story Victorian built in the late 1800s, wasn't just a house. Beth and Cary bought it when real estate in the Lafayette Square neighborhood was obscenely cheap. Most St. Louisans, except for the early gentrification pioneers, feared the inner city. Now, the house was worth close to a million bucks, nearly ten times what the couple had paid. Even after Cary had died and Debbie left for college, Beth had stubbornly rejected suggestions that she sell. Maybe it was too big for a single woman, some implied. Maybe living in the city was too dangerous, others hinted.

This was her home. She was not leaving, thank you very much. End of discussion.

Debbie always knew better than to suggest her mom should sell. Besides, if she was honest, she was relieved by her mother's stubbornness. She didn't like the thought of driving by the house, knowing it no longer belonged to her family.

"Hey," Beth replied to her daughter without taking her eyes away from her notes.

"I take it your case didn't settle?"

Beth looked up with a frown. "No. And it should have. Bastards."

Debbie set the paper bags she'd been carrying down on the table. Her mom rarely cursed. Not because she didn't believe in salty words. Instead, she appreciated their power to get people's attention—unless you overused them. So she used them sparingly, like red pepper flakes in a pasta dish.

"You're referring to the delivery driver case, right, the one where the guy was drunk and speeding? Ran a red light and slammed into the man minding his own business, just trying to get to work?"

Beth put her pen down. "Yeah. We're set for trial in a few days. We've got the evidence. We've got the black box from the delivery van. And we've got footage from all of the home surveillance cameras in the area where the crash occurred. Any idiot can see the driver was one hundred percent at fault. And then you add in the blood-alcohol test."

"So why isn't it settling?"

"This isn't about liability. It's about damages. The driver's company doesn't want to pay what we're demanding. The man who died was a doctor. He made big bucks. His wife, my client, is also a doctor. The delivery company argues that she doesn't need as much money as we're entitled to. But need has nothing to do with it. She gets to recover the lost wages of her husband. And the defendants can't make up some bogus legal theory to try to weasel out of it by pointing to her salary. It's outrageous. The law is cut-and-dried on this one. Cut-and-dried. They're just playing stupid games to see if we'll cave, if I'll sell my client out just a little to avoid putting in the extra work. They not only robbed her of her husband, but now they want to punish her for working hard and having a good job!"

"So you're gonna go all John Wick on 'em?" Debbie asked.

Beth laughed. The two women had watched the movie the previous weekend, another mom-daughter Saturday night. They'd been spending a lot of their Saturday nights together.

Debbie had moved in with her mother as a matter of efficiency and necessity. Her return to St. Louis smacked of impulsiveness. Now that Debbie had settled into her job at *River City* magazine and even got a pay bump, she was still camped out in her childhood home. Sure, there were outings to look at apartments, but none were cozy enough. Besides, Beth was just as busy as Debbie. Once the two women agreed to a few house rules to prevent the daughter from regressing and the mother from over-functioning, they'd found a harmonious existence. And though neither woman admitted it—and they dodged the topic to avoid jinxing it—the living arrangement worked.

"Do you really think they're gonna try to take that to trial?" Debbie asked.

"I doubt it. No judge will let evidence of the widow's salary in at trial. But I'm mad. I'm considering this as an opportunity. A way to channel my rage into a motion in limine to keep the salary evidence out. I have a feeling I just need to win that motion, then they'll stop playing these stupid games. But they're gonna yank me around until there's a ruling. Who knows. Maybe the defense lawyers are just trying to bill a few more hours to their client. Lord knows the company has deep pockets."

"Well, I brought dinner," Debbie said, trying to switch to a happier topic. "I think you should take a break. I got your favorite Pad Thai," Debbie said as she grabbed plates from the cupboard.

Debbie placed a plate in front of her mom. Then Beth reached into one of the bags to pull out dinner. "I also got some spring rolls," Debbie volunteered. "And Yum Beef for me." The combination of grilled beef, green onion, cilantro, and cucumber in a spicy vinaigrette was one of her favorites. "And I know it's only Thursday night; how about some wine?"

Beth shook her head as she poured peanut sauce on her plate for her spring roll. "We don't have any."

Debbie grinned. "Check the other bag."

Beth sighed. "I shouldn't. I should finish the motion. Well, just one glass. How'd your interview with Cap'n Jack go?"

"He's good at banter," Debbie answered. "It's gonna be a good episode."

"That's what Daniel figured," Beth answered.

Debbie's mom was the only one who referred to Detective Flannery as Daniel. To everyone else, he was simply Flannery.

"That so?" Debbie replied, curious about the detective's assessment.

Beth poured wine into a stemless wine glass. "Yeah. We were supposed to meet for lunch. I had to cancel because of this," Beth said as she gestured to her laptop, the wine bottle still in her hand, "this travesty of justice."

Debbie pulled out her chair and sat down. "Another lunch with Flannery?"

Beth didn't look up from the takeout as she scooped part of the contents onto her plate. Even if they didn't cook often, Beth always insisted that they use proper dishes. "We're friends. Nothing more."

"Uh-huh. Flannery's the most friendly you've been with a guy since Dad died."

"How would you know? You've been gone for quite a while. And besides, I'd have to be nuts to get involved with a cop—and a younger man. I've already lost one husband. And the way you seem to find trouble, well, I figure it's good for me to cultivate a friendly relationship with someone who can help if you go missing. Again."

"This is the twenty-first century, Mom. And since when did you give a damn about society's expectations? You moved to the city when people thought you were crazy, and you didn't change your name when you married. You've never needed anyone's approval. And besides, Mom, you're hot."

Beth, who had been taking a sip of wine, choked.

Debbie continued, "There's only, what, like an eight-year difference between you and Flannery? Why can we have a first lady who is twenty-four years younger than the president? Why can't we emulate the French? France has a first lady who is nearly twenty-five years older than her husband."

"Look," Beth said. "It really isn't about the age. I don't give a fig about what others think. It's just that I'm reluctant to get involved with someone who goes to work in the morning, and you don't know if he's coming home at night. I like my life the way it is: settled."

"Does Flannery know you feel this way?"

Beth took a bite of her food. "Mmmm. This is delicious. It hits the spot. Oh, I almost forgot. Can you hand me my briefcase? It's down by your feet."

Debbie picked up the elegant black case with a gold clasp and handed it to her mother. Beth opened it and smiled. "I got you something."

"It isn't my birthday," Debbie said suspiciously.

"Why?"

"Can't a mom do something nice without an ulterior motive?"

"Maybe some moms can," Debbie teased, "but you?"

Beth stuck her tongue out at her daughter and pulled out a box.

Debbie looked at the label. "Oooh, this is a fancy fitness watch!"

"It tracks your heart rate, your respiration. Has an EKG," Beth said. "And even a GPS to help you track your runs."

"Ah, so that's it. Another tracker," Debbie said.

"Oh, come on, don't be ridiculous," Beth replied unconvincingly. "Besides, I got myself one, too. Now that breast cancer is behind me, I thought I'd return to running."

"You?"

"Hey, you may not remember, but I ran a lot when you were a kid. And after you went off to college, then moved to D.C., I discovered a brisk jog cleared my head. And when I met Captain Jack's girlfriend, she said I looked like a runner."

"You met his girlfriend?"

"Yeah. Daniel introduced me," Beth said, ignoring her daughter's widening eyes. "She's an artist, a sculptor, I think. Daniel calls her an aging hippie. You know the type. Long gray braid, fan of dangling turquoise earrings. I thought she was lovely."

Debbie laughed. "I can see that. I can actually see that more than I can see Jack as a cop. And I'm still having a hard time wrapping my mind around the fact that Jack is Flannery's uncle."

Beth shrugged. "You know these old St. Louis families. For Flannery's Irish family, boys were either cops, lawyers, or priests. Jack probably chose cop for the same reason Daniel did; the other two were less appealing. Maybe Jack now has the time, freedom, and money to discover who he truly is." Beth paused. "You know, paying your dues early can give you the freedom to grow into who you really want to be—even in retirement."

"I suppose," Debbie answered. "Well, I'm still paying my dues."

"Yes. Yes, you are. And you may want to think about a backup plan. Journalism—dying industry and all."

Debbie shot Beth a look that said now wasn't the time

for her mom to pitch law school.

Beth pivoted. "What's your next story?"

"I'm not sure if it's a story yet. You know the Webbs, right? The ones who own a lot of real estate developments?"

Beth nodded. "Yeah. They just finished that fancy high-rise condo in Clayton. A couple of lawyers I know bought places there."

"Well, their son Caleb overdosed a couple of days ago on New Year's Eve. I think he was living in that high-rise condo development at the time."

"Heroin?"

"Heroin? Fentanyl? A mix? It's unclear right now. It'll take at least thirty days for the medical examiner's office to issue the final report. In the meantime, I don't know how much I will be able to find out. Officially, that is."

"So, what's your angle?"

"Ugh, you know I hate that question," Debbie answered. "Right now, I'm just trying to find out more about Caleb Webb's death. He's got a twin brother, Connor. They went to the same private boys' school as Chase Laclede. Chase was probably a few years ahead of 'em, but you know how it is here. Everyone knows everyone or at least has a friend with a connection. Maybe they run in the same circles."

"Interesting," Beth said, then asked cautiously, "Are you going to call Chase?"

Debbie paused and poured more wine into her glass. "Chase is still dodging me."

She'd spent nearly six months trying to rekindle their connection. But nothing had been the same after her ex-fiancé, Christian Garza, had shown up on her doorstep trying to convince Debbie to return to D.C.

"Maybe you should just figure out when he's going to be in court," Beth suggested. "Can't be too hard with Casenet," she said, referring to the online court database. "Just search his name. Find a case on the docket. Show up. Ask him about Caleb Webb."

"Ambush him?"

Beth smiled. "No. Just, um, show up."

"Earlier today, Sam warned me about being too aggressive."

"There's a difference between assertive and aggressive," Beth answered. "I don't think you're too aggressive. I think where you could improve is in strategy."

"I'm plenty strategic."

"Are you? You don't always have to force things to get a win. Sometimes, if you stop pushing against a problem or a person, they fall under their own weight. Or they come around on their own."

"How do you know when to stop pushing?" Debbie asked.

Beth shrugged. "Every situation is different. Like this case. Now is the time to push. But knowing when to start, when to stop, that requires wisdom and time."

Debbie frowned. "I appreciate that. But when you have a story deadline, there's no such thing as waiting for the right time."

3 GHOSTS

Shortly after dusk on Thursday, Tom Wilkins guided his rig 'round to the back of an aging gas station in Lebanon, Missouri, parking it next to a diesel pump.

The truck stop had seen better days. Just off Interstate 44, the low red-brick building looked more like a bomb shelter than a place of business. The unleaded gas pumps for the non-trucker folks were sheltered by an awning the color of putty. The fact that it kept the rain and snow off highway travelers was the only luxury customers would encounter. But the big rigs and the diesel pumps didn't merit shielding from storms.

The number of people pulling in to fill up had taken a dive over the past several years. The fading establishment couldn't compete with the modern travel plaza on the other side of the highway. The newer place had hot showers, arcades, and clean bathrooms with an initialed sheet on the door noting the last time the washroom was tidied up. Parents driving minivans outfitted with DVD players that could play *Frozen* preferred the selection of junk food at the big chain travel stop. For the college kids bound for the Missouri University of Science and Technology in Rolla, the travel plaza was bright and well-lit, even on the darkest night.

By comparison, the lonely truck stop from a bygone era was gloomy, even on the brightest day. The patrons were little more than ghosts, customers who materialized briefly and vanished into the rural countryside or were swallowed whole by the nearby interstate.

But for Tom, the bleak vibe was a perk, not a drawback. And he was looking forward to his first break since leaving Wichita Falls, Texas, seven hours earlier. His truck had rumbled through Oklahoma City, Tulsa, and Joplin before finally reaching Lebanon. It was his first haul since the New Year's holiday, which he'd spent home with the missus. It'd been nice to get back on the road after being cooped up in the house. But it was always the same thing; once he was driving, he couldn't wait to hunker back down in his castle, even if it was a bit shabby on account of the fact that he never got around to working on that fixer-up list that his wife had in her head.

Tom turned off the engine and grabbed the faded blue-and-white flannel jacket crumpled on the empty passenger seat. He pulled it on and patted the right-side pocket to check for his wallet. Despite the cold outside, he left the front of his coat open. It was too much trouble to suck in his belly to pull the zipper up. The trucker braced himself before opening the door and tugged at the John Deere cap covering his silver hair to ensure it wouldn't blow off. After the warm cocoon of the cabin, the outside air would be like the slap of a jealous lover.

He smiled. He was too old to remember what it was like to have a jealous lover. Once upon a time, he'd tried having a route mistress and a home wife. Once. The missus had caught on purty quick. You could call her lots of things, but fool wasn't one of 'em. She'd laid down the law. He could only have one woman. He had to choose, she said. He chose her. He hadn't stepped out since. No siree. You only crossed the missus once.

Tom eased himself down from his perch and walked toward the entrance, still stiff-legged from his journey, his gray-stubbled face bent down to ward off the wind. He opened the door and entered the shop.

"Howdy," the truck stop clerk mumbled as she looked away from the fuzzy screen of a tiny television nestled in the corner of the counter. Her gaze was just long enough to give her customer the once-over. She ran her chapped, ruddy hands through the home-dyed brownish-red hair that framed her lined face. The only trace left of her youthful good looks was her blue eyes.

"Evenin'," he said, his chin dipping slightly to tip the bill of his cap.

The clerk shoved her hands into the front pocket of her hooded sweatshirt. She hunched her shoulders against the chill the driver brought in with him, then turned her attention back to the game show she'd been watching.

The trucker made his way to the cooler in the back of the store, ignoring a shelf stuffed with packages of white laces for customers whose shoes didn't need tying. Nope, the people who bought these laces were looking for something to wrap around an arm to get a better vein before shooting up. The driver reached into the refrigerated compartment and grabbed a Mountain Dew. It'd get him through the last four hours of his trip to St. Louis to drop off furniture at a big chain's warehouse.

He grabbed a Slim Jim from an aisle display and set his purchases on the counter next to the cash register. Nearby, roses in glass tubes sat on a cardboard display. The perfect gift for the crack addict; remove the rose, and the glass becomes a pipe.

"Why don't you also give me a Mega Million?" Tom said to the clerk. "How's it goin'?"

The cashier's eyes shifted away from the television to the black-and-white monitors that received information from the surveillance cameras around the building's exterior. The only vehicle seen was the semi that belonged to her sole customer.

"Been quiet," she said as she rang up his purchase. "That'll be four dollars fifty-three cents."

The driver reached for his wallet, pulled out a fifty, and handed it to the clerk.

She punched a few keys into the register, and the drawer opened with a clang. She fished out his change. "Here you go," she said as she handed him the coins, holding back the wad of bills that made up the difference between the fifty and his purchase. That stack she stuffed into the front pocket of her sweatshirt.

They'd been acquaintances for nearly a decade, linked

together by meth. Patricia Perkins was her name, but he never uttered it. It could be easier to forget if he never said it, especially if he got busted. And she'd never called him Tom, even though she'd run his credit card many times over the years.

Patricia, or maybe it was Patty, didn't get close to anyone, as far as he could tell. Despite the distance, he'd still pieced together some details about her life from his regular stops over the years. Way back when, when he first started coming into the place pert near ten years ago, back when she was real cute, the clerk had offered him a money-making proposition. Somehow, she'd sized him up and trusted what she saw. Maybe Patricia was like his wife in that regard. She was looking for help to move the meth her boyfriend was cooking. If Tom took the side gig, he'd get a nice chunk of tax-free cash. And he never had to sell anything. He was strictly a delivery driver. The network of dealers lurking around the stops on his route was always easy to find.

It wasn't long before Tom realized that the boyfriend, in addition to being a cooker of meth, was also a beater of women. It was impossible to miss the various stages of bruising on Patricia's face and arms. It was a pity. He'd never laid a hand on his own wife. But he was also a firm believer in minding your own damn business. And what went on between Patty Perkins and her boyfriend was none of his damn business.

Everything went to shit when the feds busted the boyfriend. The jerk's mouth started flapping as soon as he was in cuffs. One of the first people he threw under the bus was his girlfriend. But she'd stayed cool. She clammed up. Smart one, that Patty. It wasn't long before her boyfriend was found dead in the Laclede County jail, a shank buried in his chest. According to the trucker gossip, the boyfriend was a snitch who planned to give up the names of his suppliers. They weren't too happy about it. So they took matters into their own hands to still his lips permanently.

But Patricia Perkins? That woman zipped her mouth up and kept her head down. Her clever federal public defender argued that his client had been forced into cooperating with the conspiracy by an abusive boyfriend. Luckily, her attorney could produce the emergency room records and photos of her injuries to bolster the claim. She won some leniency in the form of a sentencing downward departure from a federal judge. After five years in Vandalia Women's Prison, Patricia was free.

By the time she was released, even the drug world had changed. Homegrown meth had mostly disappeared. Missouri politicians had finally wised up and cracked down on pseudoephedrine sales. The Show-Me State went from America's meth production capital to barely a blip on the screen.

But while she was tucked away in the women's prison, forgotten by the outside world, Patty had caught the attention of the cartel. Her reputation for refusing to be a snitch spread. She was quiet and blended in; she didn't stick her nose anywhere it didn't belong. Even the prison brass liked her. She got things done without complaining or antagonizing her fellow inmates. A real hard worker, just like many other women from the sticks. They were hard workers who knew how to survive in tough times. It wasn't long before she was practically running the cafeteria, the shadow boss of the prison's actual cafeteria director. The cartel, like most organizations, valued trustworthy workers who achieved results with minimal fuss. Before being released from the pen, she'd been recruited to join an organized crime syndicate.

Once she was out, her former employer gave her back

her old job. She'd been a good employee, never late, never called in sick. Never stole from him or his business. She was the "don't shit in your kitchen" sort. By contrast, there were a lot of other people the owner had hired since Patty had left who couldn't even last three months showing up day in, day out, at the truck stop. Fifty percent of the job was just showing up on time. And he knew Patty would be there come hell or high water.

The paths of the trucker and the clerk crossed again. The years had taken their toll on them both. But that worked in their favor. The older they looked, the less suspicion they raised. Perfect for the new venture she brought him: Become a mule for a Mexican cartel.

"Even drugs are going to the damn foreigners," Tom recalled complaining to Patty. But money was money. Who knew how much longer he'd be able to drive a big rig. And his wife was getting on in years, too. They'd been living paycheck to paycheck after his first underground side gig had dried up. His wife had taken on watching kids for some neighbors who worked the night shift, but that had dried up once the factory closed. Patricia Perkins offered him one last chance to sock away some rainy-day cash. Maybe he could eventually stop driving; finally tackle that to-do list his wife had been yammering about for years.

Unlike the last time he'd ferried drugs, it wasn't just meth that he was tasked with moving. There was also heroin, cocaine, and fentanyl. Fent was some deadly shit. He refused to touch the stuff with his bare hands. But he had no qualms about delivering it. As far as Tom was concerned, if it killed people, it was their own damn fault. None of his business what idiots put in their bodies.

"I'll be fillin' 'er up," he announced as he grabbed his Slim Jim, Mountain Dew, and lotto ticket off the counter. He looked around. "So next door. The hotel?"

"Quiet," the clerk said as she reached for the open red pack of Marlboros and the yellow lighter next to it on the counter. She pulled the hood over her head. "I'm gonna grab a smoke. Like I said, it's quiet. Too cold. Plus, people still recovering from the beer flu they caught on New Year's Eve."

The trucker nodded. "Welp. Guess I'll be getting on my way."

The motel was so close that Tom's phone connected to

its Wi-Fi signal while still parked next to the truck stop's diesel pump.

He liked the open wireless connection. At one time he'd made the mistake of using his personal data during some of his mandated breaks and his wife—who paid the bills—had a fit. She'd accused him of using data to watch nudie movies on his phone. He denied it. But of course, he'd also never admit it. Besides, it was only that one time. And what happened through Wi-Fi didn't count.

The motel was just on the opposite side of the service road from the truck stop. There used to be a sign that advertised the motel from the highway, only it had been sheared off by a derecho. Now there was just a pole jutting up to the sky like an index finger jabbing toward an apathetic god. Another good thing about the motel was that there was plenty of room in the lot for his truck. The few parked cars likely belonged to hourly guests. The motorcycles in the front belonged to the biker gang that had adopted the place as an outpost.

Tom parked his big rig, hopped out of the cab, walked around to the back of the trailer, and opened it up. If anyone asked what he was doing, he'd just say he thought the load had shifted and needed to check for sure.

Three men in dark leather jackets emerged from the hotel. The leader, a fella with a long gray beard whom Tom only knew as Brick, was in the mix. As the men approached, Tom shoved his hands in his pockets, took several steps back from the trailer, and repeated what he'd been told when he'd stopped off in Wichita Falls to pick up the product. "Desk drawers."

One of the men noticed the driver move away. "What's the matter? Scairt?"

"There's fent in the mix. Even the DEA won't touch that shit barehanded. I hear they keep Narcan around when they're checking vehicles at the border because one whiff can getcha," the driver said as he took another step back.

"Pussies," Brick said before he climbed into the trailer and began rummaging through the desk drawers. "Ain't gonna hurt you if you know what you're doing."

"Just the same, I'll just stand back here, outta your way," Tom said while he waited, knowing they'd been done in a matter of minutes. The longer they lingered, the more suspicious the bikers appeared, hanging around the back of an open eighteen-wheeler and whatnot. And with his GPS tracking him, a long lag would raise red flags with his company's brass.

"The shipment's all here," Brick said to no one in particular as he climbed down from the trailer and handed the driver a quarter-inch stack of hundreds.

"You're damn right it's all there," Tom said. "El Duro don't know me. And I aim to keep it that way."

4 TIES THAT BIND

Chase Laclede flashed his most charming smile at the sour court clerk as the lawyer accepted a file-stamped copy of a settlement agreement from her. His handsome yet boyish grin always worked on his mother and the cashiers at the grocery store. It worked on the waiters and waitresses in restaurants. It even worked on the frazzled Homeland Security staffers stuck screening passports at the airport. But in court? With this clerk? No, nope, nada. There was no winning over this judge's assistant. She'd been around lawyers much too long, so long that she'd become fully vaccinated against all charm offensives. The best he could hope for was the absence of hostility.

Sure, the judge made the rulings. But a good clerk could advance—or delay—the path to a timely resolution. In the legal system, time always costs someone money.

And because Chase often charged a flat fee rather than an hourly rate, inefficiency hit his bottom line the hardest. Fortunately, this case was for one of his atypical hourly retainer clients. Still, in the future, he knew he'd be working with this clerk again. He'd probably be representing a client who could barely scrape together the fee. A client with no money who'd paid his attorney after begging his granny, pleading with an auntie, and scrounging from granny once more after her social security check arrived.

The misery inflicted on lawbreakers came with a huge blast radius. It always enveloped the innocent ones unlucky enough to love felons and crooks.

When he announced his plan to focus on criminal defense, his parents warned him that wins would be few and far between. They were right. For Chase, it was time to break out the champagne when a client was sentenced to fourteen years instead of forty. Sometimes he'd have a celebratory dinner when he'd successfully kept a piece of crucial evidence out at trial. The prosecutor, deprived of an essential component of the case, would be more willing to cut his client a break. Even though he'd redefined the concept of success, he still harbored a dream of freeing an innocent man or wrongly sentenced woman.

The podcasts all made it seem so easy. Of course, they cheated because they cherrypicked their stories. Chase didn't do the same with his clients. He represented people in trouble. Sometimes, his most significant contribution to society was ensuring the criminal justice system played by the rules.

His parents understood his choice, even if his dad wasn't thrilled with it. David and Dee Laclede were attorneys who'd met in law school at Northwestern University in Chicago. David, a black man raised by a single mom, grew up in St. Louis. Dee, a white woman, grew up in an upper-middle-class neighborhood in Aurora, Illinois. Despite their different life experiences, they became a couple soon after meeting. "It was love at first debate," his dad often said. After graduation, they married and moved to St. Louis. Dee landed her dream job in the public defender's office. David started at a top-tier law firm, eventually becoming corporate counsel for one of the Fortune 500 companies in St. Louis. After Chase was born, Dee worked with legal services, helping low-income clients. Eventually, she transitioned to a volunteer lawyer. She was now a respected and sought-after board member for several local organizations.

David Laclede had wanted his son to join a fancy silk stocking firm and make a lot of money. His financially insecure childhood convinced him that a fat wallet was a safety shield. And he didn't think his son appreciated it. Perhaps Chase had been too sheltered, attending private schools, having the right connections, and yes, even drawing from a modest trust fund.

There was one other person who understood where Chase was coming from: Debbie Bradley. Even though she wasn't a lawyer, she was the product of an attorney union. A law firm was already waiting with her name on the letterhead.

What a disaster she'd turned out to be, Chase thought as he packed up his briefcase and headed toward the courtroom exit.

As he stood in front of the elevator that would take him to the courthouse's first floor, Chase winced when he thought of Debbie. He'd been trying hard for the past several months to forget her. But for some reason, he couldn't stop himself from reading her articles and listening to her podcasts. She was smart. She was pretty.

She was funny. She was fearless.

And, he realized as the elevator doors were closing, she was riding it down with him.

"Chase!" Debbie said, her eyes just a bit too wide. "What a surprise!"

"Debbie Bradley," Chase said politely as the doors closed. Good God, she was a terrible actor.

The elevator lurched, then descended briefly before stopping one floor below. As more people entered, Debbie and Chase were forced to the back of the car—and closer together. She smiled a few times, even as he tried to keep his gaze focused on a greasy smudge on the elevator doors.

After five stops, the elevator reached the lobby. Debbie stepped off first and waited for Chase, knowing he'd take longer because he always let women go first. But as soon as he was out, she was next to him, flashing the most charming smile she could muster.

Before she had a chance to open her mouth, Chase cut her off. "I've known you long enough to know meet-cutes don't exist, not that I'd call running into one another in a courthouse a meet-cute."

Debbie's smile faltered. "C'mon, you don't answer my calls. You ignore my texts."

"I'm swamped," Chase said.

"Please," Debbie said as she touched his arm. "Please. How about lunch?"

Chase looked at his phone, which also shook her hand from his arm. "I've got lots of appointments today."

"Dinner?" Debbie persisted.

"You didn't stalk me to talk about lunch or dinner, Debbie. You're working. What, pray tell, do you want?"

"That's not true, Chase. I really do want to get together."

Chase gave a half smile that didn't reach his eyes. "To make this much effort, you must either have a hot story or a dud going nowhere."

"Fine," Debbie replied. "There is a story. But that doesn't mean I haven't been trying to connect with a friend."

When he heard the word "friend," his lips turned downward, but only for a moment. "Debbie, as I said, I'm in a hurry."

"I'm looking into the death of Caleb Webb," Debbie

blurted out. "I know he went to the same high school you attended, even if he was a few years after you. I thought you might know him. He died of an overdose a couple of days ago."

Chase pushed the revolving door to the world outside. Debbie stepped into the space right behind him.

"Yes, I heard," Chase said after they'd exited. "I met him a few times at some fundraisers my mom coerced me to attend. He was even glummer than I was about being forced to show up. His twin, on the other hand, Connor, I think? That guy could work any room; he seemed to get along with everyone. Caleb was more of a loner. The brothers reminded me of, um, cilantro and parsley. They look very similar but are, er were, distinctly different."

"Did you know about the drugs?"

"What do I look like, Debbie, a partier?"

"No, I didn't mean that. I just thought maybe, as a criminal defense lawyer, you might've heard things."

"No, I didn't. But why in the world would I tell you if I did?" Chase paused, checking his phone. "Let me guess, heroin?"

"Probably. Or fentanyl. Or a mix," Debbie said.

Chase shook his head. "The bane of the 'burbs. How

many families with money tsk-tsked poor kids caught up in the crack cocaine epidemic in the city or the meth outbreaks in rural areas? Heroin was their tragic comeuppance. Suddenly, the get-tough-on-crime crowd was clamoring for treatment alternatives to jail."

"You don't approve?"

"Treatment for users makes sense. I don't like that the law-and-order crowd refused to empathize with addicts until those addicts turned out to be their children. Then suddenly they got all woke about addiction as a disease." Chase paused. "Look, I'm not denying that drugs are a problem. Coming into St. Louis via Chicago or up from the southern border, through Interstates Forty-four and Fifty-five."

Debbie nodded. "I hear the cartels often import fentanyl from China. It arrives in Mexico, then they move it up north to their most lucrative market."

Chase shifted his weight. "I really need to get going."

"Do you think I could talk to some of your clients, you know, the ones involved in the drug trade?"

Chase stared at her. "Unbelievable. You're really asking for a favor? From me? Such a," he stammered, "such a Debbie Bradley move."

"Oh, come on. You let me talk to Joshua Lucas," Debbie said, reminding him of the profile she'd done on Chase's juvenile client. "That turned out better than just fine. You helped me. I helped your client."

"Nope. Even if I wanted to be nice to you, which I don't, it is a terrible idea. Look, I don't work for the cartel. But don't be stupid. Paramilitary narcos and journalists don't go together."

"But we're in the U.S.," Debbie argued. "They're in Mexico."

Chase shook his head. "These organizations have long tentacles that can reach even here. I don't think it's safe for you to snoop around."

"Well, if lawyers can defend them, why can't I talk to them? I don't frighten easily. And I'm no dummy. Over a hundred journalists have been killed in Mexico in the past twenty years. Some of those deaths were gruesome. A reporter investigating a drug turf war wound up decapitated. And another was shot while investigating human remains in one part of Mexico. But in case you haven't noticed, being a reporter in the U.S. isn't a freakin' picnic either. We're the 'enemy of the people.' If I cover a protest, I could end up getting shot with rubber bullets, not in spite of being a reporter but because I'm a journalist. Go to a political rally, and I've got a target on my back. Working at my desk can get me killed, like those four journalists working at that Maryland newspaper. You can't even begin to believe some of the hate emails I receive."

Chase looked at Debbie's feet.

"What?" she asked.

"Nothing, just lookin' for your soapbox. Why not talk to your fiancé? He's up in D.C. Garza's got access to the head honchos at the DEA. He covers a lot of the narco-cartel stuff."

"You know he's not my fiancé anymore," Debbie said.

Chase noticed that she stomped her right foot as she spoke. He'd realized that she did that when she wanted to add emphasis to a statement.

Debbie continued, "I've been trying to explain to you that me and Christian, um, well, we talked through things. Truth is, the relationship wasn't working for either of us. I just didn't want to admit it."

Chase looked at his phone again.

"Anyway, Chase," Debbie continued, "I needed to work through some of that stuff myself."

"Look, none of that changes the fact that he's got access to higher-level intel than I do. And I'm assuming that you two still talk."

Debbie sighed. "Sure, we talk occasionally. Mostly just to bounce ideas off one another. As a lawyer, you know how important it is to have a sounding board for your cases. The same can be said for journalists."

"I thought that's what your editor was for," Chase said before looking at his phone for the last time. "Now, I really do have to go."

Chase left Debbie standing outside the courthouse. He didn't look back until he'd made it to his car, parked a block away. When he finally turned around, she'd vanished.

He tossed his briefcase onto the back seat and climbed into his black convertible BMW. Before driving away from the meter, he reached into the cupholder to his right, pulling out a business card.

Printed on the front in gold: Connor Webb. Webb Real Estate Development. Chase flipped it over to look at a handwritten phone number Connor had scrawled on the back of the card a few months earlier.

The card had been in his car since September. It had become minor clutter in the otherwise clean vehicle that had been a present from his parents when he'd graduated from law school.

After being a renter since he'd moved back to St. Louis from law school, he was toying with the idea of finally becoming a real estate owner. His mom suggested searching for a condo. She'd mentioned the Webbs' building. She thought new living quarters might do him good. He'd moped about too long after the summer debacle with Debbie. Then a client who dabbled in real estate also mentioned the building, claiming it was a good buy.

"I can get you a discount on a place," his client had said. "I know about some unadvertised deals, early buyer specials to certain types of buyers."

"Certain types?" Chase had asked.

"You know, young, professional, good-looking. The influencer types who'll post on Instagram."

Chase had laughed. "I'm not an influencer."

"Yeah, but you must know some," his client said. "Handsome dude like you. There's got to be a bevy of lovely ladies from good families who'd be delighted to post a selfie from one of those fancy balconies. A real thirst trap."

"Naw, man," Chase had said. "That's not my scene. But I will take a look."

The Clayton condos were as sleek and modern as he'd been led to believe. It was a significant change from the 1930s-era apartment building where he lived, a building so old that it was still serviced by an elevator with a vintage Otis scissor gate.

A thin blonde in a tight skirt working in the sales office gave him a tour of the building and one of the units for sale. "Can't you imagine opening a bottle of wine and entertaining in this kitchen? And how about this balcony? You can see downtown from here. On a clear day, you can even make out the Arch," she'd said as she swept a manicured hand out over the city. Then she'd led him into the master bath. "As you can see, no expense was spared. There's plenty of room in the shower for you. And," she said, looking at him with a smile, "a guest."

An image of Debbie wrapped in a bath towel crystallized in his head. Chase cleared his throat and headed back to the living room. "I'll have to think about it a bit."

"Don't think too long. This building is hot," the agent said as they exited the space and she locked the door.

A door down the hall opened. Two men were shouting at one another. Chase turned toward the noise. That's when Connor Webb appeared, his jaw clenched.

"Just stop," Connor said a little too loudly.

"I can't. I won't," said the voice concealed behind the door frame.

"You're playing a dangerous game, Caleb," Connor said before he noticed Chase and the sales agent standing in the corridor.

"You're the one," Caleb said as he stepped into the hall and toward his brother. The arguing stopped when they realized they weren't alone.

The sales agent, doing her best to ignore the spat, summoned her perkiest voice. "Connor and Caleb, I'd like you to meet a prospective buyer, Chase Laclede."

Connor flashed a quick grin. "I thought I knew you. We played hockey together, right?"

"Yeah, back in the day," Chase answered.

"You remember my brother, Caleb?" Connor said.

Of course Chase knew Caleb. When they'd played

youth hockey, the Webb brothers were a threat to anyone who opposed them. The two boys always anticipated the other's move, making them formidable opponents. But Caleb was a pale and gaunt shadow of his former athlete self.

"Forgive us," Connor volunteered. "Me and my twin brother, well, we may be grown but we still bicker."

"Nothing like brotherly love," Caleb mumbled. "Good to see you, Chase," he said before stepping back inside and shutting the door.

Connor reached into his pocket and pulled out a business card. "Here. We'd love to have you in the building. I'll talk to my parents. They know you and your family. I bet they'd be happy to give you a friends-and-family discount."

Chase had taken the card. When he got to his car, he'd placed it in the cup holder. In the first week or two after the visit, he thought about calling Connor. But it just never felt right. Now Caleb was dead and Chase wondered whether he should call Connor to offer his condolences.

He picked up the card, looked at the phone number on the back, then filed it in his glove box for safe keeping.

He couldn't imagine Debbie Bradley sitting in his car, but she did have an annoying habit of surprising Chase in places where he least expected to see her. It would be safe from prying eyes in there.

5 CHICANERY

Debbie drove her battered Honda Civic to Clayton to see the building where Caleb had died. Even if she couldn't access his condo, a visit might yield something, although she had no idea what.

She'd done her homework last night. The Missouri Secretary of State's corporate records revealed the three legal entities the family used to build, own, and operate the place. A move meant to insulate their fortune from liability and, presumably, minimize their taxes.

Behind every high-value client was a lawyer tasked with shielding assets.

Debbie tried to shake off the funk she'd felt since Chase had walked away from her earlier that morning. A few months before, her mom had counseled leaving him alone for a bit. "I bet he comes around," she'd said. "His pride has been wounded. I don't think he's used to competition." Well, for once, her mom had been wrong. Time had only hardened Chase's heart; space had simply allowed him to thicken his armor. That much was clear after their conversation outside the courthouse.

Debbie drove around the block looking for an empty parking spot with a meter. She circled the block a second time. The third time, she whispered: Fuck.

She then spotted an elderly couple dressed in long wool coats and sensible winter shoes climbing into a Cadillac parked on the street. Debbie noticed that the car was too shiny and clean. It had to be a garaged car taken out for an errand. Perhaps, Debbie mused, they were visiting their lawyer's office, reviewing the details of their last will or trust. After all, this was Clayton, the seat of the St. Louis County government. You'd be hard-pressed to enter any office building without seeing a law firm's name, Bradley & Hughes among them.

Before anyone else noticed the soon-to-be vacant spot, Debbie had maneuvered her car adjacent to, but still behind, the Caddy. The driver could depart, but a jerk would have difficulty squeezing into the space before her. It was always a delicate balance, defending yourself from assholes without becoming one.

She was rewarded for her patience with a meter with twenty minutes left. If she was lucky, she could visit the condominium building and return to her car without running out of time. Debbie glanced at the ticket on her passenger seat, the one she'd received downtown that morning. She didn't need a second parking ticket that day.

She left the car and tried to make a mental to-do list. More than likely, she'd just take a quick walk around the outside. Jot down notes about the curb appeal of the place. Take some pictures that would help her later as she tried to describe scenes for a story she still wasn't sure would be written. After all, the building's exterior would be different once winter passed and spring arrived. If she couldn't rewind time, she could at least freeze it.

Two men wearing matching black jackets and tan cargo pants were removing holiday lights and garlands. One appeared to be in his forties; the other was probably nineteen or twenty.

Debbie forced a smile to her face. "Hi there," she said.

The men stopped unwinding the evergreen rope laced with a two-inch-wide red ribbon twisted around the columns in front of the entrance.

"Hi," the younger worker answered reflexively.

"All done with Christmas?"

"Yep," said the same man.

"I bet it was pretty," she said.

The young man nodded.

The older man frowned and resumed dismantling the decorations. "*Venga.*"

"Sorry. My dad wants me to get back to work."

"I understand," Debbie said. "I stopped by because I'm trying to find out when the memorial service for Caleb Webb might be held."

The older man worked even faster.

"We're just here to take down decorations," his son said. "You'd have to ask the people inside."

The combination of warm yellow and dimmed white lights gave the lobby the feel of a ritzy spa or an opulent hotel. A fountain burbled in the corner. Dark wood and gray tones signaled luxurious serenity. It was a stylish refuge with a prestigious address.

A woman in her early thirties, her blond hair pulled back into a sleek, shiny ponytail hitting the base of her neck, sat behind a dark wooden desk.

"May I help you?" the woman asked. She smiled with perfectly painted lips, her black turtleneck sweater hinting at a well-toned body underneath.

"Hi," Debbie said. "I was just talking to your employees out there, and they said you might be able to help me."

"Oh, they aren't our employees. Contractors. They take care of our grounds year-round. They're the best."

"I see," Debbie said.

"Are you interested in looking at one of our condo units?" the woman asked.

Debbie paused. She had a choice to make. Taking a tour would get her further inside the building. But there was no guarantee that the model unit would be like Caleb's. And if she waited to ask about Caleb, the woman might resent having her time wasted.

"This is a bit awkward. But I was a high school friend of Caleb Webb. I was wondering if you knew when his funeral or wake would be. I haven't been able to find anything online."

The woman nodded, pulling out her somber face, more suited to the turn of the conversation. "I'm afraid it

79

is a private affair. The family didn't want to announce the information publicly. They've just been inviting close family and friends."

Debbie nodded. "I understand. It's a pity. I would've liked to have paid my respects."

The woman nodded again. "I'm so sorry I couldn't be of more help."

Debbie turned to leave, then stopped. She knew she shouldn't turn around or say what she was about to say. But she just couldn't help herself.

"You know," Debbie began, "this is the first time I've been able to visit your building. I'd heard this place was beautiful, but I didn't realize how striking it would be."

The woman, unsure about which expression was appropriate for the exchange, put on a hesitant smile that matched Debbie's. "It is quite impressive, I have to admit. We're very proud of the work that was done here. We've already had some important people buy a place. Very important. Of course, I'm not at liberty to disclose who."

"Oh, of course," Debbie said. "I understand. I shouldn't tell you this, but I'm, uh, connected to *River City* magazine. I think they should really do some sort of spread on this place. Maybe a cover feature."

"That would be wonderful, of course," the woman said eagerly. "Would you like the contact information for the owners?"

"Not yet. I wouldn't want to get their hopes up. Can we just keep it between us?"

"Certainly," the woman said, nodding as if she were a co-conspirator planning a surprise birthday party.

"Would you mind if I took a few photos with my phone, just a little something to show my people?" Debbie asked.

The woman paused for a moment. "I can't see what it would hurt. But we have photos online of our lobby already."

It was too late. Debbie's phone was already out and, without waiting, she snapped a few images and then spoke again. "You know, if you have a card, I'd love to get it. If I can make a successful pitch, I'd like to give you a heads-up, too. Maybe you could be around for the photo shoot, maybe even make it into the magazine."

The woman smiled, unable to suppress her delight at the thought of making it into print. "Oh, well, I wouldn't need to be in the magazine," she said as she reached for her business card. As she handed it to Debbie, she leaned in closely and whispered the name of a funeral home. "The visitation is tomorrow, three p.m. By the way, I didn't catch your name."

"Debbie. Thanks so much. I think my meter is about to expire. I'll be in touch," the reporter said quickly as she escaped.

6 BAGMAN

Brick left Lebanon shortly after the trucker had delivered the drugs to the motel. About two and a half hours later, he was steering his black Ford F-150 pickup with an extended cab and matching topper through the quiet residential street in Spanish Lake.

He didn't worry about the Confederate flag decal on the left bumper or, on the far right bumper, the sticker with the outline of a naked woman in a provocative pose. Truth be told, he got a thrill out of poking people in the eye. So what if there was a confrontation? He could handle himself.

And it wasn't like he was driving through a lah-de-dah St. Louis suburb.

Mid-century modern madness had boosted the home values in other areas, but not in Spanish Lake. Once upon a time, it had been called Spanish Pond because of the fortification built by Spanish troops before the Civil War. It had also once been a German farming community before it was a 1950s destination for white residents fleeing the city. Then, a few decades later, white residents fled again, fearing Black St. Louisans who started moving in. Now the population of Spanish Lake was majority African-American. The family income hovered at or below the poverty line.

A garage door opened. A man with messy cornrows was standing inside, wearing a white hoodie and loose jeans. The truck inched inside, as close to the house as possible, before the door closed.

"Shit," said Cap. He'd received the nickname early in his life because he was willing to shoot anyone who got in his way. The name took on a second meaning when he was promoted to a leadership position in the criminal enterprise. Waving a Sig Sauer P239 nine-millimeter pistol in his right hand, he said, "Why the fuck you bring that Nazi ride here?"

"This baby blends in," Brick said as he climbed out of the cab. "Out on Highway 44, through Cuba, Bourbon, and Pacific, no one is gonna look at me twice. It ain't 'til I get to Antifa land that anyone pays me any mind."

"What the fuck you talkin' 'bout?" Cap replied as he put his weapon in the back waistband of his jeans. "Antifa. Shit. Right-wingers are rottin' your brain. You need to stop listening to those crazy talk radio motherfuckas. Antifa, my ass. C'mon. Let's just get this shit done."

"You got the money?" Brick asked.

"Yeah. It's all there. One point two mill in rolls. Plus, I got some size nines for ya to take back," he volunteered, referring to the .9mm pistols.

The driver opened the topper. "Here's your delivery. Lotta pills this time."

"We can process that, bro. Got a nice setup in the basement of this stash house," he said before shouting, "J.R., get out here!"

"*Un momento, Capitán,*" a voice called from inside.

"Now!"

The sound of a man running up the stairs grew louder. A thin man with an N95 mask down around his neck appeared. His parents named him José Rodrigo. But in St. Louis, folks just called him J.R. "*Qué?*"

"We got some unloading to do before you get back to

batchin'," said his boss, pointing to the back of the truck.

J.R. walked back, opened the tailgate, and grabbed the bags with each hand. The missing ring finger on his left hand didn't slow him down.

The trucker walked over to the boxes stacked along the wall and opened a lid, thumbing through the rolls.

"Better all be here," Brick said. "I don't want to end up like your amigo there."

Cap shook his head. "El Duro don't play when it comes to cash. Losing a finger ain't for skimming. Steal money, and he'll relieve your neck of the work holding up your head. Naw, man, fingers is just for being stupid, not doing what the cartel tells you to do."

"Fuck me," said Brick as he stroked his beard.

"No shit. Dumb motherfucka wanted to pick cotton and shit down in the Bootheel. Can you believe that? I mean, who wants to pick cotton?" Cap shook his head. "You know the crazy thing, though? You'd think a nine-fingered dude would be slow at mashing up H and fent. But he's fast."

Brick laughed. "Guess those cartel dudes know how to motivate."

J.R. ignored the two men even as they talked about

him. He'd mastered the art of pretending not to understand. It made his life as a drug slave easier. To be sure, he never intended to be another human trafficking statistic. In fact, he had tried to do the opposite. But he looked to the wrong men to help him, help his family. Now those men owned him. And his wife. And his daughter.

Brick threw a blanket over the top of the boxes. Then he stacked a load of firewood in his cab over the top. "I best be on my way."

J.R. disappeared into the house. Cap went over to the opener mounted on the wall. Before Brick shut his door, Cap added, "Next time, leave your Proud Boy ride out in the country."

Brick shook his head and smiled. Next time, he'd bring the truck and add another bumper sticker or two.

Brick groaned when his radio connection faded out. It always happened when the show was getting interesting. With his thumb, he tapped the station presets on the steering wheel, switching seamlessly from a St. Louis–based broadcast to the same program airing out of Rolla.

But somehow, he was still in that part of Missouri where neither station's signal was steady.

He was making good time as he drove back to Lebanon. He was always happy to leave the city. Too many freaks packed together in one place.

The monologue returned as the radio host railed against men who looked like women and women who looked like men. They were corrupting the li'l children, that was for sure. Like a Jägerbomb straight to his brain, the rants fueled Brick's rage. His nostrils flared, and his lips sneered. He shook his head at the mention of enemies from within and nodded in agreement when he heard the call for patriots to take back their country by any means necessary. The reckoning was coming. He'd be ready when he was called.

But today, he had more immediate concerns. There was, of course, the 1.2 million dollars in his cab. There was also the asshole driving the red Taurus that cut in front of him.

Brick tapped his brakes to turn off his cruise control as the Taurus with peeling paint and a dinged bumper slowed in front of his truck as they traveled down the interstate. This was his third highway waltz with that

Taurus. The driver seemed incapable of setting a consistent speed. One moment, the Taurus was speeding past Brick in the passing lane. Once clear of Brick's truck, the sedan would change lanes again, so he was in the lead. Then it would start slowing down, forcing Brick to move into the passing lane. But once clear of the Taurus and back into the regular cruising lane, the annoying car would appear again in the passing lane.

Brick snapped.

"Goddamn it," he muttered. He stomped on the accelerator, the speedometer registering ninety as his truck passed the sedan. As he flew by, Brick raised the middle finger on his right hand and mouthed "fucker" at the driver. He didn't let up on the gas pedal until he'd put a few miles between his beautiful truck and the beater.

Of course, he fantasized about cutting the guy off, forcing the Taurus into the ditch, yanking open the driver's side door, and then pistol-whipping the dipshit. But Brick was a drug money mule hauling cash that belonged to a cartel. Road rage wasn't the best choice when running an errand for El Duro. And with all the cell phone cameras, someone would get a picture of him, his truck. He'd get arrested. If the cash he was carrying was discovered, he'd go to jail, then maybe prison.

It wasn't being locked up that had him worried. It was the fact that the cartel would get to him behind bars and punish him for his crime of passion. And Brick knew that punishment would pale compared to what the nine-fingered dude cutting drugs in a Spanish Lake basement had suffered.

No, it was better to focus his attention on the task at hand, moving money back to Lebanon. Brick and his gang made the drive between St. Louis and Lebanon three or four times a week, several million dollars' worth of cash and drugs. His cut wasn't enough to buy a mansion in St. Louis—though it would make for a sweet setup in the country.

Whether it had all come from St. Louis sales, he didn't know, nor did he care. St. Louis, the Gateway to the West, was once the jumping-off spot for pioneers. Now it was one of the gateways to the southern border.

He was compensated handsomely for his trouble. A driver would get a couple thousand bucks for a round trip. Five hours of driving worked out to four hundred dollars an hour, tax-free. And because he was the leader, Brick got a taste of the action whether he drove or not.

The leader of the pack always eats first. That was the law of nature.

But even he knew his days working for the cartel might be numbered. Drug busts and Bitcoin were his biggest worries. Of the two, cryptocurrency had him the most anxious. He readily admitted that he didn't fully understand it. However, he'd heard enough about crypto to guess the benefits for *Dardos Venenosos*, the cartel headed by El Duro that he served. Bitcoin was a nearly untraceable way for the cartel to launder and move money. That made it safer. Now that the Chinese had jumped into crypto laundering, they became an increasingly important partner for the Mexican cartel. With cryptocurrency, the cartel could move more money than the network of biker gangs and over-the-road truckers could manage. It was only a matter of time before some nerdy foreigner sitting behind a computer screen would take his livelihood

Again.

But, at least for now, bagmen were still needed. Perhaps, Brick told himself, they'd always be required. Sure, El Duro was a ruthless murderer. He was also a businessman. And like any savvy investor, putting all your money in one stock—or one laundering method—wasn't the safest approach. Plus, someone still had to move the drugs around the country. It didn't make sense to deliver a product and then have the courier leave empty-handed.

The closing music played over the talk radio host's sign-off. Perfect timing. Brick was nearing his favorite roadside McDonald's. He made a point of stopping at the fast food restaurant on his way back. Indeed, he believed it was a good luck pit stop. He could take a piss in peace. Then he'd put in his favorite to-go order: Two big Macs and a large chocolate shake. Even though he liked French fries, he skipped them. Greasy fingers meant a slippery steering wheel. He loved his truck too much to disrespect it that way.

Brick turned on his right blinker to signal he was getting off at the exit ramp. He didn't need to give a cop a flimsy excuse to pull him over. He glanced into the rearview mirror to ensure no one was coming up on his tail too fast. He watched as the Taurus continued down the highway.

"Dick," Brick muttered as he slowed his truck to stop at the light at the end of the ramp. At least he knew the guy wasn't the law. Brick would've been stopped for speeding, going twenty miles over the speed limit. Plus, no cop would be caught dead in such a shitty car.

The McDonald's was just off to the right, a standalone building with a drive-thru that shared an expansive parking lot with a gas station.

Brick guided his black truck into the parking lot, selecting a spot that allowed him to keep a close eye on his vehicle. It wasn't all that necessary to be so cautious. The bumper stickers on the back of his truck made clear that he was a man who would stand his ground. That and the Bersa Thunder 380 tucked into his waistband.

Brick turned off the radio before he cut the ignition on his car. It was a habit he'd been taught by his dad when he first learned to drive.

"Take care of your battery, boy! Dumb as a brick," his dad had yelled when his son forgot to switch off the radio after a driving lesson. Almost all his childhood, his dad had thrown the epithet at him. So much so that it stuck. The putdown was accompanied by a sharp slap to the back of the boy's head. "I ain't made of money. And judging by your grades, you ain't gonna be either."

His dad had been decaying in the ground going on thirty years now, lung cancer having gotten him just shy of his fiftieth birthday. His illness lasted a little over a year. Brick's father had gone from a frightening man to a pathetic husk of a human. Brick vowed he'd never go out like his dad. He'd put a bullet in his head before he relied on others to keep him alive.

Brick had few regrets. The biggest was that he would never be able to show his father how wrong he'd been. Brick had more money and more respect than his dad ever did, a worthless old man who worked odd jobs and drank away every tiny paycheck.

Brick opened the door to his truck and climbed out of the cab. As he shut the door, three black SUVs pulled behind his truck, blocking any chance he might've had to back out.

Brick's chest tightened. He could hear his heart beating in his ears. His thumb twitched momentarily, getting ready to grasp the gun hidden under his coat.

But in a reflexive move of self-preservation, the rest of his arm wouldn't cooperate with the thumb's urge. Instead, his legs made the decision to run in the opposite direction.

Brick turned to dart away from the cars that had blocked his truck from the back. He found himself staring at a wall of cops clad in dark raid jackets, their guns drawn. They hadn't been there moments before.

"Police! Hands up!"

Brick raised his arms in the air. He could hear footsteps coming from behind.

"Come forward, away from the cars. Slowly."

Brick took a step forward, his arms faltering.

"Hands up!"

He reached higher in the air.

"Down on the ground!" a voice shouted. "Keep your hands where I can see them!"

Brick slowly descended to the cement. When he was on his belly, he lay spread-eagle. It wasn't his first time.

He felt hands patting him down. The gun was snatched out of his pants. Each arm was seized and pulled hard behind his back. The cuffs clipped.

He was pulled back to standing. As hands continued to pat him down, Brick was able to look beyond the line of cops aiming their guns at him.

The red Ford Taurus was just beyond them. A man, leaning against the beat-up car, walked forward and began speaking. "You have the right to remain silent. Anything you say can and will be used against you in a court of law.

You have a right to an attorney. If you cannot afford an attorney, one will be appointed for you."

"Says who?" Brick growled.

"Says Detective Daniel Flannery."

7 PATHS TAKEN

Once again, Debbie was at war with herself. Sitting in her car, parked in the back of a suburban West St. Louis County funeral home, she pondered her next steps. The refrain from one of her father's favorite songs from The Clash played on repeat inside her head: Should I stay or should I go?

She'd parked as far away as possible from the white-columned, red-brick building entrance. After all, the best spy was the one that went unseen.

Debbie jotted down the names of those she recognized getting out of their BMWs, Mercedes, Teslas, and Hummers. Although there were two visitations scheduled simultaneously, she figured she could circle back to figure out if they had any connection with the Webbs. Digital trails left by social media accounts made it easier to uncover relationships and reconstruct a day's activities. And old posts and photos that were either publicly available or open to friends of friends could reveal the invisible web of connections between people. For a journalist, a private detective, a cop, or a scammer, digital breadcrumbs were the modern equivalent of stumbling across a trove of handwritten letters or an unlocked diary left open on a bedside table.

Caleb's parents were well-respected and well-connected. Therefore, Debbie reasoned, it was likely that the people who clamored to be memorialized on the society pages of *River City* magazine would also attend the visitation. Today's guests wore muted, yet still elegant, attire. Dark suits with crisp button-down shirts and silk ties for the men. For the women, not-too-revealing designer dresses paired with a strand of pearls or a diamond tennis bracelet. French manicures or light pink nail polish for the matrons, black nail polish for the younger, edgier attendees.

No one expected the media to cover the visitation; that would be too crass. But many attendees couldn't resist the impulse to use dress to impress others who happened to stop by and pay their respects.

Debbie figured her chance of being recognized was slim. As the crime beat reporter, it wasn't likely that the people streaming into the funeral home followed her byline closely. The wake attendees belonged to the group of readers who liked to look at the photo spreads of charity events—and the local glitterati who attended. Debbie's fan club included those who unrolled yellow caution tape at crime scenes or watched *The Sopranos*, *Breaking Bad*, and *Goodfellas*.

The reporter pulled down the visor over the steering wheel and checked her hair one last time. She'd skipped her usual ponytail-and-glasses look, even though she was most comfortable with her hair pulled back and frames on her face. She never did get used to contacts, no matter how many times she tried as a teenager and college student to ditch the nerd-girl style. Even now, as she gave herself a final inspection, Debbie had to fight the urge to scratch the contacts covering her eyeballs with her fingernails.

And her hair? It already felt like a tangled mess. Plus, when it was down, she was more likely to fiddle with it, a bad habit that she'd never really managed to break. Cutting it all off was still on the table. But she hadn't taken the plunge and embraced a sensible 'do. She wasn't ready to morph into her mom—not yet.

Debbie applied the barest hint of color to her lips and then popped them for an even hue. She checked her dress, which she'd raided from her mother's closet. Beth had an endless supply of clothing appropriate for any somber, elegant, or fancy affair. Her daughter, even in her late twenties, did not. The few pieces that might pass muster were in a pile on the floor of her closet waiting to be taken to the dry cleaner.

Debbie inhaled deeply, then opened the car door. You didn't assemble a kick-ass story by asking permission to proceed.

"You can't be here," a man said, his hushed voice hissing with anger. The speaker was behind Debbie. She summoned an apologetic look and turned to face him. That's when she realized he wasn't talking to her.

She recognized the man. It was Caleb's twin, Connor. His quiet fury was directed toward a young man and woman who'd entered the funeral home just after Debbie.

As best as the reporter could tell, the woman was close to Connor's age; her long dark hair had a streak of blue that framed her face, dark shadows circled around her red-rimmed eyes, and her puffy lips were pale pink. There was a disturbing beauty about the woman, something forlorn. If she were depicted in a painting, the background color for the portrait would've been black. She was clad in a long-sleeved navy cashmere sweater dress paired with knee-high boots. The material was meant to flatter feminine curves, but it was loose, hanging on her body like a stretched-out sweater that had been run through a dryer too often.

The man, also around the same age, had close-cropped dark blond hair that looked like he had taken an electric razor into his own hands. He was wearing charcoal-colored dress pants with hems that scraped the floor and a shirt with cuffs that slipped down to his knuckles.

"C'mon, Connor," the young woman pleaded. "We're Caleb's best friends."

"You're the reason he's dead," Connor snapped. "If my parents see you, they'll lose their shit. They're already near the end of their rope. But seeing you," his voice trailed off, "well, it will make this nightmare even worse—if that's possible. I can't believe you had the nerve to show your faces."

"Don't be a dick," the guy in the ill-fitting trousers said. "Macie tried to save Caleb's life."

Connor shook his head and snorted. "Yeah, right. And here we are."

"You've always been an asshole, Connor," Macie said. "You should look in the mirror instead of blaming us."

"What's that supposed to mean?"

"You know what it means. You might be able to fool everyone else, but you can't fool me," Macie said before turning to her companion. "C'mon, Alex. Let's get outta here."

Debbie watched as the pair turned around and headed toward the exit. Then she glanced at Connor. He shoved his trembling left hand into the pocket of his suit pants and steadied his right by checking the button on the front of his suit coat. The self-soothing gestures took only a second or two. Just enough time to regain his composure before another group of individuals expressed condolences.

Rather than remain, Debbie slipped out the door. The wake would continue, but it was clear that Macie and Alex were leaving.

Even though her boots had heels, Macie was crossing the parking lot quickly. Her companion was having difficulty keeping up, the cuffs of his pants scraping the cement as he walked briskly across the lot. "Macie, slow down," he pleaded, trying to avoid shouting and attracting even more attention to their humiliation.

Debbie followed about fifty feet behind Alex, acting as if she was looking for a car that she couldn't remember where it was parked.

Macie abruptly stopped next to an orange Mustang with a black convertible top. Debbie guessed that the sports car couldn't have been more than a year or two old. Debbie stopped next to a vehicle and opened her purse, pretending to search for her keys, occasionally looking up.

Macie reached for the handle. But before she could open the door, her shoulders dropped. Her companion, having finally caught up to her, reached his hand out and rested it on her shoulder. When she turned toward him, Debbie saw the mascara smudged under her eyes. She pressed her face into his chest and let out a sob.

"Caleb knew how you felt about him. There's nothing

in that funeral home but an empty husk. That's not him," Alex said as he opened the driver's side door and guided his friend in. Once both her legs were inside, he shut the door and walked to the passenger side.

Debbie looked at the license plate, pulled the notebook out of her purse, and jotted the information down before it could slip away.

"Macie Holloway," Debbie heard a voice next to her say.

The reporter had watched the exchange between Macie and Alex so carefully that she didn't notice Dee Laclede standing beside her.

Debbie met Dee several months earlier at a gala fundraiser for Teen Alliance. The nonprofit gave preteens and teens a safe place to gather, learn, and have fun after school and during the summer. Dee had been on the board of directors and played an outsized role in guiding a gifted teen to an academic scholarship. Debbie was now one of Dee's biggest fans, even if the woman didn't know it. And yes, Dee also happened to be Chase's mom.

"You know her?" Debbie asked.

"Yes," Dee said, a trace of sadness lingering in the air around the one-word answer. Dee's eyes and lips briefly drooped before she spoke again. "I remember her as a little girl. Her dad is our accountant. Macie was a clever child with a sharp tongue and an iron will. I thought she'd make a good lawyer, but her true interests were math and science. She was off to a promising start." Dee's voice trailed off, and she sighed. "Heroin got in the way. I don't know the gentleman she's with. But yes, I know Macie. Always so hard to see young people self-destruct. Such a bright mind clouded by drugs. It makes my heart hurt."

Debbie said, "You here for Caleb's wake?"

Dee nodded and sighed. "Rich. Poor. It doesn't matter. Addiction doesn't care about income levels."

"You knew Caleb?"

"I remember watching Caleb and Connor play hockey when Chase was a boy. The Webb twins were a few years younger than my Chase, but you know how it is; you keep crossing paths with the same families when your kids are interested in the same sports. Spend enough time sitting on cold bleachers in ice skating rinks, and you get to know the other hockey parents."

"I see," Debbie said. "So Chase. I suppose he's here, too?"

"Chase and Dan already went in. I just wanted to say

hello. It is always nice seeing you. And frankly, I could use a happy encounter before wading into the heartbreak."

"I guess Chase didn't feel the same," Debbie said, instantly regretting her moment of vulnerability.

Dee gave Debbie a faint smile and placed one hand lightly on Debbie's arm. "Never mind him. My son," Dee said before pausing, "well, he's got his father's foolish male pride." Dee opened her mouth, closed it, then opened it again. "May I give you a bit of advice?"

Debbie nodded.

"You just do you, Debbie Bradley. If you're here, there's probably a story that needs to be told. Right now, focus on that and forget about Chase."

8 PAST OR PRESENT?

"Mace, I know your secret. Mace!" Caleb said, shaking Macie's wrist. "Mace. Wake up! I said I know your secret."

Macie opened her eyes. Her bedroom was dark and empty. The smartwatch alarm on her wrist was vibrating. She tapped it and waited for the tears to flow again, only none came. But her grief was still there, trapping her in a dark, deep well of sadness. She was a bleak soul suspended in a black abyss.

She felt isolated and alone—even if she wasn't.

Macie lay in bed and stared at the ceiling. Suddenly and reflexively, she threw off the comforter and rushed to the toilet. She clutched the seat with one hand and held her hair back with another just before the retching began.

"Oh, Mace. Shhh. They're going to hear you," Macie

heard Caleb say, even though it was a memory from long ago when they were twelve. He'd held her hair back as she threw up in the basement bathroom of her childhood home.

That time, long ago, it was the day after her parents' annual pre-Christmas bash thrown for friends and her father's clients. The party was always a swanky, catered affair with plenty of booze, tiny hors d'oeuvres on silver trays, and a dining room table covered with stainless steel chafers. At the end of the gathering, Macie's mother instructed the caterers to store the leftover food in the basement refrigerator. "I don't want it smelling up our kitchen fridge," she explained before rushing to kiss the last guest goodbye. In addition to the food, the catering staff bussed the remaining wine bottles to the basement, as well as the opened and half-consumed bottles of vodka, rum, scotch, and whiskey.

Ordinarily, Macie's parents kept track of the alcohol in their home. They were dedicated to ensuring nothing got in the way of her destiny as their perfect daughter. But parties were the exception. Her parents were more concerned with impressing their friends and cementing the loyalty of their clients than policing Macie.

The day after, her parents remained in their darkened bedroom nursing hangovers even if Macie's mom insisted, "We're just tired from last night." Macie's parents expected her to keep quiet and stay out of sight. The only problem was that there was nothing to do. A restless Macie irritated her mother. It was that irritation that Macie leveraged in her lobbying effort to have Connor and Caleb over to the house.

"I promise we'll play video games in the basement. We'll keep the door shut. There's food from last night we can eat if we're hungry. We won't make a mess. There are lots of paper plates. Mrs. Webb will drop them off and pick them up, so you don't have to do a thing. You won't hear a peep," Macie had promised. Relieved at the prospect of having her daughter entertained and too weak to argue because of her headache, her mother simply mumbled from her darkened bedroom, "Fine."

But as any enterprising twelve-year-old will tell you, it is possible to keep a promise and still break the rules.

The three friends started with video games after shutting the basement door. But the afternoon took a turn when Connor spotted the open bottles of alcohol next to the refrigerator. He zeroed in on the vodka.

"Ooh, ooh, what do we have here? You know I heard vodka doesn't stink up your breath," Connor said as he opened the bottle, took a sip, and passed it to Caleb.

Caleb looked at the bottle and lifted it to his lips, but, Macie suspected, he didn't actually drink before handing it to her. The girl, accepting the implicit dare, wiped the mouth of the bottle off with her hand and took a long gulp. She wouldn't let the Webb boys beat her in a drinking game.

So the rounds began. Macie swigged while Connor sipped, and Caleb pretended. Macie was the one to get sick, barely making it to the bathroom before she started throwing up. Caleb had rushed in behind her to help. Connor only laughed.

Even now, years later, Macie could still hear Connor's sadistic laugh.

Caleb, on the other hand, had a laugh she thought of as more sardonic, especially when they played the butt-dial challenge. It started by accident. They'd been teenagers. She'd accidentally butt-dialed Caleb while her dad was yelling at her. They spent hours imitating her father based on that one unintended phone call. After that, they'd perfected the art of secretly dialing one another when they were getting reamed out by a parent. All it took were two well-placed taps. It had become a contest on two levels. Who could be the sneakiest when it came to dialing and who got the worst tongue-lashing. But now was not the time for games.

I'm losing my mind, Macie thought as she emptied the last of what little was in her stomach. The past and the present seemed to be collapsing into one another. Her memories were her reality. Her reality was a nightmare. Grief and guilt were so powerful that they bent time.

Macie spat into the toilet and stood up. She wanted Caleb to be standing behind her. She wanted to see the hint of concern around the corners of his eyes.

When they were twelve, Caleb urged Macie to brush her teeth and rinse her mouth with mouthwash. "Just avoid your parents. They're too out of it today to notice you. Use that to your advantage. Just steer clear of them, and they'll never suspect a thing."

The grown-up Macie looked into the mirror above the bathroom vanity and whispered to the boy who wasn't there: "Fine. And by the way, fuck you."

If she didn't get a move on, she'd be late for work. Her father would be waiting. And the last thing she wanted was to encounter him.

Macie's Mustang weaved in and out of traffic on the interstate. She was fifteen minutes from work and already ten minutes late.

"Jesus Christ, do you have to drive so fast?" Another memory of Caleb from the past had pierced the present. He clutched the passenger door armrest with one hand while the other was on the dashboard. After all, he had said it once. When she'd picked him up just after her parents had given her the Mustang.

"Sorry," Macie said to her ghost passenger. "I forgot about your PTSD. That car accident and all."

"I don't have PTSD," Caleb answered defensively. "It's just that you make me anxious. So your parents get you out of criminal charges for stealing chemicals from your company. Then they give you a car? That's fucked up."

"I'm not sure if my parents were more worried about me going to jail or having me tarnish their reputations," Macie said. "The car was my reward for being a good girl and going to rehab. And here's the kicker."

"There's more?" Caleb said.

Macie nodded. "They said if I stayed clean another sixty days and pass a piss test, they'd get me in an apartment."

"Parents. No wonder we're so fucked up."

"Oh, one more condition they dropped on me. I gotta go work for my dad. That way, they can keep an eye on me and pretend to their friends that their daughter is doing well. You know the speech. Got her own apartment. Working hard. Hit a rough patch, but now she's on the right path. Blah, blah, blah."

"You'd think we were fuckin' racehorses or something. The lengths they'll go to to save face in the who-has-the-most-accomplished-kid competition with their friends."

"At least your parents have Connor to brag about," Macie had said. "Since I'm an only, I get all the pressure."

Macie glanced over to the empty seat next to her. Connor was an only child now, too.

Macie veered off the highway and onto the exit ramp, accelerating rather than slowing, hoping to make the green light before it changed. She turned right onto Lindbergh, her tires squealing as she rounded the corner.

Macie sped through an orange light and made it to the parking lot of her dad's accounting firm. Once again, she turned fast, barely missing a car exiting.

Macie parked and reached for the earbuds in the console, popping them in and hitting play on her phone. The song that had been on repeat ever since Caleb died was ready to go.

Tuning people out was easier with music.

Macie had just slammed her door and started walking to the front door when she felt a tap on her shoulder. Startled, she turned to see a woman with a ponytail and glasses.

"Excuse me," she heard the woman say loudly over Lana Del Rey's "Video Games."

Shit. I don't have time for this, Macie thought.

9 UP THE ANTE

"Excuse me," Debbie said to Macie, who was climbing out of her Mustang.

The car was hard to miss, and the woman was easy to recognize. Debbie had spent several hours the prior evening stalking Macie on social media. From the online fragments, Debbie stitched together bits of Macie's life. All the while, Dee Laclede's words kept rattling in her head: *She was off to such a promising start.*

Debbie began her research with the lamest social media site, Facebook. Macie would be young enough to declare her disdain for it yet old enough to have created a profile when she was ten, eleven, or twelve. Whatever her age, she would've lied and claimed to be thirteen when she signed up. Fear of missing out was too intense to keep away.

There were two profiles tied to St. Louis. In one Macie appeared to be in her mid-thirties and had red hair. The other featured a picture of a couple of awkward young teens smirking at the camera as if they shared a joke no one else would get. Macie and Caleb, Debbie guessed, although she couldn't rule out Connor. That was the problem with twins. The pair stood on a bluff with a river and meadow in the background. To Debbie, it looked like the young teens were in Castlewood, a popular state park in St. Louis County nestled along the Meramec River, with hiking and biking trails.

Debbie took a screenshot of the image, saved it to a folder she'd started for the story, then made a mental note to ask Macie about it if she ever tracked her down. Of course, the time had to be right. And Debbie would have to earn her trust first.

Debbie shared several connections with Macie. St. Louis was, after all, a big small town. And Macie had left her social media settings on friends-of-friends. It was probably an oversight from her teens when she tried expanding her popularity circle, pulling people in rather than culling them out.

There was a high school graduation photo of Macie.

She'd been the valedictorian of her high school class, a co-ed private high school whose annual tuition cost as much as a new car. In the picture, the young woman beamed. Her face was rounder, her cheeks plumper. Her eyes were bright, and her hair was so thick that Debbie wondered how much the tresses weighed when wet. It was a version of Macie that was both beautiful and hopeful. The gaunt and haunted woman Debbie had seen had not yet taken over Macie's life.

Debbie continued scrolling through the photos before pausing on a picture of Macie. Debbie guessed she had been thirteen or fourteen. She was standing in between Caleb and Connor. All three smiled for the camera, although Macie's grin was more mischievous. Unbeknownst to the twins, she had used her hands to create rabbit ears behind each of their heads. Debbie added another screenshot to her small but growing collection of Macies.

She opened a new tab on her browser for Instagram. Once again, she searched for Macie Holloway. She found the account. The profile picture was more recent, resembling the woman at the funeral home. However, it was private. Despite that, Debbie could still search for connections she had in common with Macie. One of the names that popped up was a high school classmate of Debbie's. They'd lost touch, and the last rumor Debbie heard was that her former classmate had been in and out of rehab.

Debbie briefly considered sending a connection request to Macie, betting that the Instagram account had more incriminating images than Facebook. But was it ethical? If Macie's Instagram account was public, Debbie would have no qualms reviewing it. After all, Macie had no reasonable expectation of privacy if she'd made it public. But asking for permission to connect to access the private posts without revealing the reason why seemed a bit too sneaky, even for Debbie.

She shelved the idea.

LinkedIn was next on her list. Sure enough, Macie had a profile. Again, it was expected. Every college encourages juniors and seniors to set up a professional profile. Holloway CPAs and Advisors was listed as her current employer, even though she had a degree in chemistry. Her profile didn't identify her job role at the family firm. As for prior work history, it listed a multinational chemical company. Debbie wondered if the young woman had a change of heart and decided to pursue a certified public accountant license or if something else was behind her job hop. Regardless, there was a good chance that Macie was still working for her dad. That was the best place for Debbie to approach her.

Debbie staked out Holloway CPAs and Advisors at seven thirty the following day. After all, the early bird lands the interview. After waiting an hour and a half in her cold car, Debbie was about to call it quits. That's when she caught sight of the orange Mustang tearing into the parking lot. Once Macie hopped out of her car, wearing a thick, puffy, dark blue coat, her hair pulled back into a messy ponytail, and sunglasses on her face, Debbie approached.

"Yes?" Macie replied.

"I know this is sudden," Debbie began slowly, "but I was hoping to talk to you about Caleb."

Macie's lips turned down, and her shoulders drooped a bit. She shook her head. "Who are you?"

"Debbie Bradley. I'm a writer. For *River City* magazine."

"I don't want to talk about Caleb. And I don't know why I'd want to talk to a writer."

"Please, we could just talk. Off the record."

"I'm late for work," Macie said as she turned to walk toward her workplace. As if on cue, her cell phone rang. "Shit, that's probably my dad's office assistant." Macie hit mute. Before she could speak, Debbie interrupted.

"Look, I know you've got to get to work. I don't want to hurt you. And I'm not here to blame Caleb. I just want to understand."

"What is there to understand? I don't even understand. And in case you hadn't heard, I killed Caleb."

"I doubt it's that simple," Debbie said. "And if that was true, we wouldn't be standing together. You'd be in jail somewhere. I gather that Caleb was a heroin addict who'd just gotten out of rehab. He was standing at the most deadly crossroads—between addiction and recovery."

Macie's phone rang again.

"I tell you what. I'll be at that Starbucks at five thirty," Debbie said, pointing to the coffee shop nearby. "I'll buy you coffee, tea, or whatever you want. I promise that I'm a good listener. Who knows, you might feel better talking. Completely off the record. What do you have to lose?"

Sam rapped on the door frame leading into Debbie's office. She'd negotiated the walls, window, and door when she agreed to stay at the magazine. Sam didn't know why it had been so important. After all, she was rarely in the space.

"What's up?" Debbie asked.

"That's my question," Sam said. "Is Caleb Webb a story?"

Debbie exhaled. "I don't know."

"What do you mean you don't know?"

"I mean, I don't know," Debbie answered irritably.

Sam frowned. He understood that sometimes writers needed space to explore a story idea. But they could also find themselves trapped by the cost of time spent sunk into pursuing something that would never work. A good editor knew when to tell reporters to break up with a lousy story.

"Why don't you elaborate?"

Debbie cleared her throat. "Well, I've got some possible leads. I just don't have anything firm yet."

"Go on."

"There's a friend of Caleb's. I think she was there the

night he died. I saw her at the wake. I caught up with her this morning as she headed to work. We didn't get time to talk, but I asked her to meet me for coffee at five thirty today."

"She agree?"

"Not exactly."

"I see," Sam said, frowning again.

"But she didn't say no."

"I shouldn't have to remind you that magazine pages don't get filled with wishes, hopes, and fairy dust. Words on a page, Debbie Bradley. Words on a page."

"I know, I know. Look, if the Caleb angle falls through, how about just a general story on the drug problem in St. Louis? Sort of a heroin-goes-high-class or fent-in-the-burbs piece?"

Sam stroked his chin as he leaned against the door frame. "Perhaps. We got a tip about a federal task force drug bust outside Rolla. A ring operating in St. Louis. Guess it was one of those partnerships between the feds and local law enforcement. Anyway, they were moving fent, heroin, all that, for the cartel. According to my source, your buddy Flannery is one of the local guys on the task force."

"Interesting," Debbie said. "There's gotta be an indictment I can dig up."

"Yeah, and I'm surprised I haven't seen a news release. These guys hide from the press until it's time to peacock after a big bust."

"I'll see what I can find out this afternoon before I meet with Macie."

"What are the odds she'll show?"

"Fifty percent?"

"Make it ten."

"Always the optimist." Debbie paused. "I have one other suggestion to push this story forward."

Sam pursed his lips.

"I know you warned me to be careful with Caleb's parents. Let me contact them. See if they'll talk."

Sam shook his head. "Not yet."

"What happened to words on a page, fairy dust and all that?"

"If that gal meets you tonight, I'll contact Radcliffe. Maybe he can put in a good word with the Webbs."

"Keep an eye on your phone," Debbie said. "I'll text you as soon as I'm done meeting Macie."

"If you meet with Macie, you mean."

10 SANTA MUERTE

The top of the outdoor shrine was level with El Duro's knees. The base rested on the dusty ground. The back leaned against the cinder block walls of a building with only four charred wooden beams for a roof that kept out neither rain nor the midday sun.

The shrine was dominated by a statue nestled inside the makeshift altar. It bore some dark similarities to the Virgin Mary. But rather than the pink cheeks, sad eyes, and perfect lips of the mother of Jesus, the icon's face was a bleached skull with black holes. Her empty gaze fixed slightly downward. Instead of fleshy youthful hands, the figure's naked slender bones were clasped in silent prayer. The idol was adorned with a green veil covered in tiny yellow stars and lined with gold piping that covered the hairless head and cascaded down around the figure.

She was draped in a red dress, and folds in the robe hinted at a bent right knee. The figure stood on a pillow with the horns of a bull on either side. Under her feet, a skull and orange flowers. Golden tendrils like the tentacles of a sea anemone or severed fingers surrounded the figure, forming a macabre halo.

Santa Muerte: The Saint of Death.

Around the statue were the remnants of offerings: Cuban cigars, skull-shaped sugar candies, an unfinished bottle of tequila. Condemned by the Vatican as blasphemous, Santa Muerte was believed to have originally been Mictecacihuatl, the Aztec goddess of the afterlife, death, and rebirth. But now, she was the patron saint of drug traffickers, prison gangs, and peasants scratching out a living from the earth while the cartel's guns fired over their heads.

"Tontos supersticiosos," El Duro muttered as he passed the shrine and entered the roofless building. Death would come for them all. It couldn't be bribed with cigars and tequila. Rosaries and candles wouldn't stop it.

El Duro, a fit man in his early forties with silver streaks in his dark, wavy, close-cropped hair, a trim goatee, and a scar above his eyebrow, didn't count himself among the saint's believers. To be sure, it wasn't due to fealty to the Catholic Church. That faith was part of his cultural heritage, nothing more. Long ago, he'd concluded that religion was just another man-made creation designed to consolidate power over others. As El Duro saw it, there were rulers and followers, and he'd bow down to no man or woman, even if they claimed to have some secret channel to the divine.

El Duro removed his sunglasses as he entered the building on a ranch a few hundred miles from the U.S. border. It had become the temporary training area for the paramilitary force that served *Dardos Venenosos*, El Duro's cartel. The owner had been unhappy about the arrangement. Still, he accepted money for the hassle rather than a bullet for refusal. It was the most rational choice. *Balas o dinero.*

Inside the four gray walls were three men, all seated on the cracked concrete floor, blindfolded, hands fastened behind their backs with zip ties. Two of them had blood dripping from the corner of their mouths. One had a gash on the side of his temple, where a red stream had dried on his face.

"So these are the ones who wouldn't cooperate," El

Duro said.

A man with an AK-47 slung over his back who hadn't shaved for several days replied, *"Sí, jefe."*

El Duro frowned. "Take off the blindfolds."

The man with the machine gun nodded. He lifted his right hand to his lips, removed the cigarette dangling in the corner of his mouth, threw it to the ground, then rubbed it out with the ball of his boot-covered foot. He stepped forward and yanked down the covering over each man's eyes. The prisoners blinked, then, as they grew accustomed to the sunlight, their eyes widened when they recognized the visitor. Each man shrank back reflexively.

El Duro paced in front of the men. "Such a pity that we couldn't be friends. I tried. You have to know that I tried."

The captives said nothing.

"We could've all just gotten along. All you had to do was ignore the Guatemalans crossing the border. We certainly offered you money for your trouble. *Idiotas.*"

"Duro, mi familia," the man with the gaping head wound started. "I have four children."

"You should've thought of them when we gave you a chance."

"But Mexico City. They're coming down hard on us. We've been told we have to stop the migrants before they get into the U.S. To keep *El Naranja* happy."

"I don't care about Mexico City. I don't care about the gringos. All I care about is business. If something's bad for my business, it's gonna be bad for everyone. But when business is good, we all win," El Duro said. "You, *mi amigos*, are my problem. All three of you. You should've been helpful. But you weren't. I'm the one who gives people problems. People don't give them to me."

A man with blood at the corner of his lips mumbled a prayer as tears streaked his cheek.

El Duro stepped forward and placed his hand on the man's head. "Shhhh. God abandoned you. God abandoned all of us a long time ago."

El Duro glanced at the man clutching the assault rifle. "Take care of them." He paused momentarily, then added, "We're moving to a new location."

"*Sí, jefe*," the man said.

El Duro glanced at Santa Muerte's altar as he left the building. A new offering had appeared while he was inside: a badge inscribed with the word *policía*.

He looked up as Kiko approached. Francisco "Kiko"

Pérez was El Duro's oldest friend and ally.

"Get rid of that," El Duro said, pointing to the shrine. "And make sure that badge is never found. Make it disappear like the guy who owned it. We need to pack up today. We're getting out. Word's come down that *federales* and the Americans are getting ready to attack. My source tells me to expect an ambush on the ranch in two days. We need to vanish. Today."

The man nodded just as the crack of the AK-47 erupted. After only a few seconds, the assault rifle fell silent.

"I want you to torch the whole place."

"All of it?"

"Yes. And give the old man some more money," El Duro said, referring to the owner. "He can rebuild this shithole. Plus, construction will give people around here jobs."

Kiko nodded.

El Duro looked toward the small runway carved into the land. "After I take off, destroy the landing strip. In a few hours, we'll be in touch to tell you where you're headed."

"We'll be ready."

El Duro climbed aboard the Hawker 800 twin-engine business jet he'd named *Halcón*. The aircraft had been purchased in 2013 from a Venezuelan company that went belly up due to that country's economic crisis. Panamanian lawyers for the cartel created a shell company to buy the jet. Once it was part of the DV assets, it had flown unquestioned and untouched throughout South America, Central America, and even North America. And the generous bribes paid to officials who could've questioned the airplane's ownership ensured no one was interested in trying to dig further.

In addition to flying the boss where he needed to be, it also transported grenades, rocket launchers, and assault rifles.

El Duro grabbed a chilled Negro Modelo from the plane's fridge. He opened it and settled into one of the plane's luxurious seats, awaiting takeoff.

The pilot entered the cabin. "*Perdón, señor.* I have some news."

El Duro took a drink, set the bottle down, and sighed.

"*Qué?*"

"Some of the mules in the States. They've been arrested."

"Where?"

"Missouri."

"What'd they get?"

"About a half million in cash, about three million worth of drugs, and several people were picked up."

"Fucking *pendejos*," El Duro muttered. He looked at the pilot, who stood meekly in front of him. El Duro felt the urge to shoot someone. But if he took out the pilot, he'd be stuck in this fucking place. Besides, he didn't want to put a hole in his favorite plane.

"*Tonto*, just get me back."

The pilot slipped away, releasing his breath only after closing the main cabin door, sealing himself off from his boss.

El Duro looked out the window of his small plane, watching the camp's inhabitants scurry about loading ammunition and weapons into trucks. At the same time, he listened to the engine ready for takeoff. He took another long draw of the Negro Modelo that was sweating in his hand. "Fuck."

11 CONFIDANTE

"Tall, skinny chai latte," Debbie said to the barista at the coffee shop, where she hoped Macie would eventually materialize. "Hot. Please."

When she rolled out of bed in the morning, black coffee was Debbie's beverage of choice: no cream, no sugar, no whipped topping, and definitely no syrup flavoring. It had to be bold, hot, and strong. Weak shit wouldn't do. But after eleven in the morning, a bracing cup of black coffee meant a sour stomach. And jitters.

The reporter arrived half an hour early for the maybe meeting. From what little she knew of Macie, Debbie guessed that, deep down, the young woman was a people pleaser. Macie had been a top student in high school, so validation and basking in the approval for achieving good grades must matter. Macie cared more about the Webbs than she let on. Otherwise, why bring up the fact that they thought she was a murderer? And when she was ambushed by a reporter, Macie remained cordial and polite.

There was more. Underneath the rebellious, aloof exterior, Macie seemed lonely. It was clear that Connor didn't want her around. Her parents didn't accompany her to Caleb's wake. And her closest friend, as best Debbie could tell, was dead. Heroin had made her a pariah. Caleb's death, persona non grata.

The barista called out her name. Debbie grabbed the tea and walked toward two oversized upholstered chairs with big backs and armrests near a window at the entrance. In between the chairs was a small table.

Macie wouldn't be able to miss her—if she showed. Otherwise, Debbie had less than twelve hours to pivot to a new story. At least a backup plan was starting to take shape.

Sam's tip about the drug bust turned out to be a promising lead. After some snooping, Debbie had learned that the partnership between federal and local law enforcement hadn't yielded just one raid. There were several choreographed closely together: A truck stop and motel in Lebanon, Missouri, and a sweep of a drug house in Spanish Lake.

Debbie sat down and swept crumbs off the small table. When she looked up, she could see Macie walking across the parking lot. It was ten minutes past five; Macie was early. Debbie guessed that was on purpose. If Debbie wasn't there, Macie could still say she'd shown up but also have an excuse to leave.

When Macie entered the coffee shop, Debbie raised her hand. Macie's lips turned downward in disappointment for a microsecond before her lips assumed a polite, slight smile.

"Can I get you something?" Debbie offered as Macie walked over.

"Naw, I got it," Macie answered, waving her hand as if the physical gesture erased the verbal offer. "I got so many gift cards for Christmas since my parents don't like to give me cash. I don't know why they don't realize I could just sell them. I'll just use one. Besides, I just want bottled water."

"Okay, sure," Debbie said. "Is this spot good?" she asked, gesturing to the chairs she'd preselected.

"Yeah, great. I can't stay long, though."

"No problem," Debbie chirped.

As Macie grabbed a water from the refrigerator case at the counter, Debbie pretended to look at the art on the wall, then directed her gaze out the front window. Because it was nearly dark out, Debbie could covertly study Macie's reflection in the glass.

"I've got an NA meeting at six," Macie said. "If I don't go, my parents will know. I'll be in trouble. Showing up at Narcotics Anonymous is one of their rules."

"I understand. I'll make sure you don't miss it. And thanks so much for meeting me."

"I'm not sure if I'm doing the right thing," Macie said, setting her bottled water on the table before taking off her coat. "My friend Alex told me I was stupid to talk to a reporter."

Debbie nodded. "I understand. I assure you, this is off the record. That means anything you tell me is secret and confidential. I can't use it in a story. I can't write about it."

"Why should I trust you?"

"That's a good question. I've been doing this job for a while. I've never burned a source. If I had, you'd have heard about it. I don't want to destroy my reputation for one story. Not if I want to keep working as a journalist."

Macie sighed. "I'll admit I did a little research on you."

"Some people may not like what I write, but no one has claimed I lied to them." Debbie paused. "You never know. Some people find talking to me rather cathartic. I'm a good listener."

Macie sat down in a chair, took her phone out of her coat pocket, and placed it on the table. "You know, I still can't believe he's gone. I keep looking at my phone. Expecting a text from him. Usually, a comment about something or someone stupid he's seen. You know, he really noticed things. And he recognized people's bullshit. He was probably too perceptive. I don't think his insights ever made him happy."

Debbie nodded. "Sounds like he was a student of the human condition."

A slight smile lifted Macie's lips. "Yeah, you could say that. Honestly, sometimes it could be annoying, especially if you were the one he was examining. As he got older, he learned to keep his observations to himself. I was one of the few he felt comfortable truly being himself."

"What about his brother? They're twins. I imagine they were close. And probably a lot alike."

"They used to be tight. I've known Caleb and Connor for a long time. We grew up together. The three of us were thick. Once upon a time. But as Connor and Caleb bumped heads more and more, I found myself siding with Caleb."

"Why was that?"

Macie pursed her lips, and her eyebrows squeezed closer together as she considered the question. "Maybe, um, because I tend to root for the underdog."

Debbie waited, letting silence fill the space as Macie's last words hung between them.

Macie continued, "At some point, Connor decided to be the goody-goody one. And if he was the good twin, that meant Caleb got stuck with the bad twin label. It wasn't enough that Connor was always sucking up to any adult in the room; he worked hard to undermine Caleb with their parents, teachers, and with coaches. The more you're labeled as aloof and difficult...self-fulfilling prophecy, right?" Macie took a drink of her water and screwed the cap back on. "Connor was always more extroverted than Caleb. And maybe Caleb was a bit too contrarian for his own good."

"Is that why Caleb turned to drugs? Rebellion?"

Macie again unscrewed the cap from her water bottle, took a sip, then replaced the cap. "I mean, we all smoked pot. Me, Caleb, Connor, all of our friends in high school. I don't count marijuana as a drug."

"Okay, so heroin. How'd Caleb get into it?"

Macie set her bottled water down on the small table, then pushed herself as far back into the chair as physically possible and crossed her arms in front of her body.

"Connor will tell you that I got Caleb hooked."

"I want to know what you say, not what Connor says."

"But who are you going to believe? Him or me?"

"I'm here to listen, not judge."

Macie looked across the room and let out another loud sigh. "Caleb and Connor were in a car accident," Macie began. "They were college students at Mizzou, junior year. They'd been drinking with their frat buddies. Connor was driving, and Caleb was in the front passenger seat. Connor blew through a red light. Their car got T-boned by a pickup truck, which slammed right into the spot where Caleb was sitting. Connor walked away with some bruises and scratches. Caleb broke an arm and started having a lot of back pain a few weeks later."

Debbie grimaced. "That's not good."

"No, it wasn't. Anyway, Caleb had to go to the hospital. His parents were freaking out. Connor got charged with a DUI, which his parents made disappear by hiring a high-priced lawyer; got it knocked down to a littering ticket. So much for the good twin. Anyway, Caleb's arm was put in a cast. His blood alcohol would've been through the roof, too. But he was twenty-one and wasn't driving, so whatever. Anyway, doctors gave him oxycontin. Not much, just a little. He went through it and then stopped. But that's about the same time his back started hurting. He had MRIs and CT scans, but they couldn't pinpoint the problem. Doctors figured it would go away. After all, he was a young guy. They gave him another prescription to get him through the pain. And then they gave him another prescription. But after that, the doctors cut him off. Only it was too late. He was hooked. By the time he came home for the summer between junior and senior year, he was stealing oxy from the medicine cabinets of friends' homes. And he was trying to buy it. Well, he was eventually caught by his parents. They yelled. Cut off his allowance, hoping that no money meant no drugs."

"But it didn't work that way, did it?"

"No. He was really struggling, you know? And I was already using H—thought I could control it because of my fancy chemistry major. My drug counselor says my knowledge made me arrogant." Macie picked up the bottled water and then put it back down without sipping. "Anyway, heroin is cheaper than oxy but gives you the same nice high. I felt bad for Caleb. He was doing risky stuff to get his hands on cash. And he was meeting up with some sketchy people. I had a good supplier, a trustworthy one I met through Snapchat. Anyway, I suggested that heroin might go easier on his trust fund allowance."

"And it clicked with him?"

Macie shifted the bottled water from one hand to the other. "Too much. He was smoking it at the beginning of the summer. By the end of the summer, he was shooting up."

"Did Connor join you two?"

"Naw. We had to sneak around him. It wasn't that hard because Connor was busy working for his parents."

"Were you buying the drugs for him?"

"At first, yeah. But then his habit exploded. He was buying on his own. I kept warning him that there was a lot of bad stuff on the market. Shit that would kill him."

"Like fentanyl?"

"Yeah. There's a lot of dirty heroin. I kept telling him to stick with my supplier. Trust my judgment. You know, chemist and all. But it wasn't enough. He kept chasing the high. By the end of the summer, Connor had figured out what was going on. He ratted Caleb out. Caleb's parents sent him to rehab for the first time but made sure he was out in time to finish his senior year. Instead of paying for him to go to Mizzou, the Webbs made him stick around home and finish his degree at UMSL."

"And Connor?"

"He went back to Mizzou and lived large his senior year. And he made sure to chronicle his good times on Snapchat. He did it just to twist the knife into Caleb a bit more. You know, Caleb definitely had FOMO."

"And you?"

Macie shook her head. "I went back to school as well. I was able to keep a firewall between school and drugs."

"So you all three graduated?" Debbie asked.

Macie nodded her head. "A miracle, at least for Caleb and me. I got a big pharma gig; they had a program for promising women in chemistry. Caleb and Connor went to work for their parents. But within a year, things got fucked up."

"How so?" Debbie asked.

"Off the record?"

"Absolutely. We've been off the record. We're still off the record."

"Well, me, I fucked up. Hard. Started experimenting with chemicals for, um, personal use. The company noticed controlled substances missing. I got fired. They were gonna prosecute, only my parents patched it up. My dad may be an asshole, but he handles the money for some clever lawyers."

"What about Connor and Caleb?"

"They were fighting all the time. Caleb still blamed Connor for the accident, the addiction, and missing his last year at Mizzou. Connor blamed me. Their parents were always taking Connor's side."

"So, a lot of resentment?"

Macie sipped her water. "Oh yeah. His household was toxic. Not that mine was any better. But we always had each other."

"Were you two ever, well, um, more than friends?"

Macie paused. "We were always friends. Good friends.

Close friends. But that was it—except once. The night before."

"Before what?"

"Before he went to rehab that last time. I'd come over. Caleb suspected his family was going to force him into treatment and he was so upset. Crazy upset. I was fucked up. One thing led to another."

Macie's voice trailed off. She dug her fingernails on her right hand into her forearm. "Stupid, stupid, stupid."

"Don't beat yourself up. It happens."

"You don't understand. It shouldn't have happened." Macie paused. "That night. The night we met him after he got outta rehab. I was gonna tell him."

Debbie waited.

Macie lifted her hand from her forearm, fingernail marks embedded into the skin.

"Tell him what?"

"I'm pregnant. Can you fuckin' believe that shit? The chances of that happening were, well, I shoulda bought a Powerball instead of hooking up with Caleb. Anyway, it was eight weeks since my last period when Caleb died. Nine weeks now. I got pills that I can take up to ten weeks." Macie looked away for a moment. "I don't know what to do. I wanted him to tell me what to do. He was supposed to tell me what to do. Asshole."

Debbie reached her hand across the table and rested it on Macie's forearm. "Oh, God. I'm so sorry."

"Sorry don't fix nuthin'. I'm so sad about Caleb. And so mad at him. And then I feel awful because I'm mad. He's in the ground. I'm not."

"Have you been to a doctor?"

Macie nodded. "I went to the clinic across the river. On the east side."

"Are you, um, still using?"

"No. I've been clean since before Caleb came home. Don't ask me how. Freakin' miracle I haven't used. But I don't know. I just don't have the cravin' right now."

"Anyone else know?"

"Just you. And my friend Alex."

Debbie took her running shoes off and left them by the front door. After the meeting with Macie, Debbie needed to burn some energy, even if it was dark. A few miles around Lafayette Park, just across the street from her home. It was safe enough.

There was a lot to process and nothing to use. Debbie hadn't even decided whether to tell Sam about the pregnancy. Off the record didn't mean a reporter couldn't confide in her boss. But she didn't have to reveal secrets, either.

However, she had texted Sam to let him know Macie showed. Now, it was his turn to make things happen.

Debbie walked in her socks to the kitchen for a glass of chocolate milk, her go-to for post-run recovery. Sure, dairy was controversial, but she wasn't a fan of sports drinks. Besides, she was under no obligation to disclose her preference.

The alarm system beeped. The front door had been opened.

"I'm home," Beth called out. "Daniel is with me."

Debbie drained her glass and placed it in the sink. It was time to get back to work. "How was the gardening class?" Debbie called out as she walked to the living room, knowing she'd find them there.

"It was really informative," Beth said. She was wearing the same black turtleneck she'd had in the morning. However, the skirt had been replaced by a pair of slim-fitting jeans, and she'd swapped her sensible heels for

145

black Chuck Taylor All-Stars. "I can't wait to get started on a raised bed this spring."

"Who's going to build them?" Debbie asked, looking at Flannery.

Flannery gave Debbie an awkward smile. Over the past several months, Debbie had detected two sides to Flannery. The detective at work was confident, gruff, and in control. In his uniform, he was tall, handsome, and commanding. And he'd once saved her life. But whenever he was around Beth, he turned into a doofus. It was the uncomfortable, off-center version of Flannery with a crush on her mother that Debbie could squeeze for information.

All was fair in love and journalism.

"You know I'm pretty good with a hammer and nails," Beth answered. "But Flannery is going to help me. He's got a truck to move lumber."

"And dirt," Flannery added.

"How was your day?" Beth asked.

"Productive," Debbie answered as she turned to Flannery. "It just so happens that I was going to call you."

The detective groaned. "Don't you ever take a break?"

"I am my mother's daughter."

"Don't bring me into this," Beth said.

Flannery squared his shoulders. He may have been wearing cargo pants and a jacket, but he tried to regain his cop composure. "What you need?"

"I heard you were part of that big drug bust with the feds. The one with cartel ties."

"Yeah," Flannery said. "Nothing secret about that. I was part of the contingent that took down the leader of the biker gang. I was undercover, driving a Taurus. Followed him from Spanish Lake to just outside of Rolla. Kept a visual on him."

"Interesting. How big a role does St. Louis play in the drug trade?"

"Track down the Midwest HIDTA," Flannery said.

"The what?"

"The Midwest High-Intensity Drug Trafficking Areas report. They issue a threat assessment annually. It isn't classified. That report flags the movement of drugs. St. Louis is a hub for trafficking, money laundering, and sales."

"Who'd a thought?" Debbie said. "We're certainly no Miami."

GERI L. DREILING

"Maybe not. But as my uncle pointed out, St. Louis has always attracted criminal syndicates."

Debbie suppressed a smile. Flannery listened to her podcast after all.

When Macie's purse hit the dining room table, it sounded like a bag filled with apples and metal bits had landed on the wood surface. The table had been a gift from her parents when she moved into the apartment. Instead of an eating place, she used it as open storage.

I'm so tired, she thought as she entered her empty place.

"Of course you are," she imagined Caleb saying. "You've been gone all day. You haven't eaten anything except those crackers this morning. Not healthy, especially in your condition."

"You're a fine one to talk about healthy habits," Macie mumbled as she kicked her shoes off and then rummaged in her cupboards for the last protein bar. "And if we keep having these chats, they'll lock me in a loony bin."

"Would that be so bad?" Caleb asked. "No more decisions to make. No more groceries to buy. No more work to do. Just drawing pictures and sitting in therapy."

"Oh good gawd, not therapy. I just got done with my NA meeting. Bunch of whiny little fuckers," Macie said as she filled a glass of water from the tap.

"You really gonna put that water in your body straight from the faucet?"

"Hey, I've put worse in. Besides, St. Louis has pretty good water."

Macie sank down on the couch and looked up at the painting next to the television. "You know, I still love that art piece."

"Of course you do. I gave it to you," Caleb said with a smile, sitting on a chair beside her.

"You know, you could be a generous shit when you wanted."

"Only with the people I care about."

"I met someone today. A reporter."

"Oh yeah. Do you think that is a good idea?"

"It was off the record. It felt good to talk."

"You know talking can be overrated."

"But the only people I have are you and Alex. And Alex is still using. Can be kinda hard to stay clean when you hang out with someone on H."

Macie stretched out on the couch, still wearing what

she'd put together for work. "Anyway, I kinda liked her. Told her about you. About my problem."

Macie imagined Caleb reaching for the gray fuzzy blanket at her feet and pulling it over her body.

"You're too trusting, Mace. Be careful."

12 TANGLED WEBBS

The long road, perfectly paved and pothole free, was the only way in or out of the exclusive neighborhood. The trees lining the street artfully shielded manors on each side of their green curtains in the summer. In winter, the multimillion-dollar homes were easier to spot. But the estates surrounding the houses were so vast that privacy was never compromised.

The suburban enclave was unlike Debbie's city neighborhood, where you could look out your bathroom window and wave at your neighbor while you each brushed your teeth.

Sam had come through. Shortly after she'd finished grilling Flannery the previous evening, he'd texted her. The Webbs agreed to meet with her the next day. Debbie still wondered how Sam had managed to pull it together so quickly. There had to be more to the story. There always was.

She drove past one-word signs that stated: Private. It was the province of the rich-rich, the middle of three affluent categories Debbie had created in her head. There was the rich of her parents, more upper-middle class than anything else. Then there were the Webbs, a step above. And finally, obscenely wealthy. That was her publisher.

It was such a St. Louis thing to do, sort people by income. Well, it wasn't just her hometown, Debbie forced herself to admit; it was the whole planet.

The reporter guided her battered Civic into a semi-circular driveway. The home was red brick with white columns. It was the sort of house that wouldn't have a cleaning lady; it would have a full-time housekeeper. A dedicated gardener would tend the grounds rather than a lawn service. It was a space where phrases like east wing and west wing were bandied about.

Debbie parked her car just past the Italian-style fountain, bereft of water. Whether it was because of the frigid temperature or as a sign of mourning, Debbie didn't know. She didn't bother locking her car after she got out. It was hard for car thieves to sneak into the neighborhood. And if they did, why would anyone bother with her rusted heap when many more attractive options worthy of a Gone in Sixty Seconds whiteboard checklist could be boosted?

The massive white front door underneath arched, leaded glass opened before Debbie could ring the bell. A young man smiled, his dark blond hair, brilliant blue eyes, and dimpled chin perfectly framed in the door frame: Connor Webb. He wore khakis and a button-down white oxford with blue stripes that strained against his shoulders and neck muscles. He was an eerie reminder of how Caleb would've looked if drugs hadn't exacted their price.

"Debbie, I presume?" Connor said warmly.

Debbie lifted her right hand to the side of her eyeglasses before nodding. "That's me. Connor, right?"

"Guilty," he said as he stuck his hand out to shake hers. He was charming, Debbie had to admit.

"Come on in. My parents are waiting for us in the living room."

The foyer floor was a dark gray marble, and a contemporary chandelier was suspended overhead. Near a white curved staircase hung oil landscapes. Debbie didn't recognize the artist but guessed it was someone expensive.

"Did you have any trouble finding our home?" Connor asked, using small talk to fill the void as they walked. The path to the living room was a long one.

"No, no. Not at all," Debbie said as she followed behind. You could see it from outer space. The estate took up a large chunk of real estate on Google Maps.

Connor walked through a doorway and stopped. "Debbie, I'd like to introduce my parents, Matt and Sarah Webb. Mom and Dad, Debbie Bradley."

The pair rose from an oversized, cream-colored couch. The room was covered in dark wood flooring. A walnut shelf lined the expanse of one wall, filled with books, beige vases with tasteful faux greenery, carefully spaced photographs, and small statues.

"Pleased to meet you," Debbie said as she extended her hand to each.

Sarah stood about the same height as Debbie, a woman who was neither thin nor heavy. Faint amber highlights were blended subtly into her brown hair, worn shoulder length with wispy bangs.

Matt reminded Debbie of a bulldog on stilts. His

closely shaven hair drew attention to a prominent widow's peak. His face was round with a small nose and ever-so-slightly drooping at the jowls. And like a bulldog, Matt Webb had a thick neck and broad chest, though his gut gave his body a boxy shape. But when he was young, Debbie guessed, he'd probably possessed the inverted pyramid physique of his son.

"Won't you please sit down, Debbie," Sarah said, gesturing toward a chair facing the sofa in front of the Webbs. Connor grabbed the armchair next to Debbie.

Debbie sat down carefully, worried her pen might ink up the chair. "Let me say how sorry I am about losing your son—and brother—Caleb."

Sarah looked down at her lap and nodded.

Matt's broad chest expanded as he inhaled before delivering a speech he'd recited often since Caleb's death. "Thank you. Yes, it has been so very hard for all of us. Unfortunately, when you love an addict, you constantly fear getting that terrible phone call. In some ways, it was a shock. In other ways, well, it wasn't."

"I can't imagine how hard it must be and how hard it must've been," Debbie said.

Sarah nodded, unable to conceal the sadness that

lurked behind her eyes. "It's like seeing your baby disappear a little each day. At some point, even though your son is still alive, the shell that remains is no longer the person you knew." Sarah paused and cleared her throat. "Goodness, I've forgotten my manners. Would you like something to drink, Debbie? We have coffee, tea, water, soda? Rosa would happily bring you anything you like."

"Thank you so much, but I'm fine."

Connor chimed into the conversation, attempting to brighten his mother's mood. "So I understand you're from St. Louis."

Debbie nodded. "Yes, I spent some time working in Washington, D.C., but I'm back."

"Must've been interesting," Matt said, a hint of disapproval in his voice.

"Debbie," Sarah interrupted, "I was talking to Chris Radcliffe yesterday about a possible new building project. He told me you wanted to write a story about heroin and fentanyl. He thought we might be a resource."

Debbie nodded, choosing her words carefully. "So many teens and young adults are getting caught up in heroin in St. Louis. So many overdoses. I wanted to shine a light on the issue. And I was hoping that maybe you'd share your experience in the hopes that it might help others."

Matt shifted in his chair. "The three of us agree that the idea is a fine one. We like the thought of trying to prevent another senseless death. If we could just help even one family." He shifted once more in his chair. "We just have one small request before we're willing to be interviewed."

"What's that?"

Matt leaned over to the table at the end of the sofa and picked up a folder. He opened it and pulled out a stapled document. "Given the heartbreak we've endured and our community standing, and, well, the fact that you're part of the media even if Chris Radcliffe vouches for you…we were hoping that before we began, we could get you to sign this before moving forward."

He handed Debbie the document. She studied the first page, flipped to the second, and then the third. "A nondisclosure agreement?" Debbie asked.

"Very simple, very standard."

"But how can I write a story with a nondisclosure agreement?" Debbie asked with a voice as neutral as she could muster. "A story is just that: a disclosure."

"Well, you will be able to disclose what we tell you. We just have some conditions before publication, really."

"Conditions?"

"We must have the chance to read it and approve it."

"And I assume, make changes?"

"If you're as good as Chris Radcliffe says you are and as good as my son tells me based on your reputation, I doubt it will be any problem at all."

Debbie could feel her ears getting hot. Her lips smiled, but her eyes didn't follow. "How about we just talk off the record? I'll put my notebook away."

"We talked to our lawyer. He said this is the best way. You can promise off the record, but it is just your word. And you must admit that the news media isn't trustworthy. Fake news and all."

Debbie clasped her hands together and placed them on her lap. She measured her tone carefully before speaking again. "I can't sign this."

"Why not? Even the president of the United States uses them. If he does it, it's gotta be good. Look, we're protected, and you get to write your story."

"Not if you don't like the story," Debbie said as she

flipped through the agreement. "It says here that you can kill the piece or make any editorial changes to the text, no matter how big or small. And if I run it without your permission, you can sue the magazine and me personally for damages. You can even try to stop the magazine from printing it. A prior restraint provision, by the way, is awfully bold."

"Look," said Sarah, "think of this as an in-case-of-emergency-break-glass insurance policy. If you do everything you say you're going to do and treat us fairly, this is nothing."

Debbie knew she had to leave before her temper got the best of her. "My mom, also a lawyer, tells me to be careful what I sign. If it's in writing, it can be enforced, no matter what you tell me. So I'm gonna need to talk to my editor first."

"Well, Ms. Bradley, no signature, no story. I'm sorry you wasted a trip," Matt said as he stood up from the couch. "We really appreciate that you came out today to talk to us. Why don't you take the NDA back to your office? You can talk to your editor and Chris Radcliffe. Maybe they'll be more open to it than you thought. Then we can schedule another meeting."

Sarah chimed in. "Again, thank you so much for coming out. And we do look forward to talking to you again. I think the work you're doing could help a lot of people. In the meantime, Connor, could you see Debbie out?"

"Of course, Mom," Connor said as he gestured back to the hallway. "Debbie, this way."

Debbie mustered her most gracious goodbye and followed Connor. It was a long way in and a long way back. She had to force herself to walk calmly. Her anger made her legs want to run. Or kick something. Anything.

Connor opened the front door and stepped out with Debbie, shutting the door behind him. "I'm sorry about this," Connor said. "Off the record?"

"Of course," Debbie answered.

"I told my dad it wasn't wise to give you an NDA. But he wouldn't listen. Never does. He's a control freak. The thought of not being in the driver's seat when it came to your story, well, that just isn't something he'd accept."

"You know, I meant what I said about off-the-record. My editor would fire me in a split second if I violated my word."

"For Dad, the damage would already be done. But let

me work on them a bit. And, in the meantime, because I believe you, do you want to meet for an off-the-record chat?"

Debbie looked at him carefully. "Are you sure? Won't your parents be upset?"

"They don't need to know. I'm a grown man, after all. I can decide who I want to talk to. Besides, I don't see the harm in getting together."

"Well, okay. Sure," Debbie said.

"How about six this evening? I've got your number. I'll text you later today, and we could meet in the Central West End for a drink. There's no chance my parents will venture outside the suburbs unless it's to check on a property, attend a fundraiser, or watch the Cardinals or the Blues."

"I'll be there," Debbie said.

At first, she didn't know what to do. As she drove away from the Webbs, Debbie was irritated and in no mood to brief Sam about her meeting with Caleb's family. That got her thinking about the backup story. Last night, she'd mined the Spanish Lake address from court pleadings using Pacer, the open electronic resource to obtain federal court records.

It couldn't hurt to take a look at the raided place before going to the office.

Light snow fell as she turned into the cul-de-sac in Spanish Lake. The home was halfway down a dead-end street. Yellow crime scene tape crisscrossed the front door, and a lock box hung from the knob. The living room windows on the ranch home were covered with plywood.

Debbie turned her car around at the circle, then parked across the street from the house. Perhaps the property location wasn't an accident. With only one way in or out of the court, it would be hard for police or a rival gang to catch anyone staying there by surprise. And yet, somehow, there had still been a bust.

She climbed out of her car, pulled the phone out of her coat pocket, and snapped photos as snowflakes landed on her jacket and frosted her hair.

The neighborhood was quiet; cars neither came nor went. And the driveway hadn't been roped off by police. If she walked up it, that wouldn't really be trespassing, would it?

The windows on the attached garage weren't covered. Debbie cupped her hands on either side of her eyes and peered into the empty space. The door inside the garage that led to the house had a large splintered hole in the center. Perhaps the cops had used a battering ram to force the home open and flash-bang grenades to stun. But Debbie wondered why the exterior garage door hadn't been harmed. Was it already open when they descended? Or had they grabbed the code somehow ahead of time? Or had there been a hole in the interior door before the raid?

A shadow passed the hole from inside the house. Debbie reflexively pulled back from the window. She looked around the street, but it was deserted. She pressed her face against the glass again. Nothing.

To the right of the garage was a chain-link fence. With gloved hands, Debbie reached for the metal. She wore the black high-waisted pants, cream-colored turtleneck, and dress boots chosen for the Webb interview. Not exactly fence-climbing attire. But this was no time for caution. Besides, ripped clothing was a small price when an empty street made it easy to snoop.

Debbie inserted her boots into a diamond square in

the fence. She'd scaled hundreds as a child. Maybe she hadn't done it lately, but she knew how it went. When her legs neared the top, it took a little care to maneuver over without snagging her pants. And then she was over.

Now, she was definitely trespassing.

An air conditioner compressor, a rusted lawn mower, and, she noticed, faint footprints left in the new snow were all on the side of the home. There was a basement window near the ground, just behind the compressor. Debbie dropped to her hands and knees in the snow and peered in.

A shadow moved. Debbie popped up.

She rushed to the backyard to peer around the corner of the house. From that vantage point, Debbie could see the basement window while remaining hidden.

The window opened. Two gloved hands reached out. The intruder's head hadn't yet emerged. Debbie stared at the gloves and noticed the ring finger of the left-hand glove was flat and floppy. It didn't grip the ground like the others.

A head covered in a black knit cap emerged from the open window. Slender shoulders followed as the figure's chest wriggled across the snow-covered brittle yellow grass. The zipper of a dark green jacket scraped against the bottom of the metal window frame. The figure had almost entirely extracted himself from the basement. With the bulky winter clothes, Debbie couldn't tell if it was a man or a woman.

Her phone rang.

When the person's head snapped to the right, Debbie made out the gaunt face of a man with the stubble of a dark beard across his chin.

"Oh, *Dios!*" he whispered, his surprised eyes locked with hers.

Debbie held her breath and turned off her phone. She retreated two steps, then froze. She'd have to run for it, but before her legs got the message to move, she was being pulled by her forearm toward the stranger. Unable to find her footing, Debbie's back was quickly shoved against the house. A cold switchblade pressed against her neck.

"Shhhh," the man whispered, "I don't want to hurt you. Your phone."

Debbie gave a slight head nod, signaling she understood.

"Slowly," he said.

She reached into her pocket with her right hand, saying, "Take it easy. I don't want any trouble."

"Give it to me," he ordered.

She handed it over with the slow movements of a hiker who surprised a mountain lion. He held his right hand out for the phone while his left hand gripped the knife. He'd moved the blade away from her neck, but it could quickly return.

"You shouldn't be here," he whispered.

"Neither should you," Debbie said.

He stepped back. "Please, just pretend you never saw me."

"Who are you?" Debbie asked.

"*Un fantasma.* A ghost."

He took four steps back, folded his knife, and put it in his pocket. He put his finger to his lips before turning and running across the backyard. Once he'd climbed over the fence, he retrieved her phone from his pocket, gave her a last look, and dropped it into the snow before disappearing.

13 PISO FRANCO

"We have a few, er, issues," Kiko announced to El Duro upon entering the cartel leader's office.

Sitting behind a desk once owned by a Mexican president, his boss looked up and gestured for Kiko to sit. The leather chairs for visitors had once graced the office of an American general who served in World War Two. El Duro had spared no expense when it came to his furnishings. He might be currently taking refuge in his jungle compound, but that didn't mean he had to live like a snake.

El Duro sighed as he rose from his desk and walked to the nearby terrarium. He picked up a container of live insects on the table, dumped it in, then waited for the small frog with cobalt blue legs and deep blue coloring on the back ringed with turquoise circles to react.

This was always his favorite part.

The *rana dardo venenoso*, poison dart frog, stiffened so as not to attract the attention of today's feast: young crickets. But once one ventured into the frog's striking distance, the insect would have no chance of survival.

He'd always been fascinated with the frog. Even if his name had changed over a lifetime, his obsession with the frog had endured. It existed when he was a child known as Eduardo Recio, nicknamed Dardo by his parents. After he was kidnapped by the cartel at the age of thirteen while trying to cross the border into the United States, the tiny poisonous frog gave him hope. Dardo was the scrawniest, shortest boy in the narco-paramilitary training camp. But, like the poison dart frog, he too could be lethal.

He had to be lethal. If he wanted to survive. It wasn't long before Dardo was hailed for his bravery, his persistence, and his violence. Dardo was christened with a new nickname: Duro. Tough.

His reputation for ruthlessness and his impulse to lavish rewards on loyalists attracted followers. As he aged, his influence swelled. He was no longer called Duro but El Duro, "The Tough One." He'd either outlived or defeated his rivals. And after the leader of his cartel was captured by the Mexican military, El Duro moved like the poison dart frog striking at prey. He splintered from his organizational roots, taking his followers with him rather than jockeying for the top spot of an organization that he believed had grown too unwieldy. He'd start fresh.

Dardos Venenosos, the Poison Darts, was born. El Duro seized the military equipment the old cartel had amassed. After all, he'd had a hand in the original acquisitions. He leveraged it for lightning strikes to shock and awe the small-town leaders aligned with the old cartel. The villagers could cooperate or die. He used the same strategy with police officers, military soldiers, and top brass. Those who got in line were rewarded, and those who didn't? They suffered. *Balas o dinero.*

Now he was the most wanted man in Mexico. There was a ten-million-dollar reward on his head. But the bounty was more of an inconvenience than a threat. He could still pop into luxury resorts and even Mexico City. He just couldn't remain long.

After the frog finished his snack, El Duro poured whiskey into two glasses and handed one to his oldest ally.

"So, tell me, Kiko," El Duro said as he returned to his

desk. "Tell me these problems."

"We got word that the Chinese fent shipment arrived on the coast."

El Duro nodded.

"But some of the dock workers were balking at processing. Too dangerous, they claim. More money is what they want."

El Duro studied the fingernails on his right hand for a moment. "I see. And if I give in to their demands, what do you think happens?"

"Others will follow."

"You know why I like these old pieces of furniture owned by powerful men?"

"No, *jefe*."

"Because those men didn't back down. You can go way back in time—to the European kings—even queens. Those savvy gringos and gringas knew how to chop off heads, imprison their sisters, poison rivals. You name it, they did it. A tried and true system."

Kiko shook his head. "And they think we're violent."

El Duro nodded. "When they came to the throne, if they looked weak, they wouldn't last. Neither would we."

Kiko finished his whiskey and held the empty glass in

his hand; he knew better than to set it on his boss's desk.

"You know who all the dock workers are?" El Duro asked.

"*Sí.*"

"If they think coming together as a group will save them, well," he said, "we'll stop that. Round them up. Ask them to nominate their leader who will present their demand formally. Once you've got a head, chop it off. In front of the group. I guarantee they'll shut up and get back to work."

Kiko nodded. "There's also the matter of the bust in Missouri."

El Duro waved his hand. "I already know about that one."

"There's also a reporter snooping around. A magazine reporter. Seems she writes about crime."

El Duro sniffed. "Being in St. Louis, it must keep her pretty busy. But why bother me with something or someone so small?"

"One of our contacts insisted. Her asking questions is making them nervous. And you know when people get nervous they either do something stupid or don't do what you need them to do." Kiko handed his phone to his boss.

El Duro looked at the screen. "This her?"

Kiko nodded.

El Duro handed the phone back and memorized her name. After his dinner, he'd do some more digging about the reporter. "She's meaningless. She can't hurt us."

"Piranhas are also small fish. And the poison dart is a little frog."

"The biggest threat is the one you miss, yes, I know. But if we mess with her, we're just asking for trouble. Maybe we can get away with silencing journalists in Mexico but in the U.S.? The Saudis should never have messed with Khashoggi," El Duro said.

Kiko's face remained blank.

"Never mind," El Duro said, knowing Kiko didn't follow the news as closely as he did. Or read it in *inglés*.

"What do you want me to do?" Kiko asked.

"Who do we have on the ground who's invisible?"

"By invisible, do you mean connected and embedded? Or do you mean a shadow on the fringe? We have both."

"Let's start with a shadow on the fringe."

"José Rodrigo," Kiko answered. "He managed to slip out during the drug bust."

"Where is he now?"

"At a safe house in St. Louis. Waiting on instructions from us."

"What if we had him keep an eye on her for a couple of days? See where she goes, who she sees, what she does?"

Kiko frowned. "He's good at disappearing, but I wouldn't call him a tracker. He might be clumsy. Plus, a nine-fingered hombre is hard to forget."

"But if we just use him for a couple of days, a temporary filler, until we decide how to proceed," El Duro said, musing out loud. "No more than two days. With instructions to stay far away. Never get close. Never talk to her. Just be our eyes for forty-eight hours."

Kiko shrugged. "It could work. I'm not thrilled about it. As long as he kept his distance."

"So long as our problems stay north of the border, the drug bust and the journalist are annoying, like a mosquito bite."

"But they took our money."

"I hate to lose money as much as you, Kiko. But now that our crypto laundering operation through China is running, it doesn't hurt us that much."

Kiko frowned again. "Give me a dollar or gold. I don't trust fake money."

"You don't trust it because you don't understand it. Don't worry. We're protected."

Piso franco. Safe house. But for J.R., the apartment where he'd sought refuge after the drug bust would always be dangerous. Sure, he'd sidestepped jail, and yet, he remained imprisoned. He'd managed to evade the law, but there was no escaping the cartel.

His life or theirs. The choice was simple. The consequence? Brutal. He remained tethered to his tormentors to keep the people he most loved in this world alive.

The image of his wife and daughter had sent him shimmying out of the basement window when he first heard the flash-bang grenades. Their faces were in his mind's eye as he fled the drug house before he could be swept up by the police. And his ties to them compelled him to return to the place that had been boarded up, roped off, and under surveillance. He couldn't leave his wedding ring behind in that house. It was the only touchable object he had from the woman he loved. He could no longer wear it. That finger had been cruelly removed from his hand. But he'd carried it with him in a chain around his neck. On the day of the bust he'd put it in his secret hiding place, a ceiling panel in the basement. He didn't want to contaminate it with the nasty chemicals he had to handle.

Yes, he'd risked much to get his ring back. And when he found it and crawled out of the basement window, he thought the danger was over. How did he know someone would be lurking around the home when he was there?

At least she wasn't a cop. That much he could tell by their brief encounter. She'd been as shocked and scared as he was.

It wasn't too hard to slip away from her. And by the time she crossed the lawn to get her phone, J.R. was behind the wheel of the silver 2005 Toyota Camry he'd used to drive to Spanish Lake. The hubcap on the front passenger side was missing, leaving a solid black tire with a black rim and three lug nuts exposed to the road. But the license tags were current. The headlights and brake lights worked. He'd checked.

Of course, he hadn't been given use of the car by the

cartel for his personal errands. Instead, it was easier to get him to his next assignment if he had wheels. And they knew he wouldn't stray too far. They had his family.

The safe house was in a run-down part of South City untouched by gentrification. Neighbors knew not to ask questions or be nosy. The unspoken rule: Mind your own damn business. Besides, most people were just trying to make ends meet. They didn't need the hassle of upsetting a syndicate.

He'd been in the safe house before. That was why he knew where to go as the cops banged doors down and threw men to the ground, cuffing their hands behind their backs. His first time in the safe house was when he arrived in St. Louis. Then he returned to it a year later so he could hitch a ride down to the Bootheel to visit his wife and daughter. The women who were the center of his life lived in a trailer. They worked as migrant laborers going from farm to farm. He'd been granted the brief visit as a form of psychological torture, not kindness. Seeing his family made him remember why he loved them. Leaving them made the ache in his heart almost unbearable. The more he yearned for them, worried about them, and tried to protect them, the easier he was to control.

J.R. climbed the stairs to the second floor of the brick building constructed sometime in the 1930s. Of the fifteen apartments, he knew which one was used for cartel business and where the key had been stashed. Anyone who stayed would put it back in the hiding hole. It was a community space.

And you never knew if you'd be alone when you entered.

J.R. inserted the key into the lock and swung open the door, expecting to see an empty room. Only there was a man on the gold-tattered couch waiting. He was getting to his feet when the door opened.

"Where you been?" the man asked after J.R. closed the door.

J.R. shoved his hands in his pockets and hunched his shoulders. "Food. Nothing here to eat."

The man harrumphed. "Don't see nothin' in yo hands."

"Ate it," J.R. responded. "I was hungry. And if someone was here when I got back, they might try to take it."

The man frowned. It was true that desperate men

would resort to rash acts. "There's a job for you."

J.R. sighed. Where could they be sending him now? If there was a God, it would be closer to his family.

The man held out his phone. There was a picture on the screen. "Take a look."

J.R. took the phone. He looked at the photo on it and nearly dropped the device.

"What's the matter with you?" the man said.

"*Nada*," J.R. said, waving his hand, hoping the heart thumping in his chest couldn't be heard. "I thought it would be a map, not a señorita."

The man scowled as he snatched the phone back. "They told me you weren't right in the head. Musta gone a little *loco* when they took your finger."

J.R. smiled, the sort of grin he'd learned to fake. They thought he was dim and didn't know they were making fun of him. But it was better to be underestimated.

"Here's where she lives," the man said, holding out a piece of paper. "The higher-ups want you to keep an eye on her for a few days."

"What's her name?" J.R. asked.

"Debbie Bradley. Don't let her know you're around. Don't talk to her. Stay far away. Just let us know what she's doing."

"I don't know how to do that," J.R. said.

"You better figure it out. Fast," the man said. "Here's a phone and a card for gas. You'll text a phone number that's already in there. No one will answer if you call. And the number will be disconnected in a few days. And if you try to use your phone to call anyone else, we'll know."

J.R. took the phone. "*Sí*," he mumbled.

14 CANCEL CULTURE

Debbie slammed the paper she was holding down on Sam's desk.

Whap.

"A present?" Sam said as he looked up from the text he'd been proofing.

"An outrage," Debbie answered.

Sam picked up the sheet. He frowned. "A nondisclosure agreement? Please tell me you didn't sign this."

Debbie crossed her arms. "Are you kidding? Of course not. I know better."

"Hmmm. Whatdya you do to piss 'em off?" Sam asked.

"Why do you automatically assume I was doing the offending?" Debbie said, her hands jumping defiantly to her hips.

Sam rolled his eyes. "I'm joking. Sort of."

Debbie inhaled deeply. "I was polite. And if I say so myself, charming."

Sam waved the paper still in his hand. "This document says differently."

"Seriously? Did you look at it? There was no way this was prepared on the spur of the moment. It was drafted before I ever drove my car into the Webbs' lah-dee-dah neighborhood. This," Debbie stammered, "this was an ambush!"

"Okay. Point taken," Sam said. "Sit down, please. You're making me nervous. You're as twitchy as a two-pack-a-day smoker stuck on an international flight."

Debbie sunk into the chair across from Sam's desk, but her right foot bounced with energy.

"How'd they try to spin it?"

"An affirmation of trust. Started with flattery. I'm a well-respected journalist blah, blah, blah. And if I was as good as everyone said, well, this was just a meaningless piece of paper, blah, blah, blah. They'd tell me their story. I'd write the story. They'd approve the story. By signing it, I'd demonstrate that I wasn't into dirty tricks."

"Clever," Sam replied. He fell silent as he skimmed the document. "A variation on the *National Enquirer* catch-and-kill practice. Instead of catching a story by promising a payment, the Webbs simply agree to tell their story. But the price is the NDA with an option to prevent publication. Which, of course, will allow them to kill it." Sam paused. "No story is so important that would have me yield my role as editor to the story's subject."

"I figured as much," Debbie said.

"So where does that leave us?" Sam asked. "Kill the Webb angle and just go with stats about drugs in St. Louis?"

"Well," Debbie said slowly, "let's not be hasty."

Sam frowned again. "What are you getting at?"

"Even though Caleb's parents aren't talking, his brother, Connor, wants to get together tonight for an off-the-record chat. Maybe I can glean more insight into his relationship with Caleb. And maybe he can tell me where his brother was getting his drugs. Even if I can't go deeply into Caleb's psychological profile, maybe I can learn more about how the drugs got into his hands. And Connor could be an ally who could persuade his parents to drop the NDA requirement."

Sam sighed. "You have to tread carefully. And then you'd have to be even more careful when writing. I don't want anyone claiming you used off-the-record material in the piece."

"Yeah," Debbie said. "You know what I find really annoying?"

Sam smiled. "So many things annoy you, Debbie, that I can't even begin to guess."

"The unfairness of it all. The hoops and hurdles the Webbs put up make it even more attractive for a reporter to focus on people at the bottom of the socioeconomic ladder. Those are the people who don't have the time, energy, or money to try to throw an NDA in my face. If I wanted to make my life easier, I'd just focus on the people who can't throw grenades into my path."

Sam shook his head. "Are you just now realizing that the rules for the rich differ from those of the poor?"

"I've always known they're different. But I'm just experiencing it in a new and surprising way."

Sam looked at Debbie's foot. It was still shaking. "There's more, isn't there?"

Debbie looked down. Her foot stilled. "I, uh, I did a thing."

Sam asked slowly, unsure he was ready for the answer, "What sort of thing?"

"You know that house in Spanish Lake, the one targeted for the bust, supposedly part of the cartel ops?"

Sam drew his one-word answer out in two syllables. "Ye-es."

"Okay, well, after the Webbs, I knew I was too keyed up to come back to the office. Needed to dial it back a bit."

Sam's eyes widened at the idea that this was his reporter chilled.

"So I decided to drive by that house. I had a close-enough address; figured it would be pretty easy to find. And it was."

"And?"

"The neighborhood was quiet. What could it hurt to get out and take a few pictures? And then, well, I was in the backyard."

"Don't tell me you trespassed."

"Okay, I won't tell you."

Sam grimaced. "Did you at least get something good?"

"I ran into someone. Or he ran into me. Actually, he crawled out of a basement window while I stood there and watched."

Sam leaned forward. "Who was he?"

"I don't know. We both kinda freaked. He had a knife. Took my phone but then ran across the yard and dropped it for me to retrieve. He wanted to get away from me. He wasn't interested in hurting me."

Sam rested his forehead on his hand. What a stupid thing to do. And yet, he would've done the very same thing. "You coulda been hurt. And I wouldn't have had any idea where you were."

"But I wasn't."

"Why do you think he was there?"

"No idea. Maybe the guy was getting something he left behind. Or maybe he thought a vacant house presented a plunder opportunity."

"Did he have anything in his hands?"

"Apart from the knife? Not that I could see. All I know is that the dude had a slight build and a strong accent. Oh—and he was missing a finger."

Sam sat back in his chair. "You've got to be more careful. If something happens, our publisher is going to have my head."

"You gonna to tell him?"

"Tell him what?" Sam asked. "Just keep me in the loop a bit better."

Debbie shrugged. Her foot had stopped its nervous twittering. "Well, I'm meeting Connor tonight. After that, I have no idea."

Rather than rendezvous in the city's Central West End, as they had initially planned, Connor sent a text about half an hour before the meeting suggesting a trendy upscale bar in downtown Clayton, just around the corner from where Caleb died.

The watering hole was a gathering place for all the usual suspects. Lawyers in their courthouse attire. The business-casual crowd; men in their button-down shirts and khakis and women in black slacks and cardigans. A few overdressed interns, just barely legal.

Some were there to unwind with coworkers after a long day. Others wanted to delay their return home, where the night shift meant supervising homework or dealing with a cranky spouse. To be sure, there were also people on the prowl for a soul mate or a quick hookup. They were the ones who almost always suffered sunrise regret.

Debbie pushed the door open. A hot, moist blast collided with the frigid air, leaving her momentarily disoriented as she gazed into the soft yellow light. It took her eyes a few moments to adjust before she spotted Connor at the bar. He was leaning into the conversation with a blond woman in a black turtleneck stretched tightly across her ample chest. She had one hand resting on his forearm.

"Connor," Debbie said when she reached him. He'd been so engrossed in his chat that he hadn't noticed her.

"Debbie!" Connor said, abruptly pulling away from the woman whose grip on his arm had tightened. "Thanks so much for meeting me here. I was needed at the condo building. Paperwork. Always paperwork. And issues. Mom and Dad had dinner plans in Chesterfield. This was easier."

"Not a problem," Debbie said. "It was convenient for me too." Looking at the woman beside Connor, Debbie held out her hand. "I'm Debbie Bradley."

"Oh, sorry, this is, um," Connor stammered.

"Britney," the irritated woman volunteered.

"Britney," Connor repeated.

"Nice to meet you," Debbie said.

Connor turned to Britney. "It has been lovely catching up, but I'm afraid I'm going to have to cut this short."

"Fine, but I'll be at the bar if you need me," she said, frowning while her eyes scanned Debbie from head to toe. "You look like you should be carrying a clipboard or something."

Debbie's mouth opened, closed, then opened again. "Thanks?" It was good that she didn't have one because she'd be tempted to whack Britney over the head with it.

Connor cleared his throat. "Debbie, can I get you a beer?"

"Just a tonic water. With lime," Debbie said.

She didn't drink when she was on the job, and even if Connor might have other ideas, this was work for her.

Connor raised his hand, quickly catching the busy bartender's attention.

He must be a regular, Debbie guessed. And a good tipper. She reached into her wallet to pull out a twenty.

"No, no, I got this," Connor said before turning to the bartender. "Just put it on my tab and have someone send over another beer in five minutes."

"You got it, boss," the man said.

"Boss?" Debbie asked.

"Figure of speech," Connor said. "There's a table opening up. Why don't we grab it?"

They snapped up the table with drinks in hand a millisecond before another couple reached it.

"So," Connor began, "tonic water. I thought reporters all drank scotch or whiskey or some shit like that."

"That was last night. You shoulda seen me," Debbie joked, "drinking, smoking a pack of cigs, at the manual typewriter, *clack, clack, clack, ding.*"

"Very funny," Connor said as he drained his beer.

"Seriously, I've got to be in court in the morning. For a story."

It was the truth. The defendants swept up in the recent sting were scheduled for their first hearing in federal court. It was Debbie's first chance to check them out.

"What sort of story?" Connor asked.

"Oh, just another crime story," Debbie said vaguely. There was no way she would hint that it was her backup piece in case her story about Caleb fell through. Never tell your potential targets that there's an escape pod available. They'd never cooperate if they didn't think a story was inevitable.

"Thanks again for meeting with me," Debbie said, trying to change the subject.

"The least I could do after my dad's performance. I told him that it wouldn't work. And I'm assuming that your editor said no."

"That'd be correct," Debbie said, taking a sip of her drink.

Connor flashed an easy smile and placed one arm on the back of his chair, spreading his body more fully to take up the empty space. "Well," he began, "I've been reading your stuff. Nice piece on the mafia in St. Louis. Listened to your podcast. Entertaining. Cap'n Jack sounds like a character."

Debbie laughed. "Ah yes, Jack Flannery is an interesting man. He certainly makes for a good on-air guest. Livens things up. I'm going to have him back."

"I thought you did a pretty good job yourself. You really walked the listener through some complicated family and business connections without losing the good bits," Connor said. "I envy you. You must live an exciting life."

Debbie shrugged. "Me? Not really. Sure, some

moments are less boring than others, but I mostly just sit behind a desk and type words on a computer screen."

"No typewriter, then? Seriously, you get to meet all sorts of interesting people, even not-so-fascinating people like me. Must make your boyfriend jealous."

Debbie shifted in her seat. Did the guy really think he was being subtle? "No boyfriend."

"Girlfriend?"

"No. No girlfriend."

"Well, I don't see a ring. So I'm assuming you aren't married."

Debbie smiled. "Nope. Almost. Once. But I managed to squirm out of that trap."

"So, do you ever go out with people you meet on stories?"

Debbie smiled and took another sip to pause the conversation. An image of Chase popped briefly into her head.

"My editor says I'm one of the most annoying people he knows. And many of the people I interview agree with his assessment."

"I don't find you annoying."

"Oh, give me a little time," Debbie said. It was time to

take control of the conversation's direction. "So, how are you doing? It must be rough."

Connor's arm came down from the back of his chair. It was his turn to shift uncomfortably. "You know, I lost my brother a long time ago. He was gone before his body gave out." Connor paused, looked around the room, then continued. "I mean, we were so close." He stretched his arms out on the table and clasped his hands together, his shoulders drooping slightly. "I don't know if you've ever watched someone you love slip away like that, but it's awful. And you go through so many stages. You want to believe the lie: they've changed, they'll never do drugs again, they're clean. But as long as they hang out with people who enable that sort of life, it is nearly impossible to get them back."

"And your brother had someone like this in his life?"

"Yes. Yes, he did. She was a friend of his. And mine. Because we both have the same friend, and Caleb is my twin, my mom is a mess. She's terrified that I'm going to become an addict. If Caleb had some sort of genetic predisposition to addiction, well, we're identical. So she freaks out when I drink a beer, get a painkiller prescription."

He paused, draining the last of his beer. "It's bad enough that I'm trying to deal with my own grief, I've got to deal with my mother's terror about losing her only living child."

"What about your dad?"

"My dad? He's so buttoned up that you'll never get past his armor. The only thing he's scared of is losing control, whether it is the story of our family or your story."

"You mentioned people in Caleb's life that weren't healthy. Anyone in particular?" Debbie asked.

Connor let out a disdainful snort. "Someone we thought of as a member of our own family. A childhood friend."

Debbie sipped her drink and waited.

"I blame Macie," Connor said, the three words almost spitting from his mouth in anger.

"Macie?" Debbie repeated without betraying the fact she knew the woman.

"Yeah, Macie Holloway. Mace, as Caleb used to call her."

"Who is she?" Debbie asked as much to hear his side of the story as to test Macie's claims.

"We were all friends as kids: me, Caleb, and Macie. But she was bad news. Always sour and dark. I think she rubbed off on him. He got more distant. And eventually, she got him into heroin. And," Connor said as he leaned forward and grasped Debbie's one free hand before closing his mouth.

Debbie waited, restraining from asking, "And?" It was better to let the words unwind at their own pace.

"I think Macie killed Caleb. Who else coulda given him that last dose?"

"What makes you think she was the supplier?"

"Because she'd been his supplier in the past."

"Even if she did, do you really think it was on purpose? Or just an accident?"

"Does it matter? He's dead. And she gave him the lethal weapon. That was so Macie, always pushing Caleb. Besides, the law doesn't care if it was an accident. If you supply the drugs and someone dies, you can be put behind bars. A guy in St. Louis was sentenced to twenty-three years in prison for distributing fentanyl that ended in someone's death."

Debbie frowned. "Why haven't the police arrested her?"

"Oh, they've interviewed her. They're just gathering evidence. It has to be a rock-solid case. Her parents have money, so the cops only get one shot at doing it right. There isn't a lot of room for error. Her folks kept her from getting charged in the past. They'll do it again."

"But didn't I read somewhere that she had Narcan? Doesn't that undercut the argument that she was trying to kill him?"

"That's one of the hurdles the cops have to overcome. But if you're giving someone fent-laced heroin, you know one Narcan dose isn't enough." Connor paused. "Mark my words. Any day now, they're going to lock her up. Just you wait and see."

One hour and three beers later, Debbie suspected it was time to leave. When Connor's fourth drink arrived, she knew she had to go. The longer the evening wore on, the less meaningful the conversation became. And the more he drank, the bolder he got.

She'd be better served by retreating, resetting, and retrying another time—before Connor did something foolish that would force her to put him in his place.

Debbie resented having to think about the sexual undertones. It wasn't something that Christian ever considered. But like many women in their twenties trying to build a career and professional reputation, letting her guard down wasn't an option.

In the trenches, you've got to trust your instincts. And Debbie's gut said nothing good would come from staying.

"I really appreciate that you agreed to meet with me," Debbie said, rising from her chair and grabbing her bag.

"Oh, don't go," Connor begged. "The night is young. You're fascinating, Crime Beat Girl."

Debbie winced. She still hated that moniker.

"Unfortunately, I've got court in the morning. I need to work more tonight to prepare, but I hope we can try another interview with your family."

Debbie spotted Britney, eager to take Debbie's place. "Oh look, I think your friend Britney is still here."

Connor frowned. "Ugh. I'd rather spend time with you," he said as he watched Britney pick up her drink and walk toward him. "Oh well. I know how it goes. Duty calls. We'll do this again. Hopefully, when you don't have court. Call me."

"I've got your number. I'll be back in touch," Debbie

said as she retreated from the table in the bar where the after-work crowd was already thinning.

Outside, the sky was dark, even if it was only six. Short days could be cozy and hygge-like. Or depressing. It depended on whether you had someone to snuggle with.

Debbie sighed and texted her mom, whose office was only a few blocks away. Perhaps they could go grab a bite for dinner. With her trial looming, Beth was likely sitting in a conference room with stacks of paper piled around her.

As if connected telepathically, Debbie's phone vibrated. A text message from her mom.

"Case settled," Beth wrote before attaching a *Seinfeld* meme with Elaine, George, and Jerry doing a celebratory dance in the doorway of Jerry's apartment. Debbie smiled. If there was one thing she could count on, it was her mother's fondness for lame memes.

"Yay! U want to have dinner? I'm in Clayton," Debbie messaged. A few seconds later, her phone rang.

"Hey," Debbie said to her mom. "Congrats."

"Thanks. It was that wrongful death case, where the bastards didn't want to pay damages to cover the husband's lost wages because they said the wife didn't need it."

"I remember. Guess they had a change of heart?"

"More like the judge destroyed them in a settlement conference today. We finally got a serious offer. My client is happy. The judge is happy. I'm happy. What are you doing down here?"

"Had an off-the-record interview with Connor Webb."

"Interesting. Very interesting."

"Yeah, it was. I'll fill you in on the crazy day I've had when I see you. You want to grab a bite?"

"Um," Beth said, "well, Flannery happened to text after the case settled. Caught me in a weak moment. I already agreed to go to dinner with him. Why don't you join us?"

Debbie groaned. "My well of niceness is bone dry. Drained by Connor. Besides, three's a crowd."

"It's just dinner."

"Uh-huh," Debbie answered.

"Really," Beth said.

"Okay, okay. I believe you. But I'm exhausted. Freaking crazy day. Wait until I tell you about the NDA that Matt Webb wanted me to sign."

"He didn't!"

"He did!" Debbie said. "Look, I'm at my car. I'll tell you all about it when you get home tonight."

"Okay, you sure you don't want to join us?"

"I'm positive. I'll talk to you when you get home. Oh, and Mom, I know you know this, but don't mention Connor or the NDA to Flannery, okay?"

"Of course not."

"Love you."

"Love you, too."

Lafayette Park was the perfect nighttime surveillance spot. Just across the street from Debbie's house, the trees provided enough cover so that even the dogs being walked by their humans at the late hour overlooked J.R. So long as he stayed still.

Going undetected turned out to be one of his superpowers. It had gotten him across the border and helped him slip through more than one raid. Now, it could help him with his latest assignment.

Getting out of the car wasn't originally in his plans. At first, he thought he'd just nail down the location. He'd been given the address and a burner phone. But after sitting alone in the safe house for more than an hour, J.R. couldn't take staring at the walls with nothing to do. He might as well scout out the place.

It was easy enough to find—only fifteen minutes from his hideout. But once he found what he was looking for, J.R. had no desire to return to the bleak apartment. It might be a cold night, but being outside was better than locking yourself in a dingy solitary prison cell.

J.R. parked. His car was one of many on the street, so it wouldn't attract attention. From there, it was easy to hop out and find a place to observe the journalist. The home had windows that were at least the height of one and a half men. The drapes were open to a sitting room on the first floor. J.R. could see the young woman sitting in a chair, watching television when she wasn't checking her phone. Eventually, she got up and turned out all the lights save for one table lamp. A few moments later, a second-floor light came on. After what he guessed was twenty minutes, that light went out too.

Even though it was bitterly cold, he couldn't remember the last time he'd been outside alone, without a minder. In the solitude of the empty park, there was no one to make fun of his hands. There was no one shouting at him to work harder, faster. The yellow glow from the distant street lamps provided just enough light to let him see his breath curl up and away as it left his body. He warmed his hands in his pockets, flipped the collar up on his jacket, and looked heavenward at the stars in the night sky. It was an alien sky, different from the one over his village. At home, the night sky was brighter, more beautiful. Here, in this foreign land, the city's lights drained the universe of its sparkle. He wished someone had warned him that he'd surrender his sky if he left his land. Then again, the younger version of himself wouldn't have listened. Stubborn bull.

As he mulled over one ill-fated choice after another that had brought him to this moment, J.R. noticed that the lights had turned back on in the house. A middle-aged woman with perfect blond hair and a smile passed by the same window where the reporter had been. Rich American women, with their money to spend on beauty treatments and access to medical care, always looked younger than the hardworking women in his village. J.R. wondered if the woman he was looking at was the reporter's mother. But wasn't it odd for children to live with their parents after they were grown, at least in *Los*

Estados Unidos? Even from afar, he could tell there was a kindness about her. For most of his time in the United States, he'd encountered people with hollowed-out eyes, faces lined by deep creases and covered in splotches, or they had mouths that twisted with anger, menace, or spewed threats. No, this woman was radiant. A happy halo seemed to surround her face. This woman, he guessed, was in love.

A pity. The Bible lied when it said love was the greatest gift of all. Love was a curse, and curses don't bring happy endings.

15 PLEAS AND PLOTS

"Ms. Perkins, do you understand the charges against you?"

The United States magistrate judge with silver hair and a ruddy face dipped his chin slightly to look at the defendant over the top of his wire-rimmed glasses.

A woman, her brittle, dry, and faded red hair pulled back in a small ponytail secured by a rubber band the color of a mushy banana, brushed the thin bangs away from her face and said softly, "Yes, sir."

"And you understand that I've appointed a lawyer to represent you?"

"Yes sir," the defendant answered respectfully as she looked at the lawyer standing to her right, a woman in a navy blue suit and crisp white blouse with long, shiny blond hair pulled back tightly in a ponytail at the base of her neck.

It was Patty's first time being represented by a lady lawyer. And a young one at that. But man or woman, old or young, it made no difference to Patty. Fucked was fucked. She wasn't wriggling outta this one. There was no piece-of-shit boyfriend to blame. The best she could hope for was a ticket back to Vandalia Women's Prison. And it wouldn't be so bad. She got on with the people who ran it. Maybe she could even get her old job back. If she kept her mouth shut and head down, the inmates wouldn't pay her much attention. After all, no one wanted to mess with the cartel.

Plus, she was a survivor. But ol' Tom Wilkins? Patty had her doubts. They'd been snatched at the same time. Put in the same cop car together. When the handcuffs went on, he started crying. And it seemed like he'd been bawling and sniffling ever since.

Pussy. It was always the same with the men, even the ones who'd been through hard times. Faced with losing everything and spending a lifetime locked up, they unraveled. But women? No. Women knew from the time they were little girls what it meant to be trapped, powerless, afraid. They'd felt the intense terror that came with a man wrapping his hands around your neck and squeezing 'til you passed out. They knew that nagging, gnawing sort of fear, the kind that made you hold your breath, search the shadows, and grip your keys while walking to your car on an empty street at night. Women were cursed to live in jails all their lives: the homes ruled by their alcoholic fathers, the apartments they shared with their deadbeat boyfriends, the trailers that belonged to their two-timing husbands.

Real prison? Piece of cake. But for men? Take away the precious privilege white men didn't even know they had, and they turned into weak, angry, crying babies.

"All right," the judge said as he shuffled the stack of papers on his desk and studied them for a moment before looking back up at the defendant. "If you haven't had a chance to talk to your lawyer yet, the U.S. Marshal's office will keep you in the holdover cell for a little while longer before taking you back to the jail where they're holding you. Have you talked to her?"

"Only for a few minutes," the defendant answered.

"Okay, we'll make sure you get a chance to talk today," the judge said, looking directly at the U.S. Marshal standing in a corner to ensure the order was received. The armed marshal nodded.

"And, Ms. Perkins, how do you plead today?"

Patty looked at the stern Barbie by her side for direction.

"Your honor, my client pleads not guilty."

"Duly noted, Counsel. You may be seated, Ms. Perkins. Thank you, Counsel."

Patty, clad in an orange jumpsuit, shuffled back to the jury box where all the defendants were seated. A marshal replaced her handcuffs and then moved to one side to let her pass as the judge called out the next name on his list. "Mr. Tom Wilkins."

Patty watched as the sullen man, who'd seem to have lost a vertebra or two since they'd been taken to jail, got his cuffs removed then made his way to the podium. Patty noticed he locked eyes with a tight-lipped woman in the courtroom. Probably his wife. Patty knew some bits and pieces about the missus because Tom had been unloading his woes to her on the bus that had taken them from the Laclede County Detention Center to the federal courthouse. Somehow, she got stuck sitting next to him. And once he had her cornered, that man just didn't stop yammerin'.

He made Patty squirm. If Tom couldn't shut his pie hole, he was gonna end up shanked.

He said his wife had been yelling at him about the money. How was she going to live? Was the government going to take their house, their car, and her Precious Moments? "That hag cares more about those stupid figurines than me. After all I've done for her," Tom raged.

But Patty knew the score. The ol' lady was scairt, she could lose everything. And starting over as an old woman was nearly impossible. She was probably worried that her husband would try to shave time off his sentence by telling the feds where they'd hidden their drug money. Patty figured they'd buried it somewhere. After all, putting it in a bank woulda raised flags. And if they were like most of the people Patty knew, there was always some creditor just waiting to swoop in and garnish an account. But it was hard to garnish a coffee can.

A hole in the ground was the safest place for the side hustle money.

If Patty was the missus, she'd dig up those Folgers tins. But maybe, Patty realized, the wife didn't know where her husband had buried the money. Shame on her.

Never trust your man. That was Patty's motto.

The missus better wise up fast, better track down the buried treasure. The chances that her ol' man was going to live much longer were decreasing by the day. Patty could see it in Tom's eyes: He was a desperate man about to crack.

As Patricia Perkins sat down, Debbie scribbled a few notes about the woman. The indictment and press release indicated that the defendant was forty-five. Yet the hollow eyes, the brown skin spots, and the deep ruts in her cheek told a different story. Despite her hardened appearance, Patty's voice had been soft, demure.

Including Perkins, eight people had been brought before the judge, charged with the same drug conspiracy. All eight wearing matching orange jumpsuits. They'd been led into the courtroom, cuffed together, and seated in the jury box. Two marshals stood guard at each end of the area generally reserved for those deciding fates, not the ones whose destinies would be decided.

Debbie checked each defendant off her printed press release as they were summoned before the judge.

Chenche Montez, 24, of Mexico

Deon James Sutton, 28, of Spanish Lake, MO

Cleavon DeMarco Ellis, 22, of St. Louis

Patricia Dawn Perkins, 45, of Lebanon, MO

Thomas Jeffrey Wilkins, 52, of Lebanon, MO

Isidoro Colón, 31, of Mexico

Jaidyn Heaven Hahn, 23, of Spanish Lake, MO

Javin Charles Banks, 33, of St. Louis, MO

Because the defendants had been charged with federal crimes, the case was in federal court, the Thomas F. Eagleton U.S. Courthouse in downtown St. Louis. Completed in 2001, the Eagleton courthouse was a fusion of a courthouse and an office building. At least, that's how her dad used to describe it whenever he drove past on the way to a Cardinals game. "Look, Debbie. Did you know that building is the tallest courthouse in the United States?"

"Yeah, yeah," Debbie would answer. She'd heard the lecture so often that by the time she was a teenager, she didn't even bother looking up from her phone when her dad started his tour guide speech. "I know, I know," she'd say. "And it is also the second tallest judicial building in the world. Chicago is first."

"But you know what Chicago's not first in?" Cary would ask, in a typical dad voice.

"Baseball," Debbie often muttered.

Her dad loved architecture, history, trivia, and the Cardinals. And he was guilty of repeating the same story again and again. She hated that quirk when she was a kid. Now, she'd give anything for him to tell her a story she'd heard a thousand times, just once more.

Flannery could never be Cary Bradley. Never would be. And therefore, he wasn't worthy of her mother.

Debbie squeezed her eyes shut and took one deep breath. *Focus. Focus on Thomas Wilkins.* Hadn't she been the one who encouraged her mom to date? Teased her about Flannery? Why was she being such a brat about it all now?

Her mom had gotten home after midnight. She was a woman who rarely stayed out late to have fun. For work? Yes. Social meetings? No. And when Debbie walked into the kitchen the following morning, her mom was standing in front of the sink humming and looking out the window, smiling. Beth used to do that in the before times. Before Cary died. Never after. Debbie remembered sitting at the kitchen table as a little girl while her mom bustled about to that same melody. She had a vivid memory of the young, healthy, and mischievous version of her father surprising her mother, putting his arms around her waist while her back was to him. She'd laugh and lean into his embrace. He'd kiss her neck. She'd laugh again. "Go on. I'm busy," she'd say, waving him off. Cary would look at his daughter, shrug, roll his eyes, smile, and let go while saying, "How did I get so lucky, huh? Your mom is quite the catch."

Hearing her mother hum the melody triggered that long-forgotten memory. Something had happened to her mother since they'd last talked. Debbie knew it. And she didn't want to hear about it.

"Gotta get," Debbie said as she poured herself a to-go cup of coffee and practically ran out of the house before her mom could utter a word.

But now Flannery was here. In the courtroom. He'd dashed Debbie's plans to lose herself in her work until she was ready to process her emotions. His presence was like an ocean wave slamming against her face, leaving her sputtering and gasping for breath.

Of course, he was there. A pox on her for not considering the possibility. He'd been involved in the bust, one of many officers belonging to a word-salad buffet of acronym agencies. The FBI, the DEA, and the SLMPD. There was also the St. Louis County Police Department, the Laclede County Sheriff's Department, and the U.S. Marshals Service. And spearheading the prosecution, The U.S. Attorney's Organized Crime and Drug Enforcement Task Force.

Debbie spotted him when she'd scanned the courtroom after the prisoners were seated. He'd come in after her and stood in one of the back corners, talking to a woman Debbie recognized as an FBI special agent.

Debbie turned around before their eyes met. She wasn't sure who she dreaded speaking with more, Flannery or her mother.

"All rise," the bailiff commanded. The magistrate judge, a no-nonsense jurist who liked to keep the docket moving and the cases he was shepherding fair and error-free, entered and got right to work. Two hours and eight defendants later, he was done with the docket and had brought the gavel down to adjourn the proceedings.

Debbie kept her head down and focused on her notebook. She hoped Flannery would be long gone by the time she got up. She wasn't going to turn around to check.

Debbie felt a touch on her shoulder. Her jaw clenched and her stomach seized before she looked up. Instead of Flannery, a middle-aged lawyer she recognized but had never met was speaking.

"Ms. Bradley," he began. "I'm a big fan of your work. I enjoyed the Mafia Wars podcast that you recently aired."

"Thank you," Debbie said.

"Are you working on a story about this case?" he asked.

Debbie shrugged. "I might be. I thought I'd check it out. I'm interested in how heroin and fentanyl are impacting our metro area. You represent the lead defendant, right? Mr. Montez?"

"Yes. Yes, I do. I was retained yesterday. Anyway, let me know if I can be of help in anything, off the record, of course," the lawyer said, handing her his business card.

"Thanks, I will," Debbie said. Tucking the card into her purse, she noticed that the only person left in the courtroom was an assistant U.S. attorney slowly gathering documents together and shoving them in a folder. Debbie got up to leave. Just before she reached the courtroom door, she heard someone say, "Ms. Bradley, right?"

Debbie turned to the assistant U.S. attorney and smiled. "Please call me Debbie."

The prosecutor cleared her throat. "You know that I can't talk to you."

Debbie nodded. "Of course. I know I've got to go through your public information officer." PIO. Or, as Sam called them, pain in the orifice.

"Yes, that's the protocol. But if you're following this case, again, I can't talk to you, but you may want to pay attention to the motions to suppress evidence. What the defendants don't want to come before a jury can always make for an interesting read."

"Thanks," Debbie said. "I appreciate the tip."

The burgundy scarf made it easier to track the reporter. In some ways, it reminded J.R. of a bullfighter's cape. When he was a small boy, he dreamed of being a matador. He imagined wearing the *traje de luces*, the suit of lights. It would be the color of Rioja wine, embellished with gold thread. Gold-fringed pads would double the size of his slender shoulders. Silk stockings would show off his bulging calf muscles. Spectators in the stands would adore him. And the bull, proud and noble, would put up a fight worthy of the fierce beast. Yet, he alone would emerge victorious from the ring. "He killed it well," the people in the stands would proclaim.

But those were the fantasies of a boy. As a man, J.R. no longer believed bullfighters were heroes. He'd come to see it as a bloody sport rewarded with applause. And the more he was forced to live in a brutal world, the more he realized how often people confused cruelty for bravery. The truly courageous man was the one who clung to kindness in the face of savagery.

J.R. finally understood a simple truth: He was the bull, not the fighter, forced to battle for his life in an arena he would never leave alive.

He'd followed the journalist for several hours that morning, arriving at the house before the first lights came on. Parked a half-block down the street, his car backed into a diagonal space next to the park. He saw her as soon as she stepped out of the house. She bounded down the steps, oblivious to the possibility of black ice, a cup of coffee in one hand. She was wearing the same face he'd spied the night before, the one he guessed she only displayed when she assumed no one was looking, part sadness, part longing. Yearning for someone or something just out of reach. J.R. recognized that face because he'd seen that same look reflected back at him when he looked in the mirror.

16 ROAD TO LEBANON

There was something soothing about the scenery when driving out of St. Louis and heading west on Interstate 44; rolling hills, yellow grass, naked trees. But to make the most of the tranquil landscape, a driver had to tune out the plethora of roadside billboards advertising the Fantastic Caverns, antique malls, and Russell Stover candies. The one sign Debbie couldn't ignore was a black billboard with hand-painted white letters that declared: "USA for Sale Call Bill or Hillary."

Must be an ancient sign, she thought as she drove past. Had to be. Outrage over the Clintons was as outdated as the iPod. Now it was all about Biden and Trump. And the media. Left, right, or center, it seemed everyone hated the press. She'd have to be careful about disclosing she was a reporter.

As Taylor Swift sang, "You're on your own, kid. You always have been."

It was early afternoon. The morning's hearing in federal court had left her restless. Dread, the sort that was hard to identify, stalked her. Perhaps it was the looming deadline and the fact that she still needed to settle on a story. Then there was her mom and what would surely be an uncomfortable chat in their future.

When the going gets tough, the anxious hop in their car and speed away.

Debbie glanced at the empty McDonald's bag on the passenger seat. Her hands were still greasy from the French fries. Tasty on the way down but not so satisfying as they marinated in her stomach. And salty. Sam's bad habits were rubbing off on her. She picked up the soda that came with the crispy chicken sandwich meal and sipped through the straw, reminding her that she needed a bathroom break. Liquids imbibed meant liquids that would need to be expelled.

Fortunately, the truck stop she wanted to visit, which the feds alleged to be an important hub for the cartel, was located at the next exit. Debbie flipped on her blinker and veered off the highway, slowing her car as she reached the top of the ramp. To her right was the dingy and empty truck stop where Patricia had worked; even from a distance, the place looked abused and unloved. To the left was a truck and travel stop with bright lights and bustling activity. Debbie preferred the business on the left.

She turned right.

Even though the truck stop wasn't far from the interstate, her destination felt remote and isolated. There was only one car out front, already pulling away as Debbie drove up. She recalled a sci-fi trope where the main character turns onto a lonely road and unknowingly enters an alternate dimension with only one way in and no way out. Maybe she'd suffer a similar fate. On the bright side, if she was trapped in some parallel universe for eternity, she wouldn't have to talk to her mom about Flannery.

Debbie parked next to the gas pump. She could fill up using the twenty in her wallet. The truck stop seemed like a breeding ground for card skimmer devices and the scammers who installed them. Cash transactions were the safest.

Ever a city girl, desolate rural landscapes left her jittery. Even in the most dangerous urban area, there was almost always someone around to hear you scream. Not that they'd do anything about it, but still. Out here? Poof, you could disappear, your cries for help muffled by the wind and smothered by the sound of semis rumbling down the interstate. Your only hope was your cell phone tracker, assuming it had reception.

Debbie locked her car and headed for the entrance, pulling open a single door with a silver handle that somehow managed to be sticky even in the cold. A bell clanged. A man clad in a gray sweatshirt with a dark stain on his chest, patchy silver stubble on his face, and a bald head looked up from the counter.

"I'm gonna get gas," Debbie said. "But first, can I use your restroom?"

The man used his chin to point the way to the bathroom.

"Thanks," Debbie said, her eyes fixed on a small hallway. She walked past shelves offering Cheetos, regular and flamin' hot; Lays chips, plain and barbecue; Slim Jims, regular or Tabasco; and salted-in-the-shell sunflower seeds. Along the back wall, flanking either side of the dark opening that led to the bathrooms, were coolers with sodas, energy drinks, and some low-budget bottled water.

The first door, just inside the hallway, had a figure on a plaque with a round head and a triangle for the body.

Debbie twisted a scuffed plastic gold knob. It wobbled in her hand. The bathroom was made for one. She shut the grimy door firmly, pressing her shoulder against it to ensure it closed and turned the tab inside the knob to lock. She pulled on it once again. The last thing she needed was the creepy guy behind the counter "accidentally" entering. She looked hard at the space only after she'd secured the door. A trash can overflowed with paper towels in one corner. Between the trash can and the baseboard, Debbie spotted a dead cockroach. Half of its black body was in the bathroom, while the other half remained under the wall.

She took a deep breath and glanced at the toilet. The tank on the toilet was missing the lid. The seat wasn't uniformly white.

"No. Nope. No way," she whispered to herself. She'd wait. But she had to wash her hands. She stepped to the sink and turned on the hot tap with one finger. Ice-cold water ran out. She pressed the soap dispenser. Empty. She sighed again, turned the water off, and opened the door. It was time to start asking questions.

Debbie walked to the counter. The clerk stared blankly as she fished into her wallet and pulled out the twenty-dollar bill.

"Pump number one," Debbie said.

The man grunted.

"You work here long?" Debbie asked.

The man grunted.

"Ah, well, looks like the women's bathroom needs a refresh."

"Refresh," he snorted. "Fancy. I don't go near women's stuff. That's for the women employees."

"Well, maybe you could let one of them know?" Debbie suggested as cheerfully as she could muster. She wasn't really the bubbly sort, but sometimes a big smile and girly voice worked.

"Ain't got none," he said.

"I could've sworn that the last time I was here, there was a nice gal," Debbie said. "We chatted for a bit. Patty, I think?"

His eyes narrowed. "Ain't no one here named Patty."

"Huh. Patricia?"

"Nope."

"Maybe I'm getting my stops mixed up," Debbie said.

The clerk pursed his lips, and his jaw tightened. "Pump's ready. People in these parts will steal your gas if you don't get out there and start fillin' 'er up. And I'm not the sort to stick my neck out and stop them."

Debbie put her wallet back in her purse. "Okay, then," she said, noticing another car was getting gas near hers.

As she emerged from the shop, she noticed two cars, one of which was already pulling away. At the other, a man was just replacing the handle in the slot on the pump. He looked at her briefly before getting in his car. Younger, short brownish-blond hair. He looked somewhat familiar, but she wasn't sure from where.

As he got in the car and edged away, Debbie grabbed the nozzle from the pump and began to fill her tank. She noticed something on her windshield, just in front of the driver's seat. While the gas flowed into her tank, Debbie inspected the object.

It looked like a playing card. The side of the card facing out had words in Spanish. Words she didn't understand. The title line began *La Santa Muerte*. Debbie flipped the card over, where a female skeleton draped in religious blue robes was depicted. Debbie looked around. The other car had left. The cashier appeared to be watching the small black-and-white television or the security camera monitors. It was hard to tell because they were next to one another.

Ka-chunk. Debbie jumped before realizing the noise came from the fuel pump handle, a sign that her tank had been filled. She removed the handle from her car, replaced it on the pump, screwed the gas cap back into place, and paused momentarily before marching back into the store.

"Do you know who left this?" Debbie asked the cashier, holding up the card left on her windshield.

The man squinted momentarily as he looked at the object that Debbie was waving in front of him. His lips turned downward. "I don't know nuthin' 'bout nuthin, now git on out," he said, "before I pick you up and take you out."

"You wouldn't dare," Debbie said.

The clerk stared at her for a moment. His eyebrows arched to show the bloodshot whites of his eyes, and his glance moved to the end of the counter.

Debbie weighed her options. This was a lonely place for a battle. And she was outmatched in size. "I'm not done with you," she muttered as she retreated to her car, which she'd left unlocked. Fortunately, no one had touched her bag.

Debbie sat in the driver's seat and put her hands on the steering wheel. An image of Horseshoe Jimmy and his exploded Cordoba on Interstate 55 flashed in her mind. She paused briefly, slid her key into the ignition, then waited.

She looked through the shop window and into the eyes of the clerk. *He knows something*, Debbie thought. She paused to give him time to hold up his hands to warn her. After all, she'd take out the fuel pumps if her car exploded in a fireball.

He didn't move a muscle. Debbie squeezed her eyelids together and turned the key. The engine wheezed to life. It didn't sound good, but it sounded normal. She exhaled and leaned back. She recalled Paulie Leisure and the legs he'd lost in the blast outside his mother's house. She let her car idle for a couple of minutes, allowing the Civic to warm up and for her rapid heartbeat to stabilize. Then, holding her breath again, she grabbed the gear shift, clicked the button on the handle that would let her move the stick, and put it into drive. The only sound she heard was her tires crunching the tiny bits of stray de-icing pellets still on the parking lot.

Safe, she concluded. Incorrectly, as it turned out.

Freedom was J.R.'s sole passenger. Last night, cloaked in darkness, freedom had stroked his cheek lovingly. Today, driving down the highway midafternoon, she belligerently tried to wrest the steering wheel from him. *Forget Debbie Bradley*, she urged. *Canada is where we should go.* But forgetting Debbie meant abandoning *them*. As long they were prisoners of the cartel, so was he.

He followed the reporter from a distance. Occasionally, a tractor-trailer would come between them. Nothing permanent, only a brief complication. But even a few minutes of driving behind an eighteen-wheeler made him remember how it felt to be trapped inside the claustrophobic box.

He'd come up from the border in the back of a semi, sandwiched between a hunched old man in a red-and-blue flannel shirt and a blank-faced teen girl in a yellow T-shirt and dirty jeans. They'd been pushed to the far end of the trailer, closest to the cab, then hidden by cargo encased in cardboard. What else the trucker was hauling,

J.R. didn't know. For hours, they jostled about. The silence disturbed only by a rattle that emanated from the depths of the steel beast when they hit a large bump.

There were no windows for the three grim-faced stowaways to gaze out of as the countryside rolled past. There were no bathroom breaks. No food. No water. And the only warning that their fate was about to change came when the truck stopped. The back of the trailer opened, and boxes slid across the floor, creating a narrow path down the middle. Footsteps shook the trailer, and then two men appeared. J.R. recognized the truck's driver. But the other man he'd never seen.

"Which one?" the stranger J.R. had never seen, the one he'd later call *capitán*, asked.

"Him," the truck driver said.

"You gotta be shittin' me. Those fuckers sent me a dude with nine digits? He speak English?"

The truck driver shrugged. "Don't know. Don't want to know. None of my business. Just get your guy. I got more deliveries to make," he said, looking at the other two in the truck.

"Yo," the truck driver said, looking at J.R., "let's go."

J.R. looked at him blankly, feigning ignorance.

The truck driver huffed. "*Tú!*" the driver barked while pointing at J.R. "*Vamos!*"

J.R. touched his hand to his chest as if asking silently, "Me?"

"Sí! Vamos!"

J.R. got up. His two companions also started to move.

"No!" the truck driver shouted, not the clipped Spanish *no*, but the extended American version that stretched the O out down the street, around the block, and to the next corner. "*Dos, no. No vamos.*"

Shitty Spanish speaker, J.R. had thought at the time. J.R.'s English was better. Not that anyone would know. It was better if people thought you were stupid. That you didn't understand. Increase the frustration of communicating orders, and you reduce how often people ask you to work. As an added bonus, people will say things they shouldn't if they think you don't understand. Having access to secrets could mean the difference between living and dying.

Who knows, maybe the fact he was so good at fading into the background, becoming utterly forgettable, had saved him in the raid. He'd been all alone in the basement, working, when he heard the flash-bang grenades go off. The police entered the house through the back, the front, and the garage. But the basement window wasn't a priority. Too small. Besides, the Capitán and his men were causing a scene on the floor above J.R.'s head. It was enough of a diversion to allow J.R. to slip out and slip away.

Following Debbie Bradley's Honda Civic, he recalled his two travel companions in that tractor-trailer. What had happened to them? The girl, he had a good guess. Probably forced into a sex trafficking ring, he thought as he quickly tried to push the speculation out of his mind. Linger too long on the girl's fate, and her face would morph into his daughter's.

The old man? What use was he? J.R. wondered. Maybe a lookout? Capitán could've used one. If he'd had a sentry, he might've been able to get away instead of being hauled into jail. Maybe the old man had a hidden talent. Perhaps he was someone's father or grandfather, being used as a motivator, a valuable hostage to get someone to do something they didn't want.

This spying is going to drive me mad, J.R. thought. Too much time to think. When he was batching, he was busy with his hands. His thoughts were absorbed with the manual tasks he'd been given. And if he needed a distraction, he'd set achievement goals, even if doing a job well in the service of the drug trade was a dubious distinction.

The right blinker on the reporter's car announced her next move. J.R. followed her as she left the interstate and turned onto an outer road. She pulled into the truck stop. He drove past. About a mile down the road, he made a U-turn. The reporter was already inside the truck stop by the time he'd pulled into the lot and parked at a pump in front of and to the left of the spot where the Civic had parked.

After turning off the engine, he reached into the glove box and pulled out the credit card he'd been instructed to use. Francisco Gomez, the card said. J.R. had no idea who owned the card, but he guessed that Gomez had been the victim of identity theft. And the name was missing the accent above the o. Francisco was either an American or the theft victim of an English speaker. He also had no idea how long the card would work. He swiped it at the pump, keyed in a zip code written in marker on the card, and held his breath until the instructions "lift handle" appeared on the screen.

A gringo pulled into the station and parked just across from J.R.'s car and in front of Debbie's Civic.

As J.R. pumped gas, he watched the reporter. She was speaking to a heavyset, unfriendly-looking man behind a counter. Stalling for time, J.R. walked over to a bucket and pulled out a long-handled windshield cleaner. The sponge at the end was frozen.

As he pretended to clean his windshield, J.R. caught a glimpse of the gringo who'd gotten out of the car. His hair was closely cropped to his head. He was young, just barely a man in J.R.'s estimation. He had the hollow eyes of a heroin addict. The driver inserted the gas nozzle into the tank of his car, a beat-up white Altima. The brown-haired man—in Mexico, they would've described his hair as blond—put his hands in his pockets with the gas tank filled. He looked over both shoulders. His eyes swept briefly over J.R.

The man reached toward his back pocket and took out something the size of a playing card. He walked to Debbie's car, lifted the driver's side windshield wiper, and placed it in the center. It would be hard for the reporter to miss whatever had been left. The figure then hustled back to his vehicle as the gas still pumped. He looked at

J.R. again. This time, he raised his index finger to his lips.

Debbie guessed that dinosaurs had roamed the Earth the last time a no-vacancy sign flashed at the motel in Lebanon. Well, maybe not that long ago. If truth be told, the glory days for the travel lodge probably dovetailed with the heyday of Route 66. Now, the only ones getting their kicks, at least if the feds were to be believed, were drug traffickers who repurposed the site as a distribution hub impersonating a resting place for weary drivers and their cranky passengers. It was only a matter of time before the property was seized as part of a drug forfeiture unless the feds saw the old motel not as an asset but as a liability to look after.

The Civic's tires crunched over gravel. The nose of her front bumper frequently dipped as her car encountered crater after crater in the parking lot. The place wasn't completely deserted. A naked semi, sans trailer, was parked in the distance. Five Harleys were lined up out front. Cigarette butts, empty cigarillo packets, and broken Jim Beam bottles littered the ground.

Debbie climbed out of her car, snapped a few photos,

and headed toward the main entrance. She half-expected Sarah Connor and Kyle Reese to emerge from one of the rooms with a backpack full of pipe bombs.

Christian was the one who'd introduced her to the *Terminator* movies. They'd been dating for about five months and had moved past the stage of disclosing big secrets. Now, they were in that relationship phase of small but surprising discoveries. "You've never seen *The Terminator*?" he'd asked incredulously one day when they'd debated Arnold Schwarzenegger, Maria Shriver, and the housekeeper.

Debbie smiled sheepishly. "I've seen snippets. But I never watched it all the way through." She didn't admit that she preferred *Harry Potter*, *Pirates of the Caribbean*, and every cheesy *Twilight* film over big action movies. As a young teen, she hadn't been immune to the charms of Robert Pattinson and Taylor Lautner. She could never make up her mind if she was a member of Team Edward or Team Jacob.

"Well, we've got to beef up your film education," he told her. "I mean, I'd have sworn you'd be a fan of Sarah Connor. We'll watch the first and the second. T2 is better. But you need to see the original to appreciate the whole story," he claimed. "As for the rest of the movies, Eh. So-so."

They agreed on a Saturday movie marathon. They started the first movie at four. Then they paused for pizza, beer, and a passionate bedroom intermission. Then it was on to the second movie. Christian had made Debbie promise to withhold her film review until after seeing both. When the last of the credits rolled, Christian turned to her and asked, "Well?"

"Well," Debbie said slowly, "well, I have to disagree with you. The first movie was the best. Definitely. More original. More surprising."

Christian shook his head. "It's so dated. Raw. The second movie, the effects. So much better. Slicker."

"But the love story between Kyle and Sarah," Debbie argued. "The transformation of Sarah Connor from fumbling waitress to on-your-feet soldier badass."

"I knew you'd like Sarah Connor," Christian said triumphantly.

Debbie let out a small sigh as she approached the motel lobby. She hadn't thought about that Saturday in a long time. Like Sarah and Kyle, Debbie and Christian weren't meant to be together forever and ever, amen.

Sarah had her gun, a German shepherd, and a kick-ass red Jeep. Debbie had her notebook, a creepy prayer card of the saint of death in her back pocket, and a Civic that would die any day now.

At least she wasn't pregnant like Sarah Connor. Or Macie.

The front desk was topped with an avocado-colored Formica counter. A wheezy ice machine sputtered and coughed in one corner, much like an old man with post-nasal drip trying to clear his throat. Wallpaper, once green-and-white, was now faded and yellowed, missing in some spots, corners peeling away in others. The floor was covered in a gold shag that had probably been last cleaned during the Bicentennial.

A woman appeared from a doorway just behind the counter. Her once-black hair was splotched with bits of silver, which she wore in a loose ponytail. Dark circles gave her eyes a haunted air. The ligaments on either side of her neck drooped. There were traces of a younger, prettier face, but it was more of a distant echo than a clear, crisp sound. Maybe she was thirty-five, perhaps she was forty-five. Stress and poverty added years onto a person's face.

"*Hola*," the woman said in an accented voice that Debbie placed south of the U.S. border.

Debbie weighed her surroundings. The woman didn't seem to be a threat. "My name is Debbie Bradley. I'm a writer for *River City* magazine, out of St. Louis."

The woman stared at her blankly.

Debbie continued. "I'm working on a story about drugs moving up and down the interstate. I was hoping to ask you some questions."

The woman shook her head no as her hand nervously played with a piece of paper on the counter before her. "*Por favor.* Go."

"Just a few questions," Debbie said as sweetly as possible. "I was just wonderin' if you own the place or if you work here."

The woman's eyes widened as her gaze wandered over Debbie's shoulder. "*Madre de Dios*," she whispered.

Debbie turned around, but she saw nothing. "Pardon?" Debbie asked.

"Please, please go," the woman said as she retreated back into the doorway from where she'd originally materialized. Then she slammed a door.

Debbie's story exhaled with another death rattle.

"*Gracias, Santa Muerte*," she muttered.

On the one hand, J.R. admired the reporter's bravery. Instead of shrinking from an iffy encounter, she hurtled toward it as if protected by some magical force field. Of course, he'd been that way once upon a time. He believed he'd been anointed with an oil of invincibility. He was the hero of his story. As long as his intentions were pure and noble, nothing bad could ever happen.

Youth was a drug, like alcohol, cocaine, heroin, or fent. Under the influence, you were reckless, your judgment whacked. And youth left in its wake wreckage you'd spend the remainder of your life trying to clean, fix, or forget.

Debbie Bradley was still under the illusion she was untouchable. J.R. hoped he wouldn't be around when her world imploded around her. Surely, the end of her charmed life was near. Picking a fight with a truck stop cashier in the middle of nowhere wasn't a good idea. And the white Altima's appearance was concerning.

He'd left the truck stop shortly after Debbie found the card under her windshield. Trying to figure out where he could watch her without being obvious took a lot of creativity. Tailing someone in the middle of nowhere was like playing hide and seek on a fallow field in Kansas.

As luck would have it, he'd pulled into the motel parking lot across the street from the truck stop. She wasn't far behind. He'd ducked down in his seat so she wouldn't spot him as she drove past and only left the car to follow her after she entered the motel.

The lobby was dark and dingy. Debbie stood alone at the counter. Behind the counter was a doorway. J.R. guessed it was to the motel's office. While the reporter waited, she looked about the room, her eyes seeming to take in every detail.

And that's when a woman appeared. An apparition crossing a doorway, stepping from one world and emerging into another.

J.R. froze. A sharp pain in his chest snatched away his breath. He bent over, pressing his hands to his knees to steady himself. He squeezed his eyelids shut and opened them again before straightening back up. His mind had to be playing a cruel trick.

He peered into the window again. It was her. A face he'd never forget. Her hair was grayer than the last time they were together. He'd always loved her hair, even when they were kids. They sat next to one another in the village grade school. Back then, she wore it in two ponytails on either side of her face. Sometimes they were low on her head, and sometimes high. He'd been tempted to tug a ponytail once or twice, but that would be mean. Unlike some bully boys in his class, he was too polite to do such a naughty thing.

It wasn't until they were seventeen that he saw her silky hair long, straight, and hanging down her back. The occasion was the Día de los Muertos parade. She wore a white short-sleeved shirt that flattered her chest and displayed her slender arms. The colorful full-length skirt complemented her narrow waist. She balanced a large wicker basket filled with orange marigolds on her head. Marigolds were tucked behind her left ear. There were two halves to her face. One half had been painted white like a skull whose flesh had rotted away. But the other half of her face, that half belonged to a young woman with dark eyes, a high rose-hued cheekbone, and half of her mouth covered in deep red lipstick. Even though part of her symbolized death, the other part was ripe with vitality and life. The girl he'd loved was now a woman he was determined to possess.

He didn't know it then, but it was the day he doomed them both. And here she was again: His wife. The mother of his daughter. The three of them suffered because of his bargain with the cartel. Was Santa Muerte finally bringing them together forever or allowing him to say a last goodbye?

J.R. returned to his car to wait. Debbie Bradley emerged and drove off. The white Altima followed. J.R. didn't care. Santa Muerte was guiding him to Marcela.

17 INCONSISTENCIES

"Macie, can you please come in here?" Her father was using his command voice. It was not a request.

"Uh-oh. What have you done now?" Caleb whispered. His sardonic commentary and bemused smile were driving her nuts.

"Fuck if I know. What haven't I done?" Macie mumbled as she rose from her chair. It sucked to be treated like a child when you were a grown woman. Even worse when it happened at work. If her parents knew she was pregnant—she didn't even want to think about it. The last shred of control she exercised over her life would be snatched away by those who said they knew better than she. Her parents. Caleb's parents. Then her parents would fight for control of the baby with Caleb's parents. "Yeah," Caleb said in her head. "They'll tell you it is all for your own good. You're just a vessel, Mace."

"Damn you, Caleb. If you were here, we could figure out what to do. You left behind such a mess." He didn't respond as Macie glanced at her purse. The window for using the pills she was carrying was now nearly closed.

If she could rewind time, there were two moments she'd revisit. And which one she'd tackle first depended on how she felt about Caleb. Right now, her number one redo was sleeping with Caleb. She wouldn't do it, no matter how shaken, afraid, and vulnerable he seemed. She'd never give him that hug that lingered too long. She'd break away before soothing him with a pat on the back that turned into a caress. She wouldn't stroke his hair or kiss his cheek to wipe away his tears. She wouldn't let herself be moved by the pain he refused to explain, even as he suffered on the couch beside her. She'd be the cold bitch that everyone but Caleb believed she was. And the second moment? That was easy. She'd stop Caleb from that overdose. Or at least she'd bring two doses of Narcan, not one.

Fuckin' Caleb, she thought before knocking on the outside of her father's door, even though it was slightly cracked.

"Come in, Macie."

She pushed open the door to her father's office. His interior designer had gone a bit crazy with mahogany. At least, that was Macie's humble opinion. His desk and the bookshelves that lined the walls of his office were saturated with reddish-brown wood. He sat behind the wood monstrosity, his thick black-and-silver hair contrasting with the tan from the cruise her parents took over Christmas. Her father's hands were clasped confidently in front of him. He projected the calm competence his clients valued. Seated across from him was a man Macie didn't recognize. He got up out of his chair as Macie entered the room. On the outside looking in, Macie's appearance mimicked the arrival of a second guest on an evening talk show, where everyone smiles at the camera and acts like they're happy to be there. Yet, underneath the grins, Macie sensed the tension.

"Umm, not good," Caleb remarked, followed by one of his nervous laughs.

"Macie, this is Detective Flannery," her father began.

The detective towered over her. Macie extended her hand as she'd been taught to do at her fancy private high school so long ago. She gripped firmly. She could still recall her chemistry teacher's admonition: "I don't want to shake a piece of boiled bacon. Flabby hands are the province of weak women."

"Dear, why don't you sit down," her father suggested.

The dutiful daughter did as she was told.

"Macie, Detective Flannery has some questions about Caleb's death."

"I already answered questions," Macie said tersely.

Macie's father nodded solemnly. "I know, honey. That's what I told Detective Flannery. But it seems he has a few more questions. I don't really know whether we can help him. Of course, we always want to help our brave men and women in blue. So let's hear what he has to say. If you can answer and clear everything up so he can be on his way, then great. If not, well, we'll hand this off to our lawyer. Okay?"

Macie nodded. Caleb, invoking one of his preteen favorites, coughed *bullshit*.

"Detective Flannery, I already told the police everything I know. I'm not sure what I can add."

"Ms. Holloway, I appreciate all the cooperation you've provided. It has been a great help to our investigation."

"How much of an investigation can there be? Caleb

244

OD'd. I tried to help him, but I couldn't. I called nine-one-one. They showed up. But he couldn't be saved. As I understand it, I'm protected by the Good Samaritan law."

"Ms. Holloway, where did Caleb get the drugs from?"

"As I said earlier, I don't know. He just said it was a trusted source."

"And it was just you two together that night?"

"Detective Flannery, I already gave my statement. What are you getting at?"

"The Webbs believe you supplied the drugs. It turns out it was heroin laced with fent, a rather sophisticated blend. You've got a chemistry background. And well, a history with heroin."

"What, a *Breaking Bad* theory? Come on, Detective. The Webbs don't have much of an imagination, do they? I'm clean. They even tested me that night. I hadn't even had a sip of alcohol."

"That makes the Webbs even more suspicious. I mean, if you knew the dose was dangerous, you wouldn't take it. So I'm wondering if there was someone else who could back your story up. It would let me remove you as a suspect."

"But the Good Samaritan law. It protects me," Macie

stammered.

"It isn't absolute immunity, Ms. Holloway. If you possessed drugs or even supplied them, you've got some exposure."

"Detective Flannery," Macie's dad interjected, "the Webbs have long blamed our Macie for their son's addiction. They believe that Caleb was pure and innocent. In their eyes, Connor and Caleb were perfect boys until they were corrupted by our daughter. I know how hard it is to accept your children have flaws. It is quite painful to realize that they've disappointed you; let you down. But the sooner you accept it, the sooner you move on. You deal with your kids as they are, not as you wish them to be. I'm sorry, Detective, but you've been sent on an errand of vengeance by the Webbs. I can assure you that the Holloways won't be dragged down into this mess. Caleb was a screwed-up kid who overdosed. It is sad but true. The Webbs need to learn to deal with it. Any further questions will have to go through our lawyer."

Reward of up to $10,000,000 USD for information leading to the arrest of Eduardo 'Dardo' Recio a/k/a 'El Duro'.

The poster left on El Duro's desk included three photos. A color picture in which he had a goatee, a black-and-white image, and another color image where he only had his mustache.

"Kiko, did you see this?" Duro asked, looking up from the flyer as his assistant entered his office.

"*Sí,*" he said, bracing himself for his boss's reaction. "They've doubled the reward."

El Duro nodded. "And there's an email address dedicated all to me: Durotips@usdog.gov. Snitches can even tweet tips!"

Kiko shook his head disapprovingly. "What happened to the good ol' days when it was just a poster in the town square and a phone number you had to call?"

El Duro picked up a pack of Marlboros, plucked a cigarette from the box, lit it, then offered the smokes to Kiko, who held up one hand. "I'm trying to cut back."

His boss shook his head. "Narcos quitting smoking for their health. Now I've heard everything. A bullet will catch us long before cancer."

"I know, I know. I promised my wife. We just found out our daughter is pregnant. So now my wife doesn't want me smoking. Says I need to think about the grandbabies. And this is our first. You'd think my wife couldn't get any bossier. But turn her into a grandmother? *Hay qué ver.*"

El Duro took a long drag of his cigarette and exhaled slowly, smoke curling into the air. "What's the latest in San Luis?"

"One of the guys in jail, an old trucker, is making us nervous. Afraid he might flip."

El Duro stroked his goatee. "Keep an eye on him. And our nine-fingered friend?"

"Following the reporter. She's boring. His reports are boring."

"Boring is good. I fucking love boring."

"We need to get José Rodrigo back to work. He makes us money batching. He's a peasant, not Sherlock Holmes."

"Worker productivity. Nice business sense, Kiko. You're coming along. But don't move him. Not yet. Journalists are unpredictable. Keep an eye on her a little bit longer. Besides, it will keep our contact focused. Let them know we're watching."

"*Sí, jefe.*"

"I've been working on a side project in San Luis."

Kiko waited. His boss had a habit of withholding information from his top lieutenants. If your second in command knows everything, then there's no more need to be second. Kiko knew this was how El Duro thought. He understood the man as if he was his own brother. It was why Kiko was still alive.

El Duro's eyes went to his poison dart frog and lingered momentarily.

"We need to own more of the supply chain, the legal stuff that goes into in-demand street products."

Kiko listened. He'd be the first to admit he wasn't gifted in the imagination department. "Not many so-called legitimate businessmen are willing to work with us."

"If you have enough money, there are ways. Start-ups willing to look the other way to grab funding. You can also be the silent owner of a business and place your own person at the top. Someone with the right pedigree. Someone who went to the right schools and has the right connections."

"Why would someone like that agree to be a puppet leader?"

"You catch them when they're desperate and

vulnerable."

"And you have such a person in mind?"

El Duro walked over to his poison dart frog and dropped a fresh box of crickets inside and nodded. "Just a little bit longer, and my choice will be running toward the safe embrace of Tío Dardo." He paused. "Have you picked a *padrino* for your grandchild?"

"We would be so honored if you would consider it."

"Well, I am your daughter's godfather. Why not her baby's, too?"

"*Muchas gracias*, Duro. My family will be delighted."

"I need to disappear. Maybe you, too."

Alex looked up from his phone as Macie paced around her apartment.

"C'mon, Mace," Alex began. His friend stopped in her tracks.

"Macie," she corrected him.

"Was it really that bad?"

"Yeah," she answered as she began pacing again.

"Will you please sit down? You're creeping me out."

"You shoulda heard that smug cop. And my dad. The

shit went down after the detective left. Mister Cool starts screaming about how I was ruining the Holloway name. How me and Caleb were selfish brats. You know he threatened to cut me off? But if he did, then how would he protect the family name?"

"What'd you say?"

"What could I say? If I argued, it would make him angrier; telling him I hadn't done anything wrong would just wind him up again. He'd start going over all the times I've lied in the past. That guy has memorized a list, and he loves adding to it. Believe me. So I just sat there. Went to my happy place." Macie didn't tell Alex that Caleb had kept her company while she tuned out.

"What'd you tell the cop?"

"You mean, did I tell them you were there?"

"In case you hadn't noticed, I don't come from a family with money who can bring in a bunch of fancy lawyers to protect me," Alex said. "I'm a nobody with nothing. They find out I was there, and I guarantee they'll pin Caleb's death on me. And I can't claim to be a Good Samaritan since I didn't stick around."

"I don't know how you could drag yourself out of Caleb's apartment. Or how you got out of the building with no one noticing. You were high as a kite."

"The last thing I remember is telling you Caleb was noddin'. Next thing I know, I'm on my uncle's couch the next morning reading your text that Caleb was dead," Alex said. "You know how it is after you shoot up. Sometimes there's a void. Anyways, did you tell the cop?"

"Are you kiddin'? I'm fucked no matter what I do. If I tell them you were there, then I lied in my original statement. And my parents, ugh, they'll find some treatment center to lock me up forever. But someone's gonna figure out I'm not telling the truth. I mean, there must be surveillance footage of us being together. Clayton is full of cameras. Not to mention our text messages. They're probably getting a warrant for my messages right now."

"Do you really think the cops would go that far?"

"Are you kidding? With the Webbs turning up the heat? Then there's that reporter."

"What reporter?"

"I didn't tell you about her?"

"No."

"Are you sure?"

"Macie, I'd remember something like that. What'd she

want?"

"She's trying to put together a story on Caleb."

"Did you talk to her?"

"Not really."

"What do you mean, not really?"

"I was polite. Nothing more."

"This is bleak, Macie. Bleak." Alex put his head in his hands before looking up. "I know some people who know some people. Maybe I can help you, er us, find a way out."

18 DOUBLE BACK

"Well, it ain't no winnin' lotto ticket. I can tell you that much," Cap'n Jack said as he returned the Santa Muerte devotional card to Debbie. "You say it was left on your windshield outside a, whadya call it? Sketchy truck stop?"

Debbie nodded and raised the bottle of Schlafly Triple IPA to her lips. Jack's girlfriend, Noreen Shanahan, had handed it to her without asking. The journalist wasn't about to say no, even if she had a strict rule against drinking while on the job. Between the trip to Lebanon and an uncomfortable conversation with her mom earlier that afternoon, a cold beer sounded pretty damn good. And besides, she wasn't working. Not really. Jack had nothing to do with the story. He was an outsider who just happened to have a vast store of insider knowledge.

"I didn't figure Cap'n Jack for the craft brew type,"

Debbie remarked.

"He isn't," Noreen volunteered as she climbed onto the couch next to Jack. Clad in black leggings and a loose-fitting white boat-necked sweater, Noreen tucked her legs lotus style underneath her body. She pulled a long silver braid over her shoulder to avoid leaning on her hair.

"Long story short, I was always Bud man, through and through," Jack admitted. "You know, rah-rah, support the home team. But then AB sold out for thirty pieces of silver," he said. "Gone like Ralston Purina, McDonnell Douglas, Famous-Barr, A.G. Edwards. The list goes on and on. When it comes to beer now, whatever Noreen's offerin', I'm acceptin'."

Noreen placed a hand with traces of watercolor paint on Jack's knee and smiled. "So, Santa Muerte?"

"Some say she was the mystical product of Aztec worship and Catholicism, very much a cult figure whose influence extends beyond the narcos. Back in the day when we'd host cops from Mexico, plenty of 'em carried a card like the one you have in their wallets. She's the image of death. But what she means can be complicated. To some, she provides protection or health. You know, it's a little easier to ask her to help keep you safe by

255

making sure your bullets go through your enemy than it is to turn to the Virgin Mary. I mean, smiting enemies isn't the Mother of God's MO, is it? But let's say your bullets don't kill your foes. Things don't work out for you as you hoped. You get whacked. Santa Muerte is supposed to make sure you cross over safely to the afterlife."

"So, is the card meant to be a blessing or a curse?" Noreen asked.

Jack took a long swig of his beer and looked hard at Debbie. "Maybe it's neither. Maybe it's an omen. Death and Santa Muerte are inseparable. But we don't know who she's got her eye on. That is, if you believe all that claptrap."

Noreen frowned. Jack didn't miss her concern. "Debbie, you sure you don't want to talk to my nephew?"

"I don't need him mixed up too tightly in my story. And I don't need to be in the middle of his investigation," Debbie answered. What she didn't mention was the connection between her mom and Flannery. If Debbie confided in Flannery, he might feel he owed it to spill the tale to Beth. It would be all levels of annoying, as far as Debbie was concerned. "You said she's revered by the cartel and cops. Who else?"

"Folks who live short, dangerous lives: the cartel, villagers caught in the middle of the war between the Mexican military and the drug paramilitary. Military guys, cops, even prison guards, lawyers, and social workers."

"That's quite a collection," Noreen added. "And journalists?"

Debbie chimed in. "I don't know how many reporters in Mexico have Santa Muerte pinned to their bulletin boards. But I do know that reporting on political corruption, the cartel, the drug trade, or all three can get you killed."

Jack nodded. "Yep. Three groups twisted tighter than a ball of mating snakes."

Debbie knew what she was doing when she shut down the idea of talking to Flannery. She'd already picked up a tip about Flannery's investigation from her mom earlier that day before she'd stopped at Cap'n Jack's. And if Flannery had known the journalist had the intel and was acting on it, he'd probably be upset. *Serves him right. Don't kiss and tell.*

Not that blaming Flannery for his indiscretion made

Debbie feel any better. Her mom was an innocent bystander. *Not my problem. If they're gonna go the distance, they need to sort out the rules of their relationship.* And from what Debbie gathered earlier that afternoon when she'd had the talk with her mom, it didn't seem like either one had thought much through.

"I don't know, Debbie. One thing led to another. He's such a good listener. We just sort of, I don't know, click."

"Kinda cliché, don't you think?"

"Maybe. But I don't know how else to say it."

Debbie shrugged. "It's hard to wrap my mind around you and Flannery. I mean, you said, over and over, that you'd never date a cop."

"Look, it isn't like we're getting married. There's been no one since your dad. And I'm not dead. Can't I live a little?"

Debbie sighed. "Of course. But Flannery? Why couldn't it be some boring appellate court judge? Somebody I wouldn't have to see on the job and at home."

"I know. When you both spend your professional lives in the criminal justice system, you're bound to have to deal with him. I mean, earlier today, he said something about interviewing Macie Holloway."

What do you call it when a reporter, a cop, and a lawyer are together in one room? A crime scene. Debbie laughed at her own joke. She'd inherited her love of lame humor from her father. Only she didn't appreciate his dad jokes until he could no longer tell them.

Dwelling on the past wasn't going to help her with the present. What did Flannery want with Macie? The Webbs thought she was a criminal. Maybe Flannery did too. But Debbie wasn't convinced that the woman was anything more than an innocent bystander to a terrible tragedy.

Still.

If Flannery had talked to Macie, there was a good chance the young woman was rattled. Flannery could unsettle a meditating Buddhist monk. It was one of his superpowers. Macie might need a sympathetic ear. And Debbie had a hunch where she could find her.

Her earlier research had included an online search aggregator for "Macie Holloway St. Louis address." The computer screen served up an information buffet stocked with morsels from Macie's life in milliseconds. Several addresses appeared. One was for a luxury home, likely belonging to her parents. There was an address in a college town. A third address matched a luxury apartment complex in West County.

After finishing up with Cap'n Jack and Noreen, Debbie swung by her home to retrieve Macie's address from her laptop. Then she made another stop at Panera and ordered sandwiches to go. It couldn't hurt to bring food to a pregnant woman. And bearing edible gifts eased Debbie's guilt about stopping by unannounced in the evening.

The journalist inhaled deeply, reached over for the bag of sandwiches, and got out of the car. As she walked up the stairs, Debbie scanned her body, forcing her shoulders back further to open her chest into a confident position. She willed her elbows and wrists to relax so that her arms swung loosely by her side. She turned the corners of her mouth upward just enough to softly crinkle the area around her eyes. She knocked only after she'd transformed into a friendly, nonthreatening figure.

Muffled footsteps approached the closed front door. The light around the peephole vanished. Debbie focused her gaze on the low-tech security device, smiled more broadly, and raised the sandwich bag in her hand.

The security bolt clacked. The door opened.

"Um, what are you doing here?" Macie said, standing barefoot on the dark wood floor.

"I figured you could use some dinner," Debbie said. "After all, you're eating for two. Plus, I thought we could maybe chat for a few minutes."

Macie's lips frowned as her eyes darted to the bag. She sighed as she opened the door wider. "Fine," she said, resignation sounding in the way she stretched out the first vowel in the word.

The apartment had been painted a trendy light gray. The wood trim was a crisp white. The dark wood floors were pristine.

"Great place," Debbie said. "And you're so tidy. Cleaning lady, or are you just very neat?"

Macie snorted. "I can't afford a cleaning lady. Or cleaning lord." Macie smiled briefly at her joke. "My parents aren't going to spring for one. But it doesn't really matter. Straightening, scrubbing, dusting, vacuuming. I consider it therapy."

"I wish I could convince myself of that," Debbie admitted. "I hate cleaning."

"Well, you're better at thinking ahead about food," Macie said, her eyes again betraying her hunger. "I was just trying to decide whether to eat some old ice cream, have a bowl of cereal—dry because I'm out of milk—or order another pizza."

"Then it's a good thing I showed up," Debbie said as she sat on the sofa.

"Let me get some plates," Macie said as she took a few steps toward the kitchen. It was an open-concept floor plan, so there wasn't much of a journey between the living room and the kitchen cabinet.

"Beautiful artwork you have here," Debbie said as she admired the rural countryside with rolling hills and a prominent oak tree.

"Thanks. That's an acrylic landscape. Painted by a local artist," Macie volunteered. "Caleb loved his work. Especially the landscapes. Probably also why he couldn't stop playing *Red Dead Redemption*. Caleb was always raving about the landscapes of that damn game. And if we were out at a park like Castlewood," Macie said, "he'd say, 'Looks kinda like *Red Dead*.'"

A wave of sadness passed over her face.

"Anyway, he bought that one for me. Actually, he bought it for me twice. The first time, it was a gift for my twenty-first birthday. The second time was to buy it back after I sold it to get cash for heroin." Macie handed Debbie a paper towel. "Sorry, don't have any napkins.

"Not a problem," Debbie said.

"Caleb has a painting from the same series in his condo," Macie continued. "Although we'll see what happens to it. I wouldn't put it past Connor to sell it. I've got my eyes on the auction houses, trying to see if it pops up. Of course, I don't know how I'll get the money to buy it." Macie rubbed her forearm nervously, a self-soothing effort meant to subdue the cravings that never went away. Like the tide, the compulsion to satisfy her addiction ebbed and flowed. Her emotions, not the moon, fueled or suppressed her desire.

Distress, Debbie could see, was a trigger. "So," Debbie said abruptly, "I have a roast beef sandwich and a veggie sandwich. Chips, apples, and a cookie. What do you prefer?"

"Veggie, please," Macie said. She looked at the chips. "I know I should have an apple. But I'd prefer the chips."

Debbie smiled. "Of course," she said, handing her the food. "You probably need some extra calories, anyway. And apples don't have much."

Macie snorted. "That's one way to spin it." Macie bit

into her sandwich, took a chip, then sipped from a can of sparkling water she'd grabbed before sitting down. "Now, I'm not naive. I can't believe you're here simply to make sure I'm eatin' three squares. What's up?"

Debbie cleared her throat. "Well," she began, "I do care whether you eat. But you're right. I do have some questions for you."

Macie looked carefully at Debbie as she took another bite. But she said nothing.

Debbie continued, "I heard a detective paid you a visit."

Macie put her sandwich down, the tremble of her hands only noticeable because of the corners of the paper towel that she'd grabbed to wipe her fingers. "How do you know that?"

"I have my sources," Debbie answered vaguely.

"I told you! I told you that the Webbs would sic the police on me. You didn't believe me."

"Who talked to you?"

Macie shrugged. "I don't know, some detective."

"Detective Flannery?"

"That sounds about right."

"What'd he want?"

264

"To go over the same stuff I've gone over repeatedly."

"What's that?"

"You know, what happened that night. The night Caleb died."

"He doesn't think you're telling him the truth?"

"The Webbs don't think I'm telling the truth."

"So what'd you do?"

"Paterfamilias stepped in. Said any more questions have to go through our lawyer."

"I see," Debbie answered. "Probably wise. So, did you tell the truth when you gave your statement?"

"Does it matter? No one ever believes me anyway."

19 RELUCTANT SPY

He knew it had been dangerous to stay behind at the motel. But how could he disappear without touching the woman who gave his life meaning? If he'd risked getting caught by the police when he returned to the house in Spanish Lake to retrieve his wedding ring, what wouldn't he risk when the flesh-and-blood woman was within reach?

"Is it you? Is it really you?" she asked when she finally opened the door to the office and pulled him inside.

"*Sí.*"

"*Madre de Dios*," Marcela whispered as she touched his face, tears welling up in the corners of her eyes.

No words passed between them as they held each other, her head resting on his chest, listening to his beating heart.

"Where's Sofía?" J.R. finally asked.

Marcela pulled away enough to raise one hand to his face, using her finger to trace an outline from his forehead, along his temple, down his cheek, and then across his jaw line. She whispered, "Cleaning rooms."

"Is it just you two?"

"For now."

"What does that mean?"

Marcela's hand dropped. She broke the embrace and broke the spell. "José, our daughter is eight. What happens to her in a few years? I've seen girls pass through here." Her voice trailed off, her eyes fixed on some image imprinted in her mind. "If we're not free, what happens? When will they take her away? How can I protect her then?"

"She's still a baby."

"You've frozen her in your memories. You rarely see her. José Rodrigo, the days may be long, but the years are short. I tell you, we're running out of time. I thought by now you'd have worked off your debt to them, *we* would have worked off the debt. I'm losing hope."

J.R. said nothing.

"We're never going to be free."

"Don't give up. I'll come up with a plan."

"I've heard that before."

"Preciosa, por favor."

"I've heard that one, too."

"Look, I'm here. I have a car. Get Sofía. We'll drive away this moment and end our nightmare."

"How did you get a car?"

"There was a raid. I escaped. They haven't decided where to put me. So right now, I'm supposed to follow a *gringa*. The one who was here."

"But you're not following her now."

"No. I saw you."

Marcela's brow furrowed. "It makes no sense. You're not a spy."

J.R. shrugged. "I'm good at fading into the background, going unnoticed."

"Well, I wish you'd been good at that when you decided to cross the border. Maybe we wouldn't be in this mess."

"*Vamos.* Get Sofía. Let's go now."

"No," Marcela said firmly. "No. Where will we go? What will we do? What's your plan?"

"Get in the car and drive."

"If we get caught, Sofía will pay the price. At least now, I have another few years to keep her safe. If I keep her out of sight, maybe they'll forget her."

"Please, please, just get her. We'll go."

"Our lives? They're nothing. But hers? She hasn't even started living."

"At least bring her to me. Let me see her."

"Too dangerous. She's too little. She still doesn't understand that she has to be careful with her words."

Marcela crossed her arms firmly, then softened her face. She kissed him. "Come back when you have a plan, José Rodrigo. I must protect our daughter. I won't gamble on the whims of a desperate man."

Her words plunged into him like the lance of a picador piercing the neck of a bull in the ring.

J.R.'s hands went up to push her away. She stumbled backward, catching herself on a desk to stop her fall. His shoulders squared. His lungs expanded with air. His nostrils flared. He could feel the bull's rage building in him. But instead of charging forward, he reached for the door and stomped away.

J.R. couldn't catch his breath. An invisible hand gripped his windpipe, squeezing the walls shut. He gulped at the air with his mouth, trying to bite oxygen like a starving man using his teeth to tear at bread. The sound of his heartbeat was deafening to his ears.

He was behind the wheel, the car flying down the interstate. He'd pass out. The car would crash. He would die. It was that simple. That tragic. And Marcela and Sofía would be left alone to fend for themselves.

It had been a long time since he'd had an asthma attack. But this one felt different. Could it be panic? But he wasn't one to panic. Not really. When the feds raided the drug house, his chest remained clear. He shimmied out the basement window and sprinted across the backyard, coatless in the cold. Not once did he cough.

But seeing his wife had caught him off guard. Her dismissiveness and distrust had shaken him. He was her husband, but she no longer believed in his ability to defend them. All these years, he'd been working hard to protect them. He envisioned himself as their guardian angel. But to Marcela and Sofía, he was the man who abandoned them.

He had to find a way out. But first, he had to fight

through the panic. Desperate, J.R. turned to the only one who could help him in his time of need. *"Por favor,"* he panted, *"Santa Muerte."* It was all he could muster, but the tightness in his lungs released a bit more each time he said it. A calm that started at the top of his head worked its way down his neck, through his arms, to the hands gripping the wheel, and down his legs.

Clarity replaced the sense of doom he'd felt.

He knew where his wife and daughter were located. He had a car. He wasn't locked in a basement endlessly processing product for the cartel. He was free. *Libertad.* He had to convince Marcela to flee. *Canadá.* That's where they'd go. He just needed a solid plan. He'd have time to come up with it while following the reporter. But first, he had to find her.

Like a bee to the hive, a chicken to the coop, or a prodigal daughter to her parents' house, J.R. knew the journalist would eventually return home. So that's where he went. Sure enough, shortly after five, when the January sun called it quits for the day, Debbie's car rounded the corner and abruptly stopped in front of the house. She hopped out, and as was typical for the reckless young woman, she cleared the front steps two at a time. J.R. couldn't help but wonder if he'd be in Illinois by now if Marcela had possessed just a pinch of the reporter's daring. But unlike Marcela, Debbie didn't have a daughter to consider. And the cartel was more dangerous than black ice.

Life was simpler when you only had to take care of yourself.

J.R. knew it was time to get his family out of their prison. But how? First, he needed a paper map—if they still existed. He didn't trust his phone. It belonged to the cartel, and he didn't know what sorts of technological voodoo they could do to review his searches. He'd try a truck stop on the way back down to Lebanon. Surely he could find something.

He'd go back for his family after Debbie went to bed. After all, his phone probably had a tracker. If he headed back to Lebanon just after returning from the town, it might raise suspicion. The cartel would worry that Debbie Bradley was on to something down there. Maybe they'd send reinforcements. And he didn't need more cartel soldiers around his wife and daughter. The safest thing to do was to follow the reporter for the rest of the evening. The cartel would expect that. Then he'd stop off at the safe house at night, leave his phone, and make his way to his family.

He'd grab his daughter first. After all, where Sofía went, Marcela would follow. He'd drive them north and east. Vermont or Maine might be the best destination. Someone had once told him that getting across the border up there was more manageable. He had a little bit of cash. He'd use that for gas. Marcela could take dollars from the motel. There had to be money in the back office. It was a business that dealt in cash. No one would even miss the tiny bit they'd take.

He considered his car. Knowing the cartel, it probably had a tracker. His car was a lifeline and a noose. The cartel would know where he'd headed if he left it at the border. Would they be able to find him? Public transportation was out of the question. Too many immigration checks.

It would be best if he could switch vehicles. He could try stealing a car. It wasn't something he'd ever done. But this was an emergency. God would forgive him. Desperate times, desperate measures. The reporter could be an easy target. No, that would be stupid, he decided. He'd have the law and the cartel on him simultaneously. If the cartel could put a tracker on his car, surely they could do the same with Debbie's. Besides, her car didn't look much better than his. Would it even make it?

Debbie Bradley emerged from her home about fifteen minutes after she'd gone inside, a look of determination on her face. She jumped in her car and drove away.

J.R. started his engine and took out again after her. I'm getting rather good at this, he thought as he weaved in and out of traffic before pulling into the parking lot of a sandwich shop. Debbie went inside and J.R. waited, his stomach grumbling. It had been hours since he'd last eaten: a candy bar and a bag of potato chips from a gas station.

His eyes settled on the trash can outside the restaurant. Americans were so wasteful with their food. He could probably find crusts of bread and parts of sandwiches that had been cast off. It was dirty business, but he'd scrounged in the garbage before. He'd do it again. If he had to.

His mother would be so disappointed. No better than the beggars in the village, she'd say. He was supposed to be the smart one in the family. Even in school, he was known as a clever child. When he was four years old, his mother would have him stand before guests and recite all the European countries and their capitals. He'd learned it studying a map that had been left by a tourist. When he was ten, he won a schoolwide competition for being able to translate the most animal names from Spanish to English. His quick mind was one reason why Marcela married him. But his intelligence gave him a confidence about the world that turned out to rest on false assumptions. And all he'd done was bring misery to their lives.

Life would be better in Canada. He could find a job in construction. He was missing a finger, but he still had a strong back and a steady hand. Marcela could get another motel job. There were always openings for people in housekeeping. He would come home after a long, honest day's work. He could make dinner and supervise Sofía while she did her homework at the kitchen table.

He'd cut up an apple and hand it to her for a study break snack. "*Toma.*"

"*Gracias, papá,*" Sofía would say as she looked up from her books and smiled at her father.

When Marcela arrived, he'd bring her water and tell her to put her feet up. Her body would appreciate the rest because another baby was on the way. A boy named after his dad. He'd get a good education. Maybe he'd be a doctor. Instead of destroying people, as J.R. had done, his son would heal them.

J.R. smiled at the thought of his son atoning for his sins. It was then that Debbie emerged from the restaurant with two bags in her hands, interrupting his daydreams.

He figured she'd turn back toward home, but she drove toward the suburbs. When would this day end?

The apartment complex Debbie Bradley finally stopped at was fancy, different from the safe house where J.R. stayed. He and Marcela could live in such a place in Canada. *Who am I kidding? We'd never be able to afford a home like this.*

Debbie climbed a set of stairs and knocked on a second-floor door. It opened and she slipped inside, leaving J.R. to wonder what he should do next. He could get out of the car. God knew how much his legs ached. But where would he go? If he tried to hide in the bushes of the megaplex, someone would spot him. It would make him even more suspicious.

Once again, it was his fear of the cartel's retribution, not police apprehension, that helped him override the pain in his back, the hunger in his belly, and the pressure in his bladder.

J.R. picked up his phone and sent a text in Spanish, a brief summary about where he'd followed Debbie and the name of the apartment complex. He hit send. As always, no one replied. The texts were all one-sided. They reminded him of prayers he whispered into the ether with no response. But in this case, there was no saintly figure on the other side—just evil demons in human form.

His thoughts turned again to his future. They could save a little money and buy a little house. They'd have a vegetable garden, just like the one in Mexico. How cold was Canada? What vegetables could you grow? J.R. wondered.

It didn't matter. He could survive the snow. He could survive the cold. But he couldn't survive being separated from his family any longer. He'd sworn to protect them. And he'd failed miserably.

Debbie had been inside for an hour before she emerged without the bags of food. She hopped in her car and peeled out of the lot. J.R. followed the oblivious reporter once again. As it became more apparent she was headed home, he breathed a sigh of relief.

Once again, Debbie parked in front of her house then disappeared inside it. He'd give her fifteen minutes. If she didn't come out, he'd leave.

He got out of the car. He needed a few minutes to stretch his legs. It was late enough and dark enough that no one was out jogging or walking a dog. He found a tree shielded from the street lamp, unzipped his pants, and emptied his bladder. His body relaxed for a moment.

He planned to get back in the car. He was going to get Marcela and Sofía tonight. Nothing could stop him.

He emerged from behind the tree only to come face-to-face with Debbie Bradley. "Why are you following me? What do you want?"

20 VISIONS

Macie switched off the light in the master bathroom and padded barefoot across the carpeted floor of her bedroom. She lifted the packed bag from the end of the bed and dropped it on the floor next to the door leading to the living room. She wouldn't forget it when it was time.

It's not one fucking nightmare. I'm trapped in sequels, she thought.

"A real fuckin' franchise, *Nightmare on Elm Street* part-God-knows-how-many," Caleb said. "Wasn't the last one Freddy versus Jason?"

"Fuck you, Caleb."

He gave her that look. The one she knew too well.

The same look he gave her on that fateful night, plunging her life into chaos. A blend of sorrow, concern, and love radiated from his eyes. A lethal hit straight to her heart. "Figured you could use the company."

Macie pulled back the bed covers and then rummaged under her nightstand for her noise-canceling headphones.

"I'm so tired, Caleb."

"I know, Mace, I know. Things are gonna work out."

"Yeah, right. My life is hit by an atomic bomb, and you're suggesting that a little sunscreen is all I need to protect myself from the mushroom cloud."

"You don't have to get all T2 on me."

"Geez-us, Caleb. Do I look like fuckin' Sarah Connor? I'm no mother of the future, that's for sure."

Caleb held up his hands. "Sorreeee."

"You're dead, I lied to the cops, your family wants me to pay for your death, I'm probably gonna face murder charges, my parents will disown me any day now, and there's the reporter."

"Put that way, well yeah, looks kinda bleak," Caleb said.

"The way I figure it, everything is connected. Once the cops figure out I lied, I'm toast. I'll probably end up sitting in jail until my case goes to trial. All choices about my body will be ripped away from me. Zero freedom on the inside, zero freedom on the outside. Just me in a cell wearing an orange jumpsuit. And you know how much I hate orange."

"You're way ahead of yourself."

"I don't think so, Caleb. I'm finally thinking clearly about what comes next. Dear Papa already said this was the end of the line if I lied."

"He's not going to leave you stranded."

"C'mon, you know how it goes. People who love addicts eventually get fed up with the lies and hysterics. I know my parents. They're at that point. Who is going to pay for my lawyer?"

"There's always public defenders."

"Who's going to post bail for me? You?"

"What about Alex?"

"The guy who sleeps on a different couch every night because he has nowhere to live?"

"Why not just come clean? You tried to help me, Macie. You're the only one who tried to save me."

"I'm not gonna throw Alex under the bus. Besides, he's my ticket out."

"You sure you want to run?"

"I don't think I've got any other choice. I could start fresh somewhere. It isn't like I'm leaving much of a life behind. And after tonight, I'm traveling light. Just me, myself, and I."

Caleb looked at the empty pill packets on the bathroom vanity. "C'mon. Let's lie down. Thirty minutes, right?"

Macie nodded. "Yeah, that's what the instructions say."

"What are we gonna listen to while we wait?"

Macie placed the headphones over her ears and scrolled through her playlist. "How 'bout 'Visions of Gideon'?"

Caleb lay beside her on the bed, even though the mattress didn't dip with his added weight. He put his hands behind his head. "Sure. I could go for some Sufjan."

21 RUBICON

Debbie had known the condo address for several months. The 1930s three-story brick building was in the DeMun neighborhood that spanned the city and Clayton borders. Despite driving by the place numerous times, she had never gathered the courage to park her car, get out, and press the buzzer at the building's entrance. The possibility of being turned away was too much rejection, even for someone used to people telling her no. Only this time, it was different. This time, it wasn't about her. Or him.

"Yes?" a man's voice answered.

"It's me."

There was a pause. "Debbie?"

"Yeah."

"Oh. My. God. Really?" He fell silent for a few seconds. "I thought by now you'd have gotten the hint that I'm not interested in you."

"Don't flatter yourself, Chase Laclede. I need your help. I mean, I'm with someone who needs your help."

"Always working an angle."

Debbie stomped her foot. "This isn't an angle. Look, I'm standing outside your building with a man."

"Pffff. My God you've got some nerve."

"No. No. Don't be ridiculous. This guy. He's in trouble. Big trouble. He needs a lawyer. He needs you."

Chase was quiet for a moment. "Make an appointment with my office. It's late. I'm done for the day."

Debbie turned to J.R. His hand was rubbing his thigh. His eyes darted left then right. He was going to bolt. "Please, Chase. Please. I'm begging here."

"How do you know I'm up here alone? What if I'm, um, with someone?"

"I don't know. And frankly, I don't care. This is more important. Life-or-death important. Just let us up so I can explain. Please."

Three more seconds of silence. "This better be good."

A lock clicked and a buzzer sounded. Debbie pulled open the door and turned to J.R. "Trust me. He doesn't like me much right now, but he's one of the best lawyers I know."

Red. That's what J.R. remembered most about the moment Debbie Bradley confronted him. His mind's eye conjured up the red of the bullfighter's cape. It was the color of danger. The color of blood. The color of death.

He didn't think when she'd blocked his way in the park. He reacted. Almost immediately, words poured from his lips. English and Spanish swirled together in a steady stream that refused to be stanched.

They stood facing one another as they'd done outside the drug house in Spanish Lake. This time, she wasn't afraid. Her face softened as he shared his story from the beginning to the end. He described his village, his wife, and his daughter. He told her about the work he'd been forced to do and all the choices he'd made that had led him to that very moment, standing before a reporter in Lafayette Park.

Maybe Debbie Bradley had a special gift that allowed her to coax secrets from people who weren't interested in sharing. If so, it would be a superpower for a reporter. Maybe he'd fallen under some sort of spell. Whatever it was, he didn't have a choice. He had to tell his story. And once told, a weight lifted from his soul. This cathartic experience left him feeling more hopeful than he had in years.

But now, standing behind the reporter in the dark as she beseeched a lawyer to let them in, he was reconsidering his impulsiveness. Why had he been so trusting? Running was still an option.

A buzzer sounded. Debbie pushed into the entryway and began climbing the dimly lit stairs. J.R.'s legs forced him to follow. An apartment door at the top of the stairs opened. The warm light inside the home sent a soft golden glow into the hallway.

"This better be good, Debbie Bradley," J.R. heard a man's voice say.

"Let me get this straight," Chase said as he ran both hands over his scalp. "J.R. is tracking you for the cartel."

"Correct," Debbie said.

"And J.R. is here illegally, brought across the border by the cartel and put to work as part of the drug trade."

"Correct again," Debbie said.

"And now you two have somehow united forces?"

"Not exactly," Debbie said. "I'm working on a story and—"

"Of course you are," Chase said, cutting her off.

"I'm working on a story. The one about Caleb Webb and heroin in St. Louis."

Chase grimaced. "Yes, I recall that piece."

"And I guess I've been poking around too much, so they're having me watched. Only J.R. doesn't want anything to do with the cartel. But they've got his family. And if he doesn't cooperate, they'll hurt his wife, his daughter."

Chase looked at J.R. "Is that true?"

J.R. nodded.

"And you believe the cartel."

J.R. held up his hand to show his missing finger.

Debbie spoke up. "He's willing to talk to the feds. Tell them everything he knows if they can protect his family."

"Why not go to Flannery with this?"

Debbie shook her head. "J.R. loses his leverage without an intermediary. Once he goes to them, the law won't have any incentive to help his family once he tells them everything he knows."

"Wow, you trust Flannery so little?"

287

"No, it isn't Flannery I'm worried about. It is the rest of them. They just want a conviction, no matter whom it hurts."

Chase nodded slowly. "Fair enough."

"And I can't do much for him. If I go to Flannery or the feds and tell them I have a source who could help, they will try to force me to disclose J.R.'s identity. And even if I promise him confidentiality, they may go to court to ask a judge to compel me to testify, arguing that I know about an ongoing crime." Debbie paused. "We both know that reporter confidentiality is a house built on quicksand. But you. You're different. You've got attorney-client privilege on your side. If you agreed to represent J.R., you could negotiate a better deal before revealing his identity."

Chase rubbed his chin. "Actually, that isn't a bad idea."

Debbie put her hands on her hips. "Of course, it's a good idea. So what should we do?"

"We?" Chase shook his head. "No. No we. J.R. and me. I'll meet with my client, and you'll have to leave so we can discuss privileged information."

"But..." Debbie stammered.

"You know the rules. Having a third party present means we run the risk of waiving attorney-client confidentiality."

"Well, I drove J.R. here."

Chase shrugged. "I can easily take him back to where he needs to go. C'mon, Debbie. You said this wasn't about us, remember?"

Debbie frowned. "Yeah, but I want to make sure he's taken care of."

"You brought him to me for a reason."

Debbie turned to J.R. "Will you be okay?"

"Sí," J.R. said. *"Sí, señorita. Gracias."*

"You're welcome," Debbie said as she headed for the door. Before pulling it open, she stopped and turned to face Chase.

"Thank you. You're right. I knew I could count on you for help."

22 KNIFE AT THE THROAT

The plan his lawyer hatched was simple. Straightforward. Foolproof. And, J.R. now concluded, utterly worthless. Only it was impossible to tell Chase Laclede the scheme was bound to fail.

J.R. should've known his situation was hopeless. From the moment the reporter confronted him to the point where he was ascending the stairs of his soon-to-be lawyer's home, he'd been a fool to think he could outrun and outsmart the cartel.

But he'd let himself hope.

From the get-go, Chase Laclede treated him with respect, stopping him from blurting out his story until a contract was signed. "I want our attorney-client relationship to be bulletproof," Chase had said. J.R. had flinched at his lawyer's choice of words.

"You hungry?" Chase asked.

J.R. nodded.

"First things first, then. Food." Chase went into the kitchen, apologizing for his barebones pantry. He emerged with a plate. On it, a sandwich. Nothing fancy; two slices of white bread slathered in mayonnaise, pressed turkey lunch meat piled between. "I've got some BreadCo bags of chips around here somewhere," the lawyer said as he rummaged through the cupboards. "I try not to eat them, but I can't bring myself to throw them away. Aha!" he said, pulling out three small brown-and-gold bags of kettle chips and setting them before his guest. "Water okay?"

J.R. nodded, his mouth full of sandwich. Sitting at a table, using a plate, having someone care. It had been a long time since he'd been treated with dignity and kindness.

After the dinner plate had been cleared and J.R.'s water refilled, Chase let J.R. tell his tale. The two sat on high-backed white cushioned chairs around a mahogany dining room table made for four. J.R. noticed there were no scratches or marks. This was no hand-me-down piece of furniture. There was only one gray-and-white placemat, which Chase moved to make way for a yellow legal pad. As J.R.'s story tumbled from his mouth, the tip of a blue ink pen scratched across a yellow page, stopping only for a sheet of paper to get flipped over the top of the pad, and a new page started.

"More water?" Chase asked, flexing the fingers in his right hand when J.R. was done.

The client shook his head no.

Chase stood up, walked to his kitchen, poured a glass for himself, and slowly walked back to the table. He sat down, took a sip, then placed the glass slowly on the table.

"So, Mr. Rodrigo, I'm hearing that your family, their safety, is the most important thing to you."

"*Sí.*"

"And you'd be willing to testify against the cartel, so long as your family is safe."

"*Sí.*"

Chase frowned. "I won't lie. Prosecutors are in the business of getting convictions. Your family's safety is secondary. My guess is that the feds will want you to be a confidential informant. The problem is that to do that, you have to continue as you are, maybe even wear a wire.

Meanwhile, your family has to stay at the motel. If they were to disappear now, it would raise too many flags. You'd be worthless to the government. And the cartel, suspicious about your family's disappearance, would exact retribution on you."

"I don't care about myself. Just them," J.R. said.

"I understand. I also know that time is of the essence. I don't trust that the government will prioritize your family's interests. But, Mr. Rodrigo, I will put your interests first. Here's what we should do. They've already got the defendants in custody from the drug house. You can testify against them. And if you saw people making deliveries, some of those folks are now behind bars, too. So you're an important witness. A witness who can convict a lot of people. A witness who might convince others to turn on the cartel to shave a few years off their prison sentence. What I want the government to do is take you into witness protection. You and your family."

"Do you think that's the best way?"

"The federal government can make people disappear much easier than you could do for yourself, your family."

"My family, Mr. Laclede. I just want to protect *mi familia*."

"I understand. Let me work out the details. I won't tell the feds where you are or who you are. I won't tell them where your family is. Not until I get some guarantees. For tonight, you need to go back to the safe house," Chase said. "Then go back to Debbie Bradley's in the morning, just like every other day. I'll get in touch with you through Debbie. Do not call me, don't text me using your phone. Too dangerous. Once I've set something up with the U.S. Attorney's office, I'll let you know. But through her."

"Do you think it can be done?"

"There's a prosecutor over there I trust. I'll start with him."

And that's how they'd left it. Chase drove J.R. back to Debbie Bradley's, where his car was waiting. It was sometime after one in the morning when J.R. parked in front of the safe house. He even let himself smile as he climbed the stairs to the apartment. He was still wearing that smile when he unlocked and opened the door. "Where you been?"

It was the nameless man who gave J.R. instructions, and keys, then disappeared again. When he showed up, it meant something was wrong.

"*Que?*"

"Don't play that *no-hablo-Inglés* game with me, *amigo*. Where ya been?"

"Where you told me to be. Following the reporter."

"Hmmm. I've been sitting here for hours. Awfully late."

"Not for *la guapita*," J.R. replied.

His visitor smirked. "Ah. I see. She with an *hombre*?"

J.R. nodded.

The man sneered. "Remember being young? We could go all day and all night and still work the next day. You catch anything good? I mean, no TV, no computer, no woman; I wouldn't blame you if you watched."

J.R.'s weight shifted from his right foot to his left. "Naw, man, I just do what I'm told. I gotta be back in a couple of hours. I need to grab a few hours of sleep."

"Well, my friend. That's what I'm here about. I've got good news for you. You're shipping out tomorrow."

The muscles in J.R.'s stomach tightened. "Tomorrow?" Not tomorrow. How was he going to save his wife? His daughter? What a *tonto* he'd been.

"Whatsa matter? You don't look happy."

Find your mask. Put on your mask. You're being too transparent. "Just surprised, that's all. I thought I was doing a good job."

His minder shrugged. "Don't have no opinions and no information about that. All I know is they need to get you back to making money for the organization."

"Where?"

"Beats me. They're coming for you tomorrow. Late afternoon, early evening. I don't think you're gonna be alone. Maybe a couple more bodies."

"So I got plenty of time to rest?"

"Yeah."

"Good. I'm beat."

His minder held out his right hand. "The keys."

"The keys?"

"Yeah, car keys. Don't want you getting any ideas about leaving."

"But shouldn't I follow the reporter a bit longer?"

"Naw, we don't need her no more. *Venga.*"

J.R. reached into his pocket with his right hand. His fingers closed tightly around the key. His chance, his last chance, his only chance, and he was meekly giving it away. One more *banderilla* plunged in between his shoulder blades.

His minders may have taken the keys to his car, but he still had legs—and the freedom to use them.

And he had something even more valuable: contacts outside the cartel. It was an accidental byproduct of his assignment to follow the reporter. All those years being farmed out as a batcher to dealers had kept him isolated. But once he had connected to people outside organized crime's sphere of influence, his options expanded.

J.R. waited fifteen minutes after his visitor left before leaving the apartment. He hustled down the interior stairwell. When he reached the entrance to the old apartment building, he flipped his hood over his head and stepped out into the frigid night, his breath curling up as it left his body. There were light fixtures attached to the brick but no bulbs. Those had been removed long ago. Whether it was because the landlord didn't want to spend the money on replacements or that tenants preferred to cloak their comings and goings in the dark, J.R. didn't know. But the darkness was his saving grace, allowing him to slip like a ghost into the night.

The route to Debbie Bradley's home was etched in his head. Sure, only a handful of days had passed since he'd started tailing her, but it was one of the few places he'd been in St. Louis. No roadmaps in his head had to compete with her Lafayette Square home.

It was just after two in the morning. Even though J.R. was traversing the heart of the city, the streets of the Midwestern town were deserted. For the most part, St. Louis was a city that slept. Sure, an occasional prostitute would materialize from a narrow corridor between two brick apartment buildings only to fade away once they realized J.R. was a man who had no money in his pockets and no interest in their services.

Besides, it was too cold to have sex without a car.

J.R. hunched his shoulders against the frigid air. All he had on was a sweatshirt, a flannel shirt, jeans, a pair of thin socks, and tennis shoes. His lack of cold-weather gear hadn't been much of a problem when he could take refuge in a car. But now, it was different. Man versus nature. Or his desire to save his family pitted against frostbite.

He pushed on.

A car slowed on the street behind him. J.R. pulled his hood down even lower and picked up the pace.

"Hey," someone yelled out a car window.

"Hey!" the voice yelled again.

J.R. didn't know if it was the cops, the cartel, a gang, or street hoods. At this hour, the rest of the law-abiding population was at home, safely asleep in houses equipped with locked doors, security systems, Ring cameras, and, increasingly, guns.

If he had to, he could run. There were plenty of homes and apartments on the other side of the sidewalk. Sure, some might have dogs in the backyard. But Americans didn't usually keep their pets outside at night in the winter. Motion detectors were the real problem. Even if he fled, it was likely that he'd trip light after light affixed to fences, detached garages, and houses throughout the city. Each would light as he passed, a flashing device aiding anyone following him.

"Hey!" the man yelled for the third time.

J.R. turned his head. An orange Camaro slowed. The windows were tinted, but the driver's side window was down. A man with a black skull cap and a gold bracelet leaned out. "Hey, you lookin' fer a fix?"

Drug dealers. They were probably selling some of the stuff he'd had a hand in packaging.

J.R. shook his head. "*No hablo Inglés.*"

The driver took another look at J.R. He wasn't much of a mark. Didn't even have a coat. The window raised. The driver stomped on the accelerator. J.R. estimated it was going sixty when it blew through the red light ahead. A moment later, it was gone.

J.R. wrapped his arms tighter around his body, tucking his hands underneath his armpits for warmth. Was it only a few short hours ago that he was warm, his belly full, and he felt safe? Now he was cold. And scared. Not just for himself but for his family.

Debbie picked up her phone to check the time. Three thirteen in the morning. She'd been awakened by something, though she wasn't sure what. It took the second alert of a Ring doorbell to realize someone was at the front door.

Debbie's feet hit the floor. As she emerged from her bedroom, she nearly collided with her mother. Both women had the dazed look of one who'd gone from deep slumber to mild panic in less than a second.

"Don't open the door," Beth commanded, even as her daughter darted ahead. "Not until we know who it is.

Nothing good comes at this hour. I mean it, Debbie."

Debbie hurried down the stairs as her mother opened an app on her phone to see who was on their doorstep.

"Slow down, let me see who it is," Beth said before declaring, "I don't know this person."

"Lemme see," Debbie said as her mom handed her the phone.

"J.R."

"You know him?"

"Yeah. He's been following me. Cartel's orders."

"What?"

"Don't worry, he's harmless."

"Unbelievable. You want me to let some guy working for the cartel in my house? And why didn't you tell me any of this?"

"Mom, please. He's freezing."

"I'm calling Daniel."

"No! That's the last person you should call. He'll just mess everything up." Debbie took a deep breath. "Please, he's in trouble. He's a victim, not a bad guy. I left him with Chase earlier tonight. Chase is trying to help him. And his family. They're basically prisoners of the cartel."

"And if you open the door, how does that help us?"

"If we don't help him, his wife and daughter could die. Do you really want that on your head?"

"Right now I'm more concerned about you."

"If he wanted to hurt me, he could've already. Heck, I drove him in my car to Chase's."

"You what?"

"Please, Mom. You've dedicated your life to helping people in trouble. You can't turn your back on someone in need now."

"But I'm responsible for your safety."

Debbie put her hands on her hips. "Mom, I'm an adult. Remember? I'm responsible for myself."

Beth looked at her phone again. The man standing outside was shifting his weight from left foot to right, trying to stay warm. His eyes darted from the camera to the street and back again. She tapped on the microphone icon in her app. "Yes?"

"Please, I won't hurt anyone. I need help. Miss Bradley?" J.R. said as he held his hands up on the front porch to show he wasn't holding anything dangerous.

Debbie grabbed her mom's phone. "I'm here. What happened?"

"I talked for a long time with the lawyer. He's going to

help me. But they were waiting for me when I returned to the safe house."

"Do they know what you've been up to?"

J.R. shook his head, his hands still raised in a surrender position. "No. I was told that I'd be shipping out tomorrow. And if I disappear again, there's no way I can help my family. Or the government."

"I'm calling Chase," Debbie said.

"Fine. You do that," Beth replied.

Debbie pushed the volume to max level, hit the speaker button, and held the phone up so her mother could hear too.

One ring. Two rings.

C'mon Chase, answer, Debbie thought.

Three rings.

"What now?" a groggy voice asked.

"Thank God," Debbie said.

"Can't I get a little sleep?"

"Um, I've got a situation."

"What sort of situation?"

"J.R.'s in trouble. He walked to our house in the middle of the night. They're going to send him away tomorrow. My mom's going nuts. And she's about to call

Flannery. Can you please talk some sense into her?"

"Ms. Hughes," Chase said, suddenly shaking off the sleep and slipping into court voice. "J.R. is my client. He's harmless. Let me throw on some clothes. I'll be right there, and we can sort it out."

"All right. I guess we can let him in."

"Unbelievable," Debbie huffed at her mother. "You listen to Chase, but you won't listen to me?"

"He's a lawyer."

"And I'm your daughter."

"C'mon, Debbie, you've got to admit that you get into a lot of trouble."

"I'm just doing my job. And if you want to help, you'll put your phone away. Flannery will mess things up."

The image of Chase collecting his client from their house, clad in gray sweatpants with his high school logo and a navy hooded sweatshirt made by some luxury designer, would remain seared in her brain, Debbie knew. It was the upscale version of J.R.'s secondhand store attire. A trained eye could distinguish between a Goodwill sweatshirt and one from Nordstrom.

Debbie could tell the difference.

Sure, she'd fantasized about spending a lazy Sunday afternoon with him wearing just such an outfit. They'd be stretched out on a couch, binge-watching *Better Call Saul*. Or maybe he was the sci-fi sort. He'd insist on rewatching *Firefly*. He might've seen it a thousand times, but it would be their first time watching it together. But no, nothing nearly so romantic. Just work. And he'd barely acknowledged her presence.

"You're a lifesaver, Beth. Literally," Chase said as he brushed past Debbie, who was holding the door open for him.

Debbie grimaced. She was the one who'd kept the police out of it.

"Coffee?" Beth asked. After Chase had vouched for J.R. by phone, Beth had let J.R. inside and busied herself with brewing coffee. Their uninvited guest now had a large mug—a splash of cream and two teaspoons of sugar—warming his hands. Debbie had drained one cup and was working on the second when Chase arrived.

"No thanks. I'm just going to grab J.R. and get out of here," Chase said, his brow furrowed with concern.

"Not so fast," Debbie said. "Don't you think you

should let me help you devise a plan before you spirit him away?"

Chase shook his head. "I had time to think about this on the way over. If someone stops by the safe house and finds J.R. missing, this is one of the first places they'll look. You're all in danger if he stays. But they don't know me. I'll take him back to my place, then I'll call the AUSA first thing in the morning. If we can strike a deal, I can have J.R. giving a statement before lunch. Sometimes you just gotta take the proverbial bull by the horns."

J.R. rose from his chair, glanced down at the tops of his feet for a moment, then looked at Beth and Debbie. *"Muchas gracias, señora y señorita. Por todo."*

"De nada," Beth answered. "And good luck."

And with that, Chase ushered J.R. out into the night and then into his car. When Debbie shut the door, her mother was already in the kitchen, unloading the dishwasher that had been set to clean before they went to bed for the first time that night.

"Why didn't you tell me about J.R.?" Beth asked without turning around, hearing Debbie enter.

"I haven't had time. I've only known about him for a few hours. Besides, you were out with Flannery. And since when do I have to tell you all the details of my work? You don't tell me."

"That's different," Beth replied. "Attorney-client privilege. And my clients aren't going to get me killed."

"J.R. isn't going to get me killed. I'm an investigative reporter, Mom. That means I dive into tough topics. I'm not going to write a three-thousand-word piece on people who don't break down their cardboard boxes before putting them in the recycling bin. I cover crime, corruption, you know, dangerous stuff. And if I'd gone to law school and become a prosecutor, I wouldn't exactly be safe. And what about a judge?"

"Debbie, I'm tired. You're tired. We never have a productive talk when we're both beat. Why don't we pick this back up in the morning?"

Even though it was phrased as a suggestion, Debbie knew her mom well enough to know it was nonnegotiable. "Fine. But what are you going to tell Flannery?"

"What can I tell him? Nothing, for now. I've got to give Chase time to work something out for his client— before law enforcement grabs J.R. Believe it or not, I do understand that Chase needs the leverage."

23 MATERIAL INFORMATION

Thump, thump, thump. Pause. *Thump, thump, thump.*

"Macie, wake up. Macie!"

Macie groaned. "Go back to sleep, Caleb. I called in sick to work today. 'Member?"

Thump, thump, thump. Pause.

"Macie!"

Macie rolled over, pulling the covers up higher. "Shhhh."

Her phone on the nightstand vibrated.

Macie finally opened her eyes. "What the fuck?" It was a text from Alex. He was at her front door.

"Too early," she muttered.

"Then don't answer it," Caleb whispered.

"I gotta."

Caleb said nothing as Macie groaned again. She rolled

her legs out from under the covers and sat up on the edge of her bed. She picked up her phone once more, squinted her eyes, and typed "brt" before tossing it back down on the nightstand. The message would buy her some time before Alex started banging on the door again.

She stood up on shaky legs and tottered toward the bathroom. So many weighty decisions had left her weak. She reached for her robe, tied it around her waist, and pulled her hair up in a high bun secured with a black satin scrunchie before shuffling to the front door. Out of habit, she peered through the peephole. Sure enough, it was Alex. He leaned against the door frame, head bent down to study his phone screen. When he heard Macie turn the lock, his head popped up. He took one big step back.

"Well?" Macie asked as she held the door ajar. "And hurry up. It's colder than death out here."

"You're telling me," he said as he crossed the threshold. "I'm the one standing out here freezing my cock off."

"Why you here so early?"

"I drove by your dad's office this mornin' but didn't see the 'Stang. No work today?"

"Called in sick. Needed a mental health day."

Alex laughed. "Whatdya tell 'em?"

"Cramps."

"Good one. You're not gonna have cramps till the big ones several months from now."

Caleb whispered, "Alex is off."

"Yeah," Macie said to no one in particular as she retreated to her kitchen for a glass of water. "You're not one for getting up early. Whatdya need?"

"We're shipping out tonight, just got word."

"You coulda texted."

Alex tapped his index finger to the side of his temple. "C'mon, Mace—"

"Macie."

"Macie. You gotta think. Text messages can be tracked. Once you disappear, someone will surely try to get your phone records. Heck, it won't be that hard. Your parents are still payin' for your phone, right? You still on their account?"

Macie shrugged. "So what?"

"They can get your records. And they're tracking their daughter with that family plan on all those iPhones."

Sure, it was true. Macie's phone was her lifeline—and her parents' leash.

Alex reached into his pocket and pulled out a new phone. "Here. Your ticket to freedom. New phone for a new life."

Macie's grip tightened on her old phone. It was the only phone number she'd ever had. The same number she'd had since her twelfth birthday. Sure, she'd upgraded the device several times since, but she'd always had the same number. Asking her to give it up? Why not ask for both her arms instead?

And this particular phone? How could she leave it behind? It had all her text messages with Caleb. Photos of the two of them over the past couple of years. Asking her to abandon it was like asking her to rip her heart out, shove it down the garbage disposal and flip the on-switch.

"You're gonna have to leave it behind, Macie."

"But," Macie objected, "it's my everything."

"Nope. Nope, you can't take it. You can't keep one foot in the old life while trying to start a new one. It won't work."

"I...I," Macie stammered, "I can't."

"You have to. You've got to let go to move on."

Tears welled up in the corners of her eyes as she placed the phone next to her heart. "But he's in here."

Alex put one hand on Macie's shoulder. "Caleb would understand. Give me the phone."

Macie took a step back. "No. Not yet. My parents might text. If I don't answer, you know how they are. They'll freak and come over. When it's time to go away for good, I'll just turn off the phone and leave it here."

"Fine. But you can't take it with you."

"I said I was gonna leave it behind. So just drop it."

Jeremy Rand leaned forward in his black leather chair. His office was on the twentieth floor of the federal courthouse, and his desk was in front of a large window with a commanding view of downtown St. Louis. As Chase sat across from the assistant U.S. attorney, he couldn't help but notice that the bright blue winter sky behind Rand looked like the omnipresent backdrop of a school photo from the 1970s.

"You really think your guy deserves witness protection?" Jeremy asked.

"Like I told you on the phone, you all missed him when you busted the drug house in Spanish Lake. He was part of that crew. He's from Mexico. He can connect the cartel directly to the operations in St. Louis. And his wife can give you details about the drug route along the way and more information about some of the human smuggling that will open up other avenues for you guys to round people up and prosecute."

"I don't know. Seems too good to be true."

"C'mon, Jeremy, it's me you're talking to." Chase gestured to the baseball autographed by St. Louis Cardinals catcher Yadier Molina displayed on the corner of the prosecutor's desk. "We played enough select ball together back in the day. You know I'm not faking a throw here. Plus, the word around the courthouse is that you've got some problems with your case. Like that truck driver."

Jeremy shook his head. "Fuck. They only just found Tom Wilkins hanging from a bed sheet late yesterday. Guards are calling it suicide. How'd it get out so soon?"

"C'mon. You know defense counsel gossip as much as old women stretching during a senior yoga class. What else are ya gonna do while waiting for the judge to get on the bench?" Chase said.

"We'd just inked a deal with his lawyer yesterday morning. Tom Wilkins was supposed to give us plenty on the cartel and more details on how they're moving product."

"Guess the feds have a problem with the rural jail you stashed him in."

Jeremy frowned. "I shoulda had him moved to a more secure location yesterday. My mistake."

"And that is precisely why you need my client, Jeremy. Not only will he help you put all the defendants in your case behind bars, but he and his wife can give you enough intel to disrupt drug and human trafficking rings throughout the Midwest. They've been in the center of it all for a few years. You save my client and his family. He saves your case and makes you look good by shining the light in other dark corners. But he needs witness protection. Same for his family. Otherwise, it's Tom Wilkins all over again. Only this time, it is a man, a woman, and an innocent child. Even you aren't so cold-blooded that you'd sacrifice a kid."

Jeremy rubbed the back of his neck. It wasn't often that ambition and a good deed overlapped. "One condition. First, he needs to come in and proffer a statement. If he's as valuable as you say, we'll work out the particulars of witness protection. But we'll probably want to keep him in the cartel longer."

"I'd rather have the agreement now."

"You know that my boss isn't going to go for that. You've got to trust I'll keep my word if you've kept yours."

"What about the wife and kid?"

"If your client is high value, I'll have immigration sweep the motel. It's already on our radar anyway because of this case. I'll have mom and kid separated from the rest of those scooped up in the raid. We'll send them to witness protection after we have what we need from the wife."

"And if you don't give my client protection?"

"Immigration still swoops in. Only mom and kid will get dumped back across the border with the rest."

"Lovely."

"Hey, at least they're back in their own country. Maybe they'll have a better chance to evade the cartel down there than up here."

"Time is of the essence," Chase said. "You gotta talk to him this morning. The cartel's looking to move him out later today."

"Do you think he'll wear a wire?"

"I don't see why not. But you're not going to have him for long. You'll need to track him somehow to see where he's headed."

"Like a catch-and-release tagging?"

"Um, he's a human, not a grizzly bear."

"How soon can you get him here?"

"It's ten a.m. now. I'll have him here by ten forty-five," Chase said. Sure, it'd take some quick driving. He'd left J.R. to wait in his office. He'd call his receptionist. Let her know he was on his way. It would be a quick turnaround. "I need you to be ready when we get back. No slow-footed government worker stuff. The cartel is supposed to collect him this afternoon. If he's not back at the safe house before then, there will be hell to pay. And you lose an opportunity to follow him through the system."

"Yeah, yeah. I can get it done on one condition. I don't get the wife and kid until he arrives at his next destination. Then we'll extract them all."

"My client isn't going to like that. Not one bit. No reason you can't make it look like an INS sweep. Just scoop them up and relocate them."

"Look, just let us follow him to the next stop. Then

we grab mom and daughter."

"I don't like it. Not one bit," Chase said. "But it's our best worst option." He paused. "Fine."

Before facing Sam, Debbie decided to try Macie one last time. Maybe some thread would shake free that could finally be used to weave together a story.

Macie's Mustang should've been parked at her dad's office, only it wasn't. It was after ten in the morning on a weekday. Relying on a hunch, Debbie drove to the woman's apartment. Sure enough, the Mustang was sitting in the spot Macie most favored. Without hesitating, Debbie whipped her car into an empty space. The reporter's hands trembled as she loosened her grip on the steering wheel. Too much coffee. Too much adrenaline. And way too much drama. It was the worst kind of drama, the sort that she didn't control, the type inflicted on her rather than being the person doing the inflicting.

She had so much to tell and nothing to write. Debbie didn't know what was worse, to be a reporter with no story or a journalist with a juicy tale that couldn't be shared. And she wasn't ready to sort out with Sam the parts that should go public and the pieces that would remain private—at least not until J.R. and his family were reasonably safe and situated. If such a thing was actually possible.

But her duty was to the story. Didn't the readers deserve to know what played out in their community daily? St. Louis had been and would always be a hub for all sorts of traffic. Let Chase watch out for his client. But she'd been the one to bring Chase and J.R. together.

Debbie knocked on Macie's apartment door. She could hear rustling inside.

"Macie, I can hear you."

No answer.

"Macie, is everything okay?"

Still no answer.

"Macie, you're worrying me."

Nothing.

"Okay, Macie, I'm going to call the landlord to make sure you're all right."

"I'm fine. Just not feeling well."

"Please, just open up."

"Go away."

"Macie, you sound different. Are you sure you're okay?"

The bolt to the front lock slid. The door opened.

"You see me now. I'm fine."

Debbie looked the young woman up and down. "You look tired."

"Well, so do you."

Debbie smiled. "You got me. I am tired. Long night."

"Can't you just leave me be?"

Debbie looked over Macie's shoulder. "Going somewhere?"

Macie looked startled. "What?"

"The suitcase."

"Oh, that? Just packing up old clothes to donate."

"Nothing else?"

"Nope."

"All right," Debbie said, sensing it was time to retreat. Macie reminded her of a wary cat who didn't want petting. She'd dodge first, swipe a sharpened claw second. "Feel better, okay?"

24 RATTLED

Macie looked at the phone on her nightstand. *Her phone.* She'd left it where Alex could see it to show him she followed his instructions. It had been turned off.

Still…

Her hands started sweating at the thought of leaving it behind. She'd left it fully charged. And for whatever reason, she'd stuffed the phone's charger into the pocket of a pair of joggers she'd rolled up and placed in the suitcase. After all, it was her favorite charger, even if it didn't work with the phone Alex had given her.

She'd already received a text from Alex on the burner phone, letting her know he was on his way and that she should grab a bite to eat if she hadn't already had lunch.

He didn't know when they'd stop to eat again. The annoying reporter had been gone for more than an hour. And it seemed she'd taken Caleb with her.

Where are you?

She'd eaten some crackers and a granola bar in her otherwise spotless apartment. Leaving it dirty seemed wrong for some reason, so she'd spent the morning cleaning while also packing.

Caleb hadn't said anything since Debbie Bradley left. He'd fallen as silent as the phone sitting on her nightstand.

C'mon, don't pout, you pussy. I could use some company, Macie pleaded.

Nothing.

Thump, thump, thump. Macie jumped at the sound, piercing the quiet. The door. Obviously, she told herself. Did she really think Caleb was making noises in her apartment?

She looked through the peephole. For the second time that day, Alex was on the other side. Instead of leaning back and gazing at his phone, he was fidgeting this time, looking over one shoulder and then the other.

"You ready?" Alex asked after she let him in.

"Yep."

"You leave your phone?"

"That's what you told me to do, right?"

"Where's it at?"

"Seriously? You're doubting me?"

"The people helping you, us," Alex said, "are taking a risk, with your criminal case and all."

"That's kinda strong. I haven't been charged with a crime yet."

"It's what you're afraid of, right?"

"Yeah."

"Well, they're taking a risk. And they want to know that you aren't going to put them in danger."

"It's in the bedroom. Along with my suitcase. I'll show you."

Macie led the way into her room. Alex followed behind. She walked over to the nightstand and gestured to the phone. "See?" She picked it up. "I even turned it off like you said."

"Good."

"So we're ready?"

"Yeah."

"Be a friend and carry my suitcase, will ya?"

"Sure," Alex said as he grabbed the handle. "Let's go. And I'm driving."

"Fine," Macie said.

"Take the phone," Caleb whispered when Alex turned his back and headed toward the living room.

With one quick movement, Macie swept it into her right hand and tucked it into her jeans pocket. Before Alex could turn around, Macie snatched her coat, which was on the end of the bed, and put it on as she followed him out the door.

Flannery didn't hide his frown. Chase knew that it meant trouble for Debbie. And Beth.

"You're telling me that your client has been stalking Debbie? And showed up on Beth's doorstep in the middle of the night? And those two let him in? And no one called me?"

Chase put a hand on J.R.'s shoulder to reassure him. Flannery's expression had gone from a frown to a glare when his eyes landed on J.R.

"Please, Detective, my client isn't dangerous."

"Your client is part of a bloody Mexican cartel,

Counselor! A man who helps put deadly drugs on our St. Louis streets."

"He's just a pawn. Nothing more. He's a family man who's done what he had to do to protect his wife and daughter. Surely you can understand that."

Flannery clenched his jaw. "So he claims. But criminals will say anything to weasel out of trouble."

Chase sighed. "Jeremy," he said to the prosecutor, "maybe Detective Flannery isn't the best choice for following J.R., given his, um, personal connections to the case. Maybe a fed would be better."

"Fuck that," Flannery responded. "I'm still a member of this task force. I can be just as professional as you. Or, as you claimed, Beth was last night."

"Look, she wanted to call you, for what it's worth. Debbie talked her into calling me first. And then I persuaded her to let me negotiate a deal. If you're this upset today, I can only imagine what sort of guns-blazing stunt you would've pulled at Beth's home last night."

Flannery shifted his weight and mulled his options. If he continued with his tantrum, he was in danger of getting pulled off the assignment. If he brought his fury under control, he could keep an eye on J.R. If J.R. got within a hundred feet of Beth, the man would regret that day forever. "Look," Flannery said, addressing Jeremy, "you know I'm not some hot-headed cop. Never been. I know my role. I won't stray from it."

"Good," Jeremy said. "J.R.'s shoe has been outfitted with a tracking device. It allows us to follow our informant to his new destination. From a distance, you can gather information about how he's moved, who's moving him, et cetera. Then, once he's in a new location, we'll find an opening to outfit him with a wire and continue our work."

"That's not going to be easy," Chase said.

Flannery spoke up. "Not easy, but not impossible. We just need to create a diversion to get him alone or wait until everyone leaves, wherever they've stashed him, to do the work. And if worse comes to worst, we'll plant a listening device in the house itself. Since your informant doesn't go out, it stands to reason that the criminal activity he knows already comes to him."

Chase nodded and looked at J.R. Had it only been last night that the two men had met? Since then, J.R. had given the government a proffer videotaped statement and inked a deal for witness protection. Every once in a while, justice will move at a quick clip. "Do you understand the plan?"

J.R. nodded.

"Okay," Flannery said as he got up from his chair. "Chase, you'll drive our informant to an area near the safe house. Then he'll walk the rest of the way. Meanwhile, I'll follow a safe distance behind."

Chase put a hand on his client reassuringly. "A piece of cake. What could possibly go wrong?"

25 TREACHERY

Debbie was still parked at Macie's apartment complex. She meant to drive away, but she couldn't shake her worry about the fragile, anxious young woman. Like a grain of sand in her shoe, one question left Debbie troubled: Why the suitcase?

A text from Sam distracted Debbie before she turned the key in the ignition. "Where are you?"

"Just leaving Macie's apartment," Debbie replied.

"I hear one of the defendants in that drug conspiracy case is dead," Sam responded.

"Who'd you hear that from?"

"I have my ways," he answered.

Of course he had his ways, Debbie thought. He may

be her editor now, but he'd been a reporter. You didn't give up your sources when you moved to a bigger office. If anything, you kept them even closer. It was an informal way to fact-check your reporters and suggest stories for them to write.

"I'll check it out," Debbie replied. "I'm heading to the office now."

Debbie rummaged through her purse. The day she'd attended the arraignment, one of the defense lawyers had given her his business card. "Call me anytime," he'd said when he wrote his cell number on the back. She didn't forget his words, even if she had trouble remembering which safe place in her bag she'd placed it. Debbie looked in the side pockets, rummaged through the bottom, and finally remembered she'd slipped the card into her wallet next to her driver's license.

She dialed the number on the back. "Yo!" the lawyer said after the phone rang once. "Make it snappy. Heading into court."

He was one of those lawyers, Debbie thought, the kind with a white earpiece fused to the side of his head. Always walking, always talking. When did he have time to think?

"This is Debbie Bradley."

"Crime Beat Girl! Glad you called. Whatcha need?"

"I heard something. I'm checking it out. One of the defendants in the cartel drug conspiracy is dead?"

"Yeah, you've got some good intel. Not my guy. Don't know much. The truck driver, Tom Wilkins," the lawyer said.

"What happened?" Debbie asked.

"The people at the jail are saying suicide," he answered.

"What do you think?" Debbie asked.

"Off the record?"

Debbie paused. Even if she agreed, it wasn't like she couldn't ever report the speculation that ensued, so long as she had solid information. She just had to get someone else to say it.

"Maybe a suicide. But I heard he was gonna flip. Help the prosecutors. Don't know for sure. 'Course, some might call helping the feds suicide. Don't know if it's true, just sayin'. Whatever. All I know is the AUSA Jeremy Rand—he needs to make sure he's helping the helpers. Doesn't sound like Tom Wilkins got much help. Dumb mistake. Rand's gonna have a helluva time convincing

329

someone else to open their mouths."

"I appreciate the help. Of course, everything's off the record, as I promised. I'll try Tom Wilkins's attorney."

"The lawyer is in my next hearing. Want me to put in a good word for you?"

Debbie didn't want to owe too many favors. "That's okay. I don't want the lawyer to suspect we talked. I really appreciate your time. I know you said it had to be quick."

"For Crime Beat Girl, I'm willing to risk the judge's wrath."

Debbie winced, still annoyed she'd let Sam talk her into the moniker that she couldn't entirely shed.

"Need anything else?" he asked cheerfully, clearly relishing his status as the source.

"That's it for now. Thanks again," Debbie said before ending the call, afraid he'd keep talking if she was too slow. So much for the guy being in a hurry.

Debbie grabbed her notebook to jot down a few questions for the prosecutor. As she stared at the blank page, she tried to summon an image of Tom Wilkins. Her recollection was hazy. A large man who looked beaten down by life. It wasn't anger she saw when he stood next to his lawyer. He seemed numb. Perhaps he didn't believe his life would come to this moment. Maybe he had been depressed, scared even, at the thought of spending the rest of his life behind bars.

Or maybe it had been something else.

When Debbie looked up, she was surprised to see Macie leaving her apartment. She was following behind a man with short brownish-blond hair. He was carrying Macie's suitcase.

He looks familiar, Debbie thought. *Where do I know him from? Aha! He was with Macie at Caleb's funeral.* Debbie did a mental check of her memory. Alex. That's who Macie said was with her that day. But she'd also seen him someplace else…

Debbie hit her fist on the console next to the driver's seat. The guy who left the Santa Muerte card. It was Alex. But why? Was Alex doing a favor for Macie? Had she been duped by Macie? All this time, Debbie believed Macie was a scapegoat, not a murderer. The Webbs may have been right. Maybe Macie couldn't be trusted. She'd killed Caleb and was now slipping out with the help of her friend. A friend who had been following Debbie.

Well, Macie Holloway, it looks like I was wrong about you.

"Is she, um, you know," Chase asked as he drove his client to the safe house, "in danger?"

J.R. knew who "she" was. He might've been in a bind, but that didn't mean he was blind. He'd noticed how the lawyer tried a little too hard to ignore Debbie Bradley when they were in the same room. How his lawyer's self-assured tone turned into icy politeness when he talked to her.

"I told the detective. I won't hurt her." J.R. paused before adding, "Or the *madre*."

J.R. could feel the tension in his hands. The meeting with his lawyer and the detective—the meeting that was supposed to revolve around the cartel's criminal enterprise—kept circling back to the two women and their safety. It happened enough that J.R. could feel angry vapor rising from his skin. These men. Worrying about their women while his wife and daughter were the ones in real danger. Men seizing the role of protector of women who didn't want to be protected because it meant being controlled. There was only one word J.R. had for the man who thought he could manage a woman: *tonto*.

"What about the other guy?"

"The one who left the Santa Muerte card?"

"Yeah, that one."

"I don't know the *gringo*. I'd never seen him before."

"Would the cartel have two different people follow one person?"

"Mr. Laclede, I don't know. No one asks me what I think, what I want. But the cartel's a business. The more people they have following a señorita, the fewer hands moving product or hauling in cash."

"Still," Chase said, his voice trailing off.

J.R. gestured to a corner up ahead of the car. "Why don't you stop there? I've only got a few blocks to walk. I don't want anyone seeing me get out of the car."

"Sure," Chase said. "Look. Just because we part ways here doesn't mean that I don't still represent you. I will do all I can to extract you as soon as possible and get you and your family into witness protection."

J.R. opened his door. "*La vida.* Life. It is short, no? If you get a first chance to be happy, don't assume there will be a second. My pride. I wanted more; I thought I deserved more. Was blind to all I had. We men, we're fools. Santa Muerte is the decider now. But if something happens to me, promise you'll get my wife and daughter."

"I swear."

J.R. nodded and slammed the door. With his head down and his shoulders rounded, he quickly created distance between Chase's car and his body, never looking back.

Chase picked up his phone. Maybe he should text Debbie. After all, she'd want an update. And if he didn't reach out, she'd probably bug him. He put the phone back down. No, let her make the first move.

Chase pressed his right foot on the brake and used his right hand to put the car into drive. He looked into his rearview mirror to see if it was safe to pull out. A car was coming up behind him. He recognized the side mirror dangling onto the passenger door. It was a vehicle that looked as though it was self-destructing one piece at a time.

A Honda Civic drove past him. *The* Honda Civic. The one that belonged to Debbie Bradley. Coincidence? When it came to crossing paths with the reporter, there was no such thing as chance.

26 CONVERGENCE

J.R. had reached the apartment but didn't have time to fiddle with the lock before the door flung open. His minder, holding a handgun, anxiously waved him inside. "Where you been, muthafucka?"

"*Comida*," J.R. answered. "Don't know when I'll eat next."

"Sit," his minder ordered, knowing full well that a trip with the cartel was no luxury cruise. It wasn't even a no-frills airline throwing a tiny bag of almonds or a half-empty package of pretzels and cheese squares. Food and water weren't part of the menu when the cartel was in charge of travel.

"Don't see no food," the minder said.

J.R. shook his head. "Ate it. Got to."

Being prepared helped you survive but made you a

target of those who hadn't thought ahead. When a man was hungry and desperate...it wasn't good. The instinct to survive turned men into monsters. Best to carb up before the trip rather than wait and have your sandwich swiped by someone bigger and meaner down the road.

"We 'bout to bounce," his minder said. "Just waiting on the last delivery. You lucky you got here before they did."

J.R. nodded his head yes and kept his mouth shut.

His minder looked through the peephole. Even though it was winter, the man was sweating. If anything got screwed up, if the deliveries weren't made according to plan, it was his head. It didn't matter if it was his fault. He was accountable no matter what.

J.R. watched his minder. The man waved his *pistola* like a *jefe*, but he was nothin' but a *peón*.

"C'mon," the minder muttered as he peered through the peephole.

J.R.'s foot began to bounce, the one wearing the shoe with the tracker.

"Dude! Yo, foot!"

J.R. stilled his leg and put his hands on his knees.

"Better."

He could hear muffled voices in the hallway. Footsteps coming up the stairs.

"Bout fuckin' time," the minder muttered.

J.R. held his breath. They'd be leaving soon. He would be farther from his family but closer to freedom. If the plan worked.

Instead of flinging the door open, the minder waited for the knock, tucking his gun into his waistband. J.R. could hear the voices more clearly now. "I don't know. Are you sure this is safe?" a woman asked.

"I know it don't look like much, but it's fine. Give it a chance."

A light knock on the door. The minder held an index finger to his lips and looked at J.R. The door opened. "Come in," he said a bit too cheerfully.

J.R. recognized the first person through the door. He'd seen the guy who followed Debbie Bradley that day in Lebanon, Missouri. Now, he was carrying a suitcase. And behind him was the woman J.R. had seen meeting with the reporter.

"Alex, I don't like this," the woman said. "I wanna go." She turned and started to back away.

"Macie," Alex pleaded. But the minder was even

faster. He put one hand on the woman's arm, yanked her inside, and slammed the door.

"Bitch, you ain't going nowhere," the minder said as he pulled the gun from behind his back. "Sit down."

Debbie watched Macie and Alex emerge from the car parked in a neighborhood that was thirty minutes—and a world away—from the luxury apartment complex where they'd started their journey.

Debbie doubted Macie ventured to this part of South City even during her heroin-using days. Upper-class suburban girls who went to prestigious high schools would've received stern lectures from their parents about the dangers lurking on these so-called "state" streets, places with names like California, Louisiana, and Nevada. And if a daughter got too bold, family-plan tracking on the cell phone and a threat to impound the girl's car would cure the thirst for adventure.

It was far from her first time in the area for Debbie, and it wouldn't be her last.

Macie walked behind Alex. Each step she took forward seemed forced. Alex stopped, turned back to

Macie, smiled, and said something Debbie couldn't hear. Some words of encouragement, she guessed.

The two entered a brick apartment building. There was no lock on the door at the main entrance. Or if there had been, it no longer existed.

Debbie reached for her phone. It could be time to call Flannery. She couldn't let Macie slip away. As she was about to dial, she spotted another person walking toward the apartment building. Debbie squinted her eyes. She knew the man.

Connor Webb flung open the apartment door Macie had entered a few moments earlier. Sure, St. Louis was a big small town. But it wasn't so small that Connor and Macie would accidentally bump into one another in this rough neck of the woods. Saks Fifth Avenue in Plaza Frontenac? Yes. But here? Unlikely.

What was Connor up to? Debbie wondered. She didn't know the answer but knew it wasn't anything good. Maybe he was here to avenge his brother's death. If so, she couldn't let that happen. Another Webb boy shouldn't throw his life away doing something stupid.

Debbie squeezed the phone in her hand. Flannery. Maybe he'd come if she called. She was about to dial when a knock on her driver's side window made her almost drop her phone.

"What the hell are you doing here?" Chase Laclede asked.

Flannery picked his phone up, paused, then put it back down as he sat in an unmarked car close enough to the safe house to see but not so close that he'd be noticed by those coming and going. He would've known he'd grabbed his phone five times if he'd been counting. But he was too distracted to keep track.

When he'd found out earlier that day that Debbie and Beth had swung open the door to their home in the middle of the night to J.R., Flannery's initial reaction had not been positive. Not at all. His first impulse was to punch J.R. repeatedly in the face, then hop in his car, drive to Beth's office, and ask her why she'd been so thoroughly, shockingly, and utterly stupid.

Of course, he'd done none of those things. He was too mature for macho theatrics. And he knew Beth wasn't into that sort of masculine performance. But it had taken more restraint than he initially thought he could muster.

Even now, he didn't trust himself to confront Beth. What were you thinking? Why didn't you call me? Not only had she not called when J.R. was standing in her living room, but Beth hadn't bothered to tell him about it when they talked earlier that morning.

A lie by omission was still a lie.

But if he came on too strong, too overprotective, he knew Beth would cut him off. Like her daughter, the damsel-in-distress shtick annoyed the shit out of Beth. He knew that. And what would make her even angrier was if he tried to tell her what to do—even though he did know what was best in this instance. After all, they didn't deal with criminals daily like he did. All they knew about the cartel was what they watched on Netflix.

Naivete, it seemed, ran in the family.

No, he couldn't call. He couldn't text. He was still angry, even if it was the righteous sort that would protect them. Nor was he happy about following the man who had brought danger to the doorstep of the woman he knew he'd fallen for. Hard. He resisted the "L" word, and lord knows he wouldn't say it to Beth. Not yet. Not so early. She'd scamper away faster than a backyard rabbit startled by a German shepherd.

But that didn't change the way he felt about her.

He'd made the decision to play along with the confidential informant plan. If he tracked J.R.'s whereabouts, he could keep Beth safe. And Debbie. If something happened to Debbie, it would break Beth. He just couldn't let that happen. He looked at the phone for a sixth time but didn't touch it.

Instead, he grabbed the clipboard on the seat beside him. He was already wearing a utility identification badge on his shirt. Utility workers and their subcontractors were ubiquitous in an aging city. Water and gas mains, old clay sewer lines; one hundred years was awfully long to go without a break.

Flannery looked down at the clipboard with a fake list of instructions, then glanced up. J.R., his shoulders hunched and head down, had the posture of a defeated man. He opened the door to a brick apartment building that had seen better days and slipped inside.

Flannery took a deep breath. He picked up his phone and typed a message to Beth, "Free tonight?" He hit send and looked up.

Another car approached. Flannery expected it to drive past. But it parked near the safe house. Two people got out. Flannery recognized one of them.

Macie Holloway? What the hell was she doing there? He didn't know her companion, but seeing Macie in this setting was like the old *Sesame Street* game, "Which of these things is not like the other?"

The pair walked to the building that J.R. had entered a few minutes earlier.

Flannery knocked his thumb nervously on the clipboard. Something wasn't right. Had J.R. been withholding information from him? Was Macie there to score drugs?

Another vehicle pulled up. A black Range Rover. Macie's dealer? The door opened. Flannery knew the driver: Connor Webb. He'd been with his parents when they ranted about Macie and claimed she'd murdered Caleb.

"What the hell?" Flannery muttered. "This can't be good."

Connor disappeared into the same apartment building that had swallowed J.R. and Macie. Was Connor here to avenge his brother?

If Flannery interfered now, he'd sacrifice the cartel investigation. But the scene didn't feel right. This was different from what they'd planned.

As he weighed his options, he noticed a Honda Civic parked far from the safe house. Then a black BMW arrived.

"Fuck!" Flannery said.

27 THE BELL TOLLS

"You're in trouble," Caleb whispered to Macie when Connor entered the apartment.

Macie shot up from the couch. "You!"

Alex grabbed her hand and pulled her back down. The man with the gun aimed it at her head. "I said, sit yo ass down."

"Please, Macie," Alex said. "No one's gonna hurt you if you just follow directions."

"Shut the fuck up," the man with the gun said. "I promised to get you where you're going alive. Didn't say nothin' about not hurtin' no one. This bitch 'bout to vex me."

Caleb whispered, *"Your phone."*

Macie felt the phone hidden in her pocket. Now was not the time for Caleb and his distracting voice.

GERI L. DREILING

"Trust me," he whispered. *"'Member our game?"*

Macie knew exactly what he meant. This was no time for games.

"Trust me. Turn it on. Let it boot up."

Macie put her hands on her hips, with her thumbs facing forward and her fingers behind, so they could slip in the pockets. Connor's attention was on the guy who seemed to be running the show.

"She's a handful, isn't she?" Connor said in his most earnest and soothing voice to the minder. As a teen, it was the tone he'd use to convince his teachers to give him just a bit more time to finish an assignment. He used it as a college student to persuade women to sleep with him. "Of course, I'll respect you in the morning." In his work life, he'd deployed it to cajole reluctant condo buyers into signing on the dotted line.

Connor continued, "Don't worry, man, we've got her under control. Don't we, Alex?"

Alex squirmed.

"Alex?" Macie said as Connor turned to her friend. He avoided her gaze.

"That's right. Alex," Connor said. "What, did you think he was smart enough to get you out of St. Louis all on his own? No, Mace," Connor said, sneering at her nickname, knowing only Caleb could say it. "I'm the one spiriting you away."

"The fuck you are," Macie said. "I'm not going anywhere with you," she said as she got up again from the couch. Connor reached out and pushed her back down.

"Unlock the phone with your fingerprint," Caleb urged. Macie fidgeted on the couch.

"Always so stubborn and self-destructive. Do that again, and there will be consequences," Connor said.

"A pussy like you? Hurt me?" Macie scoffed as she felt her phone vibrate a confirmation that it was open.

"Don't cross me, Macie, or…"

"Or what?"

"You'll end up like Caleb."

"Don't you dare say his name."

"Why not? He's my brother."

"Yeah, and he always knew you were a piece of shit."

"You got this," Caleb said. *"You know where the phone icon is without looking. Press it. Wait. Then press one of the recent callers near the top."*

Connor laughed. "I guess it takes a twin to know a twin. He was the only one who figured me out. I'll give

347

him credit for that. But who's gonna believe a drug addict? And thanks to you, he was a gold-star junkie."

"You're a monster," Macie said.

Connor laughed. "You and Caleb. What a couple of fuck-ups. But the more the attention was turned on you, the easier it was for me to do what needed to be done. Nobody notices good ol' reliable Connor when Caleb and his buddy Mace are causing all manner of drama."

"What are you talking about, you shit ass? What needed to be done?"

"You really think I wanted to be carrying the water bucket for my parents all my life? Waiting until they die before I get to be in charge? Forever a baby sucking at the teat of a trust fund? Controlled like a toddler? Fuck no. I want to be the one running the show. I'm certainly smarter than the rest of you. The rest of them."

"Jesus Christ, Connor. I knew you were a narcissistic prick. But that's a bit much even for you. I mean, you've already got everything you need. And your old man is grooming you to take over."

"Yeah, right. You know Matt Webb. He talks a good game, but he won't ever let go of control. I'll be like fuckin' Prince Charles. My dad will live into his nineties, and I won't take over 'til I'm an old coot. I mean, really. That dude was fuckin' seventy-four before he became king. No. No way. Fuck that shit. I'm not waiting. I'm gonna be like one of those tech billionaires, like Chris Radcliffe. One of those dudes flying around in their private jets, bankrolling their favorite political candidates, taking Supreme Court justices on hunting trips and shit. If I get in trouble, I'll have all the bases of government covered. Not to mention the hot chicks. And I'll go all DiCaprio. Young and tight."

"You're so gross, Connor."

"Not gross. Smart. And I deserve more. I figured out how. I just needed some investors."

"Investors?"

"You know, dummy, people who give you money that you then turn into more money."

"You shit ass. Of course I know what an investor is. But who is going to invest in a scumbag like you?"

"Unlike you, most people have a high opinion of me. Certainly higher than they have of you and Caleb. But, well, I couldn't go to a bank. My dad would shut that down faster than Usain Bolt on a track. So I had to do it on the DL. A cartel needed help laundering money."

"How in the hell do you get away with laundering money?"

"Easy peasy lemon squeezy," Connor said. "Remember when we used to say that, Mace?"

"I remember, back when you weren't so evil. Or maybe you were always evil and I was blind."

"You were high. And I'm not evil. I'm a genius. So much of a genius that I used my position selling condos and overseeing books at the condo building Caleb was supposed to manage to help the cartel. Real estate transactions are one of the easiest ways to launder money. I helped the cartel and got a nice cut of the profits. The more I prove myself, the more responsibility my investors give me. And the more likely it is that I can help sell them on future business ventures. Business ventures without Mommy and Daddy. Be my own man."

"The cartel? You're fuckin' crazy if you think you can control them."

"You've always underestimated me, Mace. But Caleb. Guess twintuition kicked in. He figured out my side hustle with the cartel. Threatened to tell Matt and Sarah. But I got the intuition, too. If he wouldn't join me, I could still control him by threatening the one thing in the world he cared more about than getting high."

Macie's hands balled into fists. Alex tightened his grip on her arm.

"You know it deep down, too, don't ya, Mace."

Macie's eyes began to sting.

"Yeah, you do. You, Macie. All I had to do was say you'd get hurt."

"Like you could hurt me."

"I'll admit I don't have an appetite for physical violence. But I have no qualms about letting other people handle it. And the cartel was ready, willing, and able. And sure, Caleb swore he wouldn't interfere. But I didn't trust him. He had to prove it. Had to agree to go to rehab without fighting it. It let me know his commitment level and got him out of my way for a while."

Macie slumped back on the couch. The night Caleb was so upset. The night he wouldn't tell her why. That night. "It was the night before he went to rehab, right?"

"Yeah, and you know fuckin' Caleb. He still fucked things up. By screwing you. A baby? What the hell?"

"How did you know that?"

Connor looked at Alex.

"You told him?"

Alex looked away.

"Alex. My useful fool. He sold his friends out for money. And he didn't even seem too bothered about it."

Macie turned to Alex. "How could you? I trusted you."

Alex concentrated on his feet.

Connor continued. "Yeah, well, a baby was a complication I didn't need. My parents woulda gone nuts. Sure, they'd have been pissed, but then the little shit woulda been raised like a brother I didn't need, threatening my inheritance. Fuck that shit. And Caleb, once he knew about your condition, he would be more unpredictable. Who knows what he woulda done to protect you. Probably some heroic shit. There was always a white knight buried under that sarcastic, seemingly indifferent, crust."

Connor paused. "So I did what I had to do. Or, well, Alex did what I told him to do. He picked up some fentanyl-laced heroin from the cartel. A strong batch."

"You were his trusted source?" Macie screamed at Alex.

"You gotta believe me, Macie. I didn't know it would kill him."

Connor laughed. "Sure, Alex. Whatever. That's why you didn't dare use from the same batch you gave Caleb."

The man with the gun chimed in. "That's some cold-blooded shit, man, killing yo own kin."

Connor shrugged. "C'mon, he was an addict. It was only a matter of time before he killed himself anyway. I just hurried it along. Before he had a chance to interfere with my future. But you, Mace—you were still a problem."

"So you were setting me up for murder?"

"That was one plan. But there was still that whole baby thing. I don't need my parents going soft for Caleb's bastard. And you know they would've taken that baby while you were stuck in prison. The better option was to get you to run away—and into the arms of the cartel."

"I'm not going."

"Yeah. You are. A smart girl like you. I already worked it out. They'll probably make you oversee the raw material they need for the drugs. And worse comes to worst, if you don't play the game right, they make you go into production. And if that doesn't work out, well, then you're expendable."

"And because I've disappeared," Macie said as she

pieced Connor's claims together, "everyone will think I killed Caleb. So I can't come home. And no one ever suspects you."

Connor shrugged. "A side benefit. Certainly. And no one knows you're knocked up. So if the kid gets placed into some rando's home or disappears altogether? No one will know, so no one will care."

"I'm not going. I'll take my chances here."

"Give me that," Connor said to the man with the gun. "If you don't cooperate, I'll shoot you. Nothing comes between me and my plans. Just one little squeeze of the trigger. And that guy," Connor said, looking at the one person in the room who'd been silent the whole time, the illegal immigrant, "that guy is gonna take the fall. Bad hombre and all. A drug addict dead because of an illegal. No tears will fall. Believe me."

J.R. thought he had been forgotten, a spectator sitting in the stands of a run-down village arena watching a bullfight. Connor was the confident matador. Macie, her nostrils flaring, was the cornered bull. The matador provoked. The bull tried to charge. Everyone else in the room waited to see what would happen next. The bull was trapped. But it could still make the matador bleed.

J.R. knew he could turn the turmoil to his advantage.

The first time Macie got off the couch and all eyes were on her, J.R. slowly stood up and positioned himself behind the sofa. Each time Macie and Connor sparred, J.R. inched closer to the kitchen. Through the kitchen, there was a back door that opened to a fire escape. All he had to do was wait for the right moment and slip out the back. He might not have been great at spying on people, but he was a superstar when it came to vanishing.

"I said you!" Connor shouted.

J.R. jumped when he realized the matador was looking at him. "Me?"

"Are you stupid? I said get over here!"

"*Qué?*" J.R. asked, trying to buy some time.

"I said, get over here."

Reluctantly, J.R. approached.

"I don't have all day!"

Alex interrupted. "Shhh. Do you hear that? Sirens?"

"C'mon, Alex. This is the city. When isn't there a siren blaring? Besides, they're a long way off."

"I don't know, man," Alex said as he scooted toward

the window and peered out, "maybe someone's coming for us."

Connor edged over to the window that faced the street below. "What the fuck?"

Alex looked more closely. "I see the reporter. Who are the other two?"

"A cop," Connor said. "And Chase Laclede? What the fuck is he doing here? Alex, did you let them follow you?"

"Dude, we were alone. I don't know why they're here."

"We gotta get out," Connor said as he aimed the gun at Macie's heart. "What's it gonna be, Mace?"

"I'd rather be dead with Caleb than alive with you."

Connor leveled the gun at Macie.

J.R. felt hands pushing him, the invisible hands of Santa Muerte. He was clearing the couch, careening toward Connor. Was it the crowd roaring or the sound of a gun blast? The audience screamed. Or maybe it was Macie. He saw red. Was it the matador's cape or blood now spreading across the center of his chest?

28 END OF THE EARTH

A gold wedding band, dangling from the end of a chain, was draped over the rearview mirror of the black BMW flying down Interstate 55. When the ring turned gently in the speeding car, Chase caught a glimpse of the side smudged with blood, the blood of a dying client who'd given his lawyer one last task.

Chase's hands trembled as they gripped the steering wheel. The tremors had started when he heard that first shot fired. And they hadn't stopped since he'd bolted out of the apartment and away from a crime scene.

Before that first shot rang out, he stood next to Debbie. She'd been arguing with Flannery, as usual. The detective wanted Debbie and Chase to leave, but she insisted on staying. "There's something off with Macie. I think Connor's in trouble," she'd said.

"And I should trust your assessment of the situation?" Flannery huffed. "What in the world possessed you to let that cartel guy into your home last night?"

"Everything was under control, wasn't it, Chase?"

Chase looked at them both. "The longer you two stand out here arguing, the more danger my client is in."

Flannery frowned. "Wait here." He walked back to his car and made a call before coming back.

"You two need to move along; that's an order. I've got backup coming. Quietly. They'll keep an eye out for Connor and Macie. I'll track J.R. We don't know if they're all together."

In the distance, they heard sirens wail.

"Not for us," Flannery said. "Fire department, I think. This time of year. Space heaters. Anyway, once I've got backup, we'll watch and wait."

As Debbie opened her mouth, presumably to debate Flannery's approach, a sound rang out from the safe house: *pop, pop, pop.*

Chase turned to see Detective Flannery pull his gun. "Shit. Stay back," he said before running to his car, grabbing a hidden radio, and saying something Chase couldn't make out.

Seemingly out of nowhere, police reinforcements materialized. Without hesitation, they followed Flannery's lead into the building. Chase noticed that he and Debbie were being joined by a growing crowd of onlookers.

An ambulance arrived. When Debbie saw it, she turned to him and announced: "I'm going in."

"You can't do that. You'll get stopped."

Debbie pointed to the lone cop responsible for keeping people out. "He's going straight for the paramedics. I'm going up."

She strode purposefully toward the building as if she somehow belonged. He hesitated and then caught up, trying to mimic her confidence. They slipped through the door and followed the noise up the stairs. Debbie entered the apartment with all of the commotion, Chase close behind. J.R. was on the floor, Flannery's hands covered the man's chest, but the blood still flowed. "Bradley! Laclede! Get outta here."

"He's my client." Chase kneeled down next to the man. J.R. gave his lawyer a weak smile. "Help them. Take my ring," he said as he motioned to the wedding band around his neck. "No time to wait."

"There's an ambulance."

J.R. coughed. "I made a deal with Santa Muerte. My life for theirs. Go."

Chase gently removed the chain from around J.R.'s neck just as the paramedics entered the apartment with a stretcher. There was nothing more to do but follow through on his client's request. He was the only one who knew where to find Marcela and Sofía. This time, he wouldn't wait for the police to act.

The cratered parking lot was mostly deserted, save for a battered pickup and a few motorcycles. The black BMW would attract attention. Chase knew he didn't have much time to find J.R.'s wife, let alone persuade her to bring her daughter and get in the car with him.

Chase grabbed a tissue from his glove box. As a criminal defense lawyer, he tried to have them handy for his clients' crying mommas, grannies, wives, and kids. Chase never thought he'd need one to wipe away a client's blood. But he couldn't show the ring to Marcela with the streak of red. He would break the news when she was in the car, and they were headed toward safety.

At least, that was the plan.

Chase stepped out of the BMW, took a deep breath, squared his shoulders, and put on his "I'm in charge, trust me" face. He really needed her to trust him.

The lobby was empty when Chase entered. He approached the counter, rang a silver bell, and waited in the dark, musty-smelling space. A woman emerged from a back room. She wasn't wearing a name tag. Chase had to tread carefully.

The woman looked at him and didn't say a word. *She thinks I'm a cop*, Chase thought. Chase flashed his most disarming smile.

"Yes?" the woman asked.

"I'm a lawyer from St. Louis. I'm trying to help a client of mine." Chase reached for his wallet. He pulled out a business card and his Missouri Bar card. "This is me, Chase Laclede."

The woman eyed him warily. "I just work here."

"My client," Chase said, looking around the room to ensure it was still empty before putting his hand in his pocket. He closed his fingers around the wedding band attached to a chain. "My client," he said again as he placed the ring necklace on the counter before the woman.

The woman gasped.

"You are Marcela, right?"

"Where did you get that ring?"

"My client is your husband."

"Where is he?"

"You need to come with me. He's done something to save you and your daughter. We have to go now. There is little time. I've worked something out with the government. I'm going to make them keep their promise. But we have to go now. Please, grab your daughter. We need to go now."

"Why should I go with you?"

"If you don't, your husband's sacrifice for you and Sofía will be wasted."

29 LAWYER UP

"C'mon, Debbie, please?" the young cop begged. "The detective will have my ass if you don't get outta here."

The officer had already removed her from the apartment and escorted her down the stairs. He was a nice enough guy, relatively new to the force. They'd crossed paths a few times at crime scenes. But never a crime scene like this one.

Chase had left before Debbie, speaking only to J.R. before he fled. Macie was sobbing while seated on a dirty couch, her cuffed hands wiping tears from her eyes. Paramedics were working furiously on J.R. And Flannery? Debbie had never seen him so determined to control the scene. Nor had she ever seen him so angry.

Ever.

"Don't worry, I don't want to get you in trouble,"

Debbie said as the young officer walked her to her car. "But I do know my rights. I'll move far enough away so that I won't obstruct your investigation. But not a foot farther."

"Miss Bradley," he said, his tone begging even if his words stopped short.

"He's mad at me, not you. You're just a convenient target," Debbie said. "Now, you should get back in. And if you feel like it, give me a call later. On background."

The officer gave her a weak nod. He didn't know who was more dangerous, Flannery or Debbie.

Debbie climbed into her car, turned on the engine, and reversed it. The car shuddered and moved about half a block. It was just far enough away from the emergency vehicles so that no one could accuse her of being in the way. Flannery could threaten her all he wanted. Even arrest her. But she was staying put.

Debbie got out her notebook and pen. Words appeared on the page. And another page. And another.

"We're losing him," she recalled hearing Flannery say when the paramedics entered. The detective was down on the ground next to J.R., his bare hands trying to stop the blood that was already spreading across the floor.

Chase kneeled next to Flannery.

"Laclede, I said get outta here. You can't be here. And you're in the way." Flannery would've probably grabbed Chase and cuffed him right then and there, but his hands were still on J.R.'s body.

Chase ignored Flannery. He bent his head down to his client. Something was said, though Debbie didn't know what. Chase pulled a necklace off his client's neck. The lawyer got up and searched the room. His eyes landed on Debbie's. Without a word, he rushed out of the apartment.

Flannery continued to apply pressure to J.R.'s chest while the paramedics maneuvered into place.

In between sobs, Macie kept saying, "He's getting away."

It was a small apartment. Debbie slowly shuffled to the kitchen. The back door, which led to a fire escape, was open.

Macie wiped her nose and looked up. "Help me, Debbie."

Flannery's head shot up. "I thought you were gone. I can't do everything myself. I said to get her outta here." Moments later, Debbie was being shown to her car by the hapless rookie.

She put down her pen. Where was Chase? Maybe he'd called. She picked up her phone. She'd missed a call. She'd felt the phone vibrate before the shot rang out— when she'd been arguing with Flannery.

Macie? How? Debbie played the recording. Then replayed it. She knew what she had to do. She dialed a number.

"Holloway Accounting," a receptionist said.

"I need to speak to Mr. Holloway."

"I'm sorry, he's busy right now."

"This can't wait. It's about his daughter, Macie. She's in trouble, serious trouble. She needs help. Now."

As Debbie uttered those words, a stretcher emerged from the building. On it, a body completely covered in a sheet.

"She's still out there, isn't she?" Flannery said to the young officer who'd escorted her out.

"Um," the officer mumbled.

"I see," Flannery said. He walked to the window and peered out on the street, noting the reporter's Civic had moved a block away. "Goddammit. Pain in the ass."

He turned to see the paramedics approach the front door, J.R.'s body loaded onto the stretcher.

"Wait a sec," Flannery said to the paramedics. He reached out and pulled the blanket over J.R.'s face. "There's a reporter down there."

The paramedics nodded.

Flannery turned to the young officer. "Go down with them. If Debbie Bradley so much as cracks open her car door, cuff her."

The officer's eyes widened. "Yes sir," he said while sending up a quick plea to the God of rookie officers to save him from the ordeal.

Flannery rubbed his forehead. What a mess. If Debbie did get arrested, Beth would come down on him hard. But he couldn't have a journalist stomping all over a crime scene or publishing stories that could disrupt a significant investigation. For Flannery, it was lose-lose. But duty came first.

Flannery went back to the officers surrounding Macie. "Any word on the ones who got away? Connor, that guy Alex, and the other man Macie mentioned?"

"No sir," one of the officers responded.

"We need to double the number of officers we've got looking. I don't want them to get away."

Flannery turned to Macie. She'd stopped crying. Flannery guessed it was only because she was out of tears, not because she felt calmer. "Look, we'll have to take you in for questioning."

"Detective, you're supposed to call the chief," one of the officers said as he entered the apartment.

Flannery frowned, turned away from Macie, and dialed his phone. "Yeah?" was all he said. He listened, nodded, and clenched his teeth before turning to Macie.

"Looks like your lawyer is on the way."

He had a good guess about who was responsible.

30 AFTERMATH

"We good?" Debbie asked Sam. It was nearly two o'clock in the morning. A few wisps of lettuce and an empty bag of salt and vinegar chips were still strewn across his desk, the remnants of an evening delivery from Jimmy John's.

"Yeah, got sign-off from legal on the first installment of your article and the podcast script," Sam said.

"And Radcliffe?"

"Just heard back from him. All good."

"Excellent."

"Go home. You've gotta be tired by now, even if you showed up here hours ago as amped as a five-year-old who'd just slammed a Red Bull."

"What do you expect? I came straight here from the safe house," Debbie said, even as she felt the long day weighing on her muscles and bones.

Putting together a story had been tricky. Like most reporters, what she knew with certainty, what she had a strong hunch about, and what could be told publicly didn't line up neatly. There were off-the-record promises to be kept, ongoing investigations that had to be respected, and defamation that needed to be avoided.

But still. It was a helluva story.

She started her first installment with the night Caleb died. She'd included the drug bust and J.R.'s escape. It closed with J.R., Macie, Connor, and Alex all entering the same place together on the same day. *What happened in between?* That was for future articles and stories. A "stay tuned" to keep the readers and listeners hooked while giving the events time to play out so that Debbie's reporting didn't get ahead of the real people grappling with the consequences in real life.

A Dickensian serial, Sam had called it, adding, "Only this one isn't fiction."

"I've still got a lot of loose ends to tie up," Debbie said.

"It'll happen," Sam predicted, "and it will likely happen fast."

Debbie felt her phone vibrate with a message

notification: "Can you stop by?"

Debbie typed a response: "Just finished work. On my way."

Chase answered the door wearing a white undershirt, suit pants, and navy socks.

"Geez, you look like hell," Debbie said as she entered his place.

"I feel even worse," he said.

Inside Chase's condo, his shoes had been left in the middle of the floor. His partially open wallet looked as if it had been tossed on the dining room table and landed somewhere in the center. A red tie and navy suit jacket coat were draped over the back of a dining room chair. A white dress shirt had been tossed on the end of the couch.

Debbie stood in the center of the room awkwardly. Chase's thoughts seemed to drift away for a few seconds. "It's been a day," she said tentatively.

"That's an understatement."

"Can I sit?" Debbie asked.

"Yeah," Chase said, shaking his head as if to cast off

the fog that seemed to have settled on his brain. "Of course."

Debbie put her bag on the coffee table and sat at the end of the couch. Chase joined her, sitting on the other end with one cushion in between. "So," she said before pausing, "where'd you go?"

"Lebanon."

"Wow," Debbie replied haltingly. "Lebanon? Why?"

"I had to get them. I promised J.R."

"Who is 'them'?"

"Off the record?"

"Yes, yes. Off the record."

"Marcela and Sofía, J.R.'s wife and daughter. I promised him."

"Just before you rushed out of that apartment?"

Chase nodded.

Choosing her words carefully, Debbie said, "I saw the paramedics take J.R. away. His body was covered. Completely. Is he…?"

Chase looked down at his feet. "You know, I had to be the one to tell his wife and daughter."

Debbie bridged the gap between them on the couch and touched his shoulder. "I'm sorry."

He sighed, then ran his hand through his hair. "What a mess," he mumbled. "I made such a mess. I should've done better by J.R."

"You did the best you could. You didn't get him into the cartel. You were trying to help him out. If there's one thing I've learned as the daughter of two lawyers, you don't create trouble. You try to extract people from it. But there's only so much a lawyer can do—even one as good as you."

Chase smiled. "You really think I'm a good lawyer?"

Debbie laughed. "Of course. I'm not the only one who thinks you've got mad legal skills."

"I appreciate that. I sure don't feel very competent today."

A silence fell between them before Chase finally spoke. "I suppose you want to know what happened to Marcela and Sofía."

"Of course I do. But see, I was able to restrain myself."

A genuine smile appeared on Chase's face, if only for a brief moment. "Off the record?"

"For the thousandth time, yes," Debbie answered.

"I got them to Jeremy Rand and struck a deal. The

wife knew how the cartel tracked product and cash that passed through the motel. And she knew about the cartel's cloud inventory management software. She had a user name, a password, and the codewords she was required to enter to describe drugs, guns, cash, and humans. She agreed to give the feds an inside look at the operations. In return for her intel, the government is putting them in the witness protection program."

"You did a good thing, Chase Laclede," Debbie said as she patted him on the leg then rose from the couch. "I should go."

He reached up and grabbed her hand gently. "Don't."

Beth was working in her home office on the third floor of her Victorian house when she received the alert on her phone that the front door had opened. The lawyer glanced at her phone to see Debbie's image captured by the camera at the door. It was past ten in the morning. The last time she'd heard from her daughter was eight hours earlier. The text at two in the morning in which her daughter said she planned to stop by Chase's. "To talk," Debbie messaged.

When Debbie didn't come home, Beth resisted the urge to text. It wasn't her adult daughter's job to relieve her mother's anxiety, after all. But why didn't anyone warn her that the worry would never disappear, even after a child becomes an adult? It was so much easier when your adult kids weren't around. You didn't know enough about their comings and goings to feel apprehensive.

Besides, Beth had troubles of her own. Daniel troubles. And she was a woman who didn't tolerate extra trouble.

He'd stopped by just after midnight. Like her daughter, Beth had been working late when Daniel asked if she was awake. He said it had been a long day, something Beth already knew after talking to her daughter about the events that had unfolded.

When he entered the foyer, he wore dark circles around his eyes. His easy smile was gone, replaced by a tense jaw and taut lips. The man before her, Beth realized, was Detective Flannery, not Daniel.

He was barely through the front door when he blurted out, "Why didn't you call me?"

"Excuse me?" She had a good idea of where he was going with the conversation, but a good lawyer never made assumptions.

"You know good and well. You let a cartel member into the house!"

"He was a man in trouble."

"A man who works for the cartel."

"He needed help."

"C'mon, Beth. Do you believe everything your daughter tells you?"

"What are you implying?"

Flannery paused, trying to choose his words carefully. "Don't you think she can be a little, er, tunnel-visioned when it comes to a story? She always manages to get herself in trouble. And now she's dragging you into it?"

"She's doing her job. And Chase Laclede vouched for him."

Flannery shook his head. "Another young do-gooder. Those two will end up in serious trouble one of these days."

"If I'd been representing that man, I'd have done the same."

"Unbelievable," Flannery said. "I thought you had more sense."

"Seriously? You know, I've done fine without your

help in the past."

"What, like the time I saved your daughter's life?"

Beth clenched her teeth. "You're not fighting fair here. Bringing up something outside this argument."

Flannery pinched his lips tighter. "Fine. I think it is fair, though, to point out that you lied to me."

"Lied to you?"

"Yeah, lied to me. You didn't mention one word about J.R. being here in the middle of the night when I talked to you the next morning. A lie by omission is still a lie, isn't it, Counselor?"

Beth folded her arms across her chest. "I had a good reason not to mention it. Debbie's a journalist. There are bound to be parts of her investigation that are confidential. The only reason I knew about it was because I was here. And Chase was representing a client. I didn't want to interfere with his work on behalf of his client. Telling you about it? Well, that would've caused professional problems for both of them."

"But what about me? What about my professional problems?" He paused. "I thought you cared for me."

"I do care for you. But I also have my duties. We all do. I took an oath. You took an oath. Chase took an oath."

"Your daughter didn't take an oath."

"She takes her work on behalf of the Fourth Estate as serious as if it were an oath."

Flannery scoffed. "Fourth Estate. Whatever."

"The right to a free press is in the First Amendment."

"And where's the right to know whether the woman I think I," he stopped before adding, "who I care for is in mortal danger?"

Beth felt her arms circle her body tightly. This wasn't a conversation she was interested in having. "You know, I once had an old lawyer who'd been married a couple of times tell me that second wives and first kids don't mix. I think I finally understand what he meant."

"Oh, come on, Beth. That's rubbish."

"Is it? I don't think so. I feel like you're asking me to choose between my daughter and you."

"No, that's not what I'm saying."

"Well, you may not be saying it, but if I understand you correctly, you think I betrayed you by doing what she asked."

"What she asked was stupid."

"You both think you have a calling of some sort. Just

as I do." Beth ran a hand through her hair. "Daniel, this, us, it just isn't going to work."

"But Beth…"

"No," she said, holding one hand up, gesturing to stop. "This can't be."

The rest of it was a bit blurry for Beth. She recalled opening the door and Flannery leaving, his shoulders sagging as he walked down the steps. She'd locked the door, trudged to bed, and spent the night looking at the ceiling until dawn.

Now, in the mid-morning light, she realized she'd been stupid to think a relationship would work between them. The trouble was that she'd gotten used to the idea of Daniel in her life. But she could move on. After all, she'd done it after Cary died. This would be easier. Surely.

"Where are you?" Debbie called from the first floor.

"Up here!" Beth replied.

Debbie clomped up the two sets of stairs. "No matter how much I run, I'm always winded when I walk up all those stairs. I don't know how you do it," Debbie said. "Here, got you this," she said, handing her mom a nonfat vanilla latte.

"The steps keep me fit," Beth said.

Debbie sat down in one of the thick chairs next to the window. "How the hell did you get this chair up all those stairs and through the narrow staircase?"

"Magic," Beth said with a smile. "And a couple of hired hands."

"I love how you've transformed this third floor. Bright and cheery."

"And quiet. You can be in the middle of the city and hear nothing." Beth paused. "So, anything you want to share?"

A sheepish grin passed over Debbie's face. "I don't think Chase is mad at me anymore."

Beth nodded. She was wading into dangerous waters with complicated currents. Her daughter was an adult. She'd already lived with her ex-fiancé. But Debbie was still her daughter. "I see. And that's a good thing?"

Her daughter beamed. "Yes."

"Well, I always have had a soft spot for Chase. As long as you're happy, I'm happy."

Debbie grinned again, then her face suddenly fell. "Oh, I'm afraid I've made your life more difficult. I imagine Flannery is upset."

Beth took a deep breath. "You could say that."

"I'm sorry, Mom."

"Not your fault. I understand why you do the things you do. I think he's more upset with me."

"But you were just an innocent bystander."

"I don't think he sees it that way."

"Well, he cares. He's probably a bit protective."

"Too protective. I don't need a protector."

"I know. You just need to get the message across to him."

"I don't think that will happen."

"Sure it will. Just repeat your message."

"You know I don't like to repeat myself. And I won't. So I ended it."

Debbie's eyes widened. "No. You were happy! Because of me?"

"Oh, Debbie, not because of you. Because of me. I take full responsibility for my choices and my actions. I just think Daniel and I see the world too differently. It is just too messy. And I don't have the energy or patience for messes."

"Mom. I'm so sorry."

Beth waved her hand dismissively. "I'm fine."

31 FINAL DESTINATION

"Señor Recio, pleased to finally meet you," Connor said, with all the confidence his privileged upbringing had given him, his hand extended across the cartel leader's desk.

"Sit," Duro said while waving away the hand. The Americano had been nothing but trouble since the disaster in St. Louis. Sure, he'd once been useful. But that was in the past. In the present? Connor was just another cocky twenty-something, an arrogant American who thought he knew better than everyone else. Duro recognized the type. The young, soft men who thought strength came from fitness powders, personal trainers, and expensive gym memberships. They'd never experienced a life without a safety net. Alex, on the other hand, struck him as more resilient.

Connor, unfazed by the rejection of his hand and soothed by the knowledge that his charm worked on everyone eventually, sat in one of the guest chairs in El Duro's office, spreading his legs apart to stake claim to all the space offered by the seat. "We had a heckuva time getting here," Connor began, motioning to Alex, seated next to him.

El Duro leaned back in his leather chair. "*Sí*, yes, I heard. And you killed one of my best batchers in the process. The *chica* got free."

"Just temporary setbacks, I assure you."

"The property we'd bought in your high-rise? Seized. Money you'd been washing for us? Grabbed by the federales. Between your failures and the bust, our St. Louis operations? *Mierda*. Isn't that right, Kiko?"

Kiko had been standing in the back corner of the office. El Duro's eyes, ears, and, if need be, muscle. "*Mierda*," Kiko said.

"Señor Recio, I can make it all up to you. I'm ready to do all I can to help you and the organization."

El Duro laughed. "You hear that, Kiko? Help us?"

Kiko laughed.

"My friend," El Duro said, addressing Connor, "the

law is looking for you across the border. And you stick out like a man in Cancún wearing a parka. Let me see your hands."

Connor held them out for inspection.

"Beautiful. Like a baby's. Nothing like the man you killed."

"The dude missing a finger?"

"Yeah. That hombre. He was a man. He worked harder than you ever could. Do you know why? He worked harder because he cared about something outside himself. He cared about his family. You? You care about you. Not only that, but you think the world owes you something. And that makes you a dangerous man."

"But," Connor stammered, "I did it for you."

El Duro laughed. "I'm no fool. You did it for you."

"Please," Connor said, "let me prove my loyalty. I've got a head for business. I could help bring efficiencies to your organization."

El Duro smiled. "You don't speak Spanish. I'm guessing you don't know any Mandarin. I've got plenty of numbers guys who are bilingual. And there's no way you can go back up north, not with every federal agent looking for you. No, you were useful in St. Louis. I don't see what you can do for me here."

"But," Connor said, still stammering, "you owe me. After all that I've done. Caleb. Macie. All of the money I helped the cartel launder."

"And you were handsomely compensated for your work, my friend. You should've stayed up north to enjoy the fruits of your labor."

"But that was impossible."

El Duro shook his head. "Your justice system up there. It's slow. All knotted up because of rights and so forth. You should've stayed, blamed the girl, and stalled long enough to move my money into something safe. Your job was to take care of my business before you ran. And sometimes, a loyal soldier goes to prison for the good of the organization. You weren't willing to make that sacrifice."

Connor's face was blank. El Duro could tell the young man wasn't absorbing the lesson. He continued. "Maybe you could learn Spanish. Maybe not. Maybe I could send you to Argentina."

"What about him?" Connor asked, pointing to Alex, who'd been too afraid to utter a word.

El Duro looked Alex up and down and shrugged. "No

one cares about him, so no one's looking for him too hard. He's more of a follower, not a leader."

Connor nodded. "Obviously. He follows me. Not the other way around."

"I see," El Duro said. "Kiko, why don't you take Alex to one of your men? Extra hands could be used for something. But," Duro said, addressing Alex, "if you mess up or use our product, you won't be around."

"And me?" Connor asked.

"A man of such importance? Kiko is going to take you to our VIP quarters. So you can relax before you make your next trip."

"To Argentina?" Connor asked.

El Duro nodded and looked at Kiko. "Sure. To Argentina."

"Let's go," Kiko grunted.

Connor and Alex got up. "*Gracias*, Señor Recio," Connor said. "You won't regret your decision."

"No, I won't," El Duro responded. "Now, I have work to do."

Kiko motioned to the door. Connor and Alex dutifully left the office. "See, Alex," Connor said once they'd made it outside, "I told you everything would be fine. You owe me five bucks."

Alex reached into his pocket and fished out a five-dollar bill.

Connor smiled as he snatched the bill from his companion. He retrieved his wallet from his pants and deposited it inside.

Kiko noticed the wallet was a fancy one. A Gucci. Kiko would offer it to Santa Muerte shortly.

32 MOVING ON

"This is Debbie Bradley, and *Crime Beat* is back with another episode about the hunt for Connor Webb and the latest developments in the criminal case against Dardos Venenosas. With me today is our recurring guest, Jack Flannery, a retired St. Louis Metropolitan Police Department captain. Cap'n Jack, welcome. And thanks for coming out on this rainy April day."

Cap'n Jack smiled at his host. "Happy to be here, Debbie." And he was. He didn't care that his nephew Daniel's face twisted up when he mentioned the writer and podcast host. "Ah, April. Showers, May flowers, and taxes. No matter the weather, there's always a reckoning with the IRS."

"Speaking of a reckoning, there are some new developments in the conspiracy case. A few of the defendants have entered a guilty plea and been sentenced. Patricia Perkins is one of them."

"The gal who was the clerk at the truck stop?" Cap'n Jack asked.

"That's the one," Debbie replied.

"Did she flip?"

"No. Ms. Perkins changed her plea. Accepted responsibility to get a downward departure on her sentence, but she didn't cooperate."

"What'd she get? I'm guessing a stiff sentence since it was a conspiracy and all."

"Yeah, and she has a criminal history which impacts the sentence recommendation."

"Ouch. That'll extend the years. Concurrent or consecutive?"

"The judge showed some mercy. Even though Ms. Perkins pleaded guilty to five counts, the judge had the sentence for each count run concurrently, twenty years on each count. A lot better than the consecutive sentence of one hundred years."

"Either way, it could be a life sentence for ol' Patty. See, kids," Cap'n Jack added, "crime doesn't pay."

"Not only that, but it can cost your loved ones dearly,"

Debbie said, "which brings us to the Webbs. Our regular listeners know that Caleb Webb died from a fentanyl-laced heroin overdose in early January. Although Caleb's friend Macie Holloway was initially a suspect, it is now alleged that his twin brother, Connor, had a hand in supplying the drugs, as did Caleb's friend Alex Underwood. Connor and Alex vanished in January. Since then, investigators have connected Connor to money laundering for the cartel. Unfortunately, he used his parents' real estate company as part of the scheme. Cap'n Jack, what steps do you think law enforcement is taking right now?"

"Well, they're combing through the accounting records. It seems condo sales at that swanky high-rise in Clayton are a prime target."

"That's where Caleb lived."

"Yep. And Caleb was supposed to be running it. But it looks like Connor was the one in charge. And Caleb, with his drug addiction and all, would make a perfect fall guy if sh…er… stuff hit the fan."

"But what about the parents?" Debbie asked. "There's been no hint of them being involved in money laundering."

"Civil forfeiture is a powerful tool that shows no mercy."

"We're talking about the Money Laundering Act of 1986, right?" Debbie said. "The one that lets the government seize property or money if it's connected to criminal activity. Even property held by a third party, such as the business organization or the parents."

"Yeah, and if civil forfeiture is pursued by either the state or the feds, instead of criminal, the prosecutors only have a preponderance of the evidence standard rather than beyond a reasonable doubt standard that there's a connection between the property and criminal activity."

"So preponderance of the evidence, kind of a fifty-one percent standard instead of a ninety-nine percent beyond-a-reasonable-doubt standard."

"That's one way to phrase it," Cap'n Jack replied.

"I guess the question then is whether the property or money should be seized if the Webbs or the business were innocent owners."

"That's where it gets trickier than driving a stretch of Interstate Seventy under construction, full of potholes and filled with eighteen-wheelers. Under the federal standard, the innocent owner defense isn't gonna fly. So if the state steps back and lets the feds take over, there's a better chance of seizing the assets. Of course, then the state gets a cut."

"But we're talking about fine upstanding members of the community," Debbie observed.

"Citizens with money. Lots of money. And lawyers. So, my humble guess is that the Webbs will work something out. They'll probably fare better than the mom or dad who gets their only home seized because their crappy kid was trafficking drugs out of it."

"Even if the Webbs hold onto everything they've worked for, one son is dead, and one has disappeared."

"Ain't no amount of riches gonna plug that hole in a parent's heart," Cap'n Jack said.

Debbie removed her headphones and sat back in her chair. "Our listeners are sure takin' a shine to you."

Cap'n Jack replied, "You're starting to talk like me."

Debbie laughed, motioned to the door, and exited the recording room. Her guest followed. Only after she closed the door did Debbie speak. "I hate to chitchat too much in there. I may be paranoid, but I always worry about hot mic moments."

"You can't be too paranoid."

"So," Debbie began.

Cap'n Jack had known Debbie long enough to anticipate where her "so" would lead. Whenever the reporter started with the word "so," she was getting ready to dive into deep waters.

"How's Flannery?" she asked.

"Mopey. Moody," Cap'n Jack replied. He didn't tell her that Flannery drove by Beth's house occasionally, late at night. "Just to see if everything's okay," he'd claimed to his uncle. But ol' Jack knew better.

"How's your mom?" Cap'n Jack asked.

"She acts like nothing happened."

"But you feel bad, don't ya?"

"Of course."

"They're adults, Debbie. They're responsible for their relationship. You're not. Don't be taking on guilt that doesn't belong to you."

"I know. But still…" Her voice trailed off. She shifted her weight from one foot to the other. "I decided it was time to move out. I was always worried about my mom giving me my space when I probably should've given her more room."

Cap'n Jack nodded, a head shake that was neither yes nor no but rather one that said he was listening; 'twas dangerous to dip too deep into the turbulent waters that swirled between adult daughters and their moms. "So when are you moving?"

"This weekend."

"Movers?"

"Naw. I don't have much. Chase is helping me with my bags. My mom has a few things she wanted to get rid of, but mostly, I'm going to furnish it myself. I never got a chance to make a place all my own. When I lived with Christian, we always had to compromise. And with my mom, of course, it's all her stuff."

"Well, once you're moved in and set up, you need to have Noreen and me over. We'll bring beer. She's been asking after you."

Debbie smiled. "When I grow up, I want to be like her."

Cap'n Jack smiled. "Me, too."

Debbie shoved a pair of joggers into a trash bag. The bag

wasn't destined for the dumpster or for donation. Instead, it was a cheap and convenient way to pack her stuff, especially since she didn't have enough boxes and didn't want to buy proper carriers.

When the reporter had left Washington D.C., she'd arrived in St. Louis with a couple of beat-up roller suitcases stuffed into her Civic. Since then, her clothing collection had multiplied, especially in the athleisure wear department. "I should probably buy more suitable work clothes," she mumbled, realizing she could no longer borrow from her mother's closet.

Her phone vibrated with an alert that someone was at the front door.

"I'll get it," her mom hollered. It was a familiar shout. The one Debbie had heard throughout most of her life. She would miss hearing her petite mom use her big voice to carry commands up three floors of the old home.

Chase, Debbie guessed. A smile spread across her lips. Things between them had been good since that night at his condo. Real good.

Beth's mom cut through her daughter's reverie. "Debbie! For you!"

Debbie dropped the T-shirt in her hand onto the bed.

"Coming!" she hollered as she left her second-floor bedroom. As she descended the stairs, it wasn't Chase who stood there waiting.

"Macie! I'm so glad to see you!" And she was. Although the reporter had reached out to Macie several times since that day at the safe house, they'd never talked. Macie never answered her phone or responded to texts. "How have you been?"

"I'm good, actually. Um," Macie stammered, "I'm sorry I didn't get back to you. My lawyer said I couldn't talk to you. And I was afraid if I tried to limit myself to relaying what the lawyer said, I'd spill my guts anyway. For some reason, it was always easy to talk to you. Too easy."

Debbie waved her hand. "Don't worry. I kinda figured that was the case. You had to do what you had to do. I get that. Do you want to come in?"

"No, I just wanted to stop by for a few minutes."

"Well, I have to say that you look great." And Debbie meant it. Macie's face was no longer sunken and yellow. Her hair seemed thicker and shinier. Even more important, Macie didn't seem jittery or nervous. Debbie wondered whether she was finally getting a glimpse of a self-assured Macie, the valedictorian who'd achieved so much in school.

"I feel better," Macie admitted. "When Caleb died, my world fell apart. When J.R. lunged at Connor, my life started to turn around. I never thought someone would have to give their life for mine, though."

Debbie nodded.

"Even though we haven't talked, I know you've been following what's happening," Macie said.

"Yes. I was so happy when you were moved from the suspect category to witness," Debbie confessed.

"Yeah. And the cops just need me to testify against Connor if they ever catch him. But I think he's long gone. Same with Alex."

"You're probably right."

"I wanted to thank you," Macie said. "I've been reading your stories, listening to your podcasts. Thanks for not revealing all the stuff I told you."

"Of course. It was off the record. I made a promise to you," Debbie said, then paused. "So the pregnancy…?"

Macie shook her head. "I came to a decision the night before I left with Alex. It was not the time to become a mother."

Debbie nodded. "What are your plans now?"

"Well, I've given it a lot of thought," Macie said. *We've given it a lot of thought,* Caleb corrected her. "I feel stronger but don't know if I'm strong enough. I get scared sometimes," Macie said, her voice trailing off. "What if something happens and I start using again? I don't want to go back to the old me."

"I'm sure it is scary."

"You have no idea," Macie said. "I've fallen into the black hole of addiction. Somehow, I climbed out. I never want to go back. And yet…"

"And yet?"

"I always feel that black hole just around the corner. If I take a wrong turn, I could fall back in. So I've decided"—*We've decided,* Caleb reminded her—"to go to rehab one more time. There's a place in Minnesota. I'm driving up there now."

"Good for you, Macie. It makes a difference if you're the one who chooses it, not being forced by someone else."

"I owe it to myself. And Caleb. I miss him," Macie said even as he whispered, *I'm still here, you dork.* "And it will give me some time to think about what I want to do with the rest of my life."

"How so?"

Macie looked at the floor for a moment. "You know, I spent so much time trying to achieve things. Win awards. Then I rejected it all. Turned into an addict. Along the way, I saw two people die. A dear friend died before me. Then a stranger gave his life for me. I think I owe them something. What that is, I don't know yet. Maybe a drug counselor? Maybe I need to do some sort of work with victims of human trafficking. I don't know. But I'm tired of being part of the problem. Maybe I won't make a big difference, but Caleb and J.R., they deserve more from me."

Debbie opened her arms and wrapped them around the girl. "I'm rooting for you, Macie Holloway."

Macie sniffed. "I know." She stepped back. "I just came to say goodbye. For now."

"For now," Debbie replied.

Macie turned to the front door, opened it, and descended the steps. She waved again when she opened the driver's side of her door. Debbie waved and then disappeared into her home.

Macie started her Mustang and synced her phone to

the speaker. They had a long drive ahead.

"You ready?" Macie asked Caleb.

"Of course," Caleb replied.

"By the way, when are you finally going to leave me?"

"Dummy, I'm not leaving you. I'm part of you. What kind of question is that?"

"All right, dick wad. I'm stuck with you. So what are we listening to?"

"How about a little Lana? 'Gods and Monsters.'"

"Sure," Macie answered as the song started. "What do you think, Caleb? Was Lana right? Does life imitate art?"

Caleb looked out the window and up at the gray April sky. *"Nah. I think she got it backward. Art imitates life."*

Patty adjusted the net over her gray hair. Now that she was in prison, she no longer had access to hair color. For her, this was the worst part of being locked up. The rest she could manage.

If she thought about it long enough, she wasn't just managing or getting by. She was doing real good, even though she was back in Vandalia. She knew the next time she left, it'd be because they were putting her in the ground.

After she'd told her lawyer she wanted to enter a guilty plea and work something out so she could return to Vandalia, he tried to push her into cooperatin' with the feds. "Patty, you'll receive a lighter sentence," he said. But he didn't understand. If she flipped, she'd end up like ol' Tom Wilkins. At least his missus hadn't been as dumb as her husband. Last Patty heard, the wife found the stash of money. Sure, the feds took her house and car, but they couldn't get their hands on the cash. Not long ago, Tom's old lady rented a trailer in a mobile home park in Florida and took a job as a waitress in a dive breakfast place. If she was smart, she'd spend her money real quietlike; never buy property in her name, at least not until the feds forgot about an old woman living in a mobile home.

Things might not have worked out for ol' Tom, but they did for his wife. Patty was on a different path.

Sure, she was back in. But the woman who ran the cafeteria was delighted Patty was back.

And the inmates? They wouldn't pay Patty no mind. If they did, someone would deliver a shank into their gut. The cartel appreciated her sacrifice. And from her perch inside the prison, she was the perfect recruiter.

As Patty walked through the kitchen, checking on the breakfast preparations, she thought about the rich boy, the Webb fella. She'd never met him, but she knew his kind. Why did men always think they could take what they wanted and escape the consequences? Patty shook her hair-netted head. The police might be lookin' for him, but the cartel would make sure no trace of him would be found.

"Okay, get the food out," Patty bellowed.

What was the old saying? Better to rule in hell than serve in heaven.

33 SOMEWHERE OUT THERE

Julia looked up from her laptop when the front door opened. She'd been typing out a five-paragraph essay in English—and trading messages with school friends—when her mother arrived home.

Going to school, having friends. Julia loved everything that Sofía had missed. Experiences that would've scared Sofía were nothing for Julia. When Sofía was given the new name and identity, she decided Julia would be fearless. So what if she couldn't join her friends on social media? Too dangerous, her mom had warned. If someone from Sofía's life recognized Julia, then Julia would disappear. She'd go back to being Sofía. And that was a twist Julia couldn't bear.

"I'm home!" Julia heard her mother call from the living room.

"In here," Julia called out.

"Where's here?"

"The kitchen."

Even though Marcela was now Carla, she was still Mom. But adopting a new identity had also changed her mother. She'd taken a job at a call center, where her bilingual abilities were prized. She'd swapped the long ponytail for a businesswoman bob. Her hair no longer showed signs of gray.

Her mother loved getting a paycheck and going to the bank. But Julia also noticed her mother's brow would furrow when a car drove past too slowly, or there was a knock at the door, and they weren't expecting visitors.

Carla walked into the kitchen and began taking food out of the refrigerator. When they moved into their small two-bedroom home on a quiet street in the Pacific Northwest, Carla rejoiced at having a kitchen to herself.

"Homework?"

Julia nodded. "I have to write a five-paragraph essay about what I want to be when I grow up. I've got to give three reasons for the choice."

"What did you choose?"

"Nurse," Julia answered.

"Why not doctor?" her mother asked.

"Ugh. You've got to go to school forever," Julia said, stretching out the last word.

Carla sighed. "What seems forever to you now will be a blink of an eye when you're my age."

"Whatever," Julia said, mimicking her friends. "I'm almost done with the assignment."

"Julia," Carla said, "look at me."

Julia sighed.

"This is important."

"Fine."

"Remember, you can always change direction. No matter how far down the road you think you are, you can always change your mind and direction. Don't confuse not wanting to redo something for being stuck. Understand?"

Julia nodded, even though it would take another twenty years to grasp what her mom was trying to say. "I'm still not changing my essay. I'm almost done. When's dinner?"

"I'll have it ready in an hour. Your dad will be home soon."

As if on cue, the front door rattled and opened.

"We're in the kitchen," Carla called out. "Take off your shoes so you don't track dirt around the house."

"*Sí, señora,*" the voice called back.

"Michael! English, please," Carla called out, even if she too, was guilty of slipping up occasionally and calling him José.

"Yes, ma'am."

Carla hummed as she bustled around her kitchen. Julia's mother had started humming after her father joined them in the house. Carla and Julia had spent their first four months alone in the space before Michael arrived.

Michael was her dad. But he was different from her dad. This dad had ten fingers rather than nine. The extra one was just decoration, he'd explained. He also wore a wedding ring.

Michael walked into the kitchen. "Smells good," he said as he grabbed a glass from the cupboard, filled it with water, and sat beside Julia.

"How do you like your new job?" Carla asked.

"I'm learning. But I think I'll like being a delivery driver. I hate being locked up in one place all day."

Michael leaned over to read his daughter's essay. As he

pondered her work, he played with the medal hanging on an old chain around his neck and under his shirt. Julia had noticed the habit soon after he moved in with them. "Santa Muerte," he'd said. "She takes good care of us."

Michael sighed. "A nurse? Funny, I always pictured you being a doctor."

Julia rolled her eyes. "Ugh. Dad!"

ACKNOWLEDGEMENTS

A book begins with a vague idea. A notion. A possibility. Soon after, words appear on the screen. Eventually, there's a first draft, then a second, a third, and sometimes even a fourth. The journey is arduous, but it isn't solitary.

Thank goodness.

My gratitude list begins, as always, with my husband, Enrique Serrano Valle. His help is invaluable. He's the sounding board for my story ideas. He reads early drafts and writes helpful notes in the margins of the printed pages he's given. A native of Spain, Enrique was my go-to resource for help with the language and fact-checking information about bullfighting. (For the record, although he grew up around bullfighting, he is not a supporter.) And finally, he is the creator of the cover images for all my books. *Te quiero mucho.*

My sincere thanks to my editor, Christine LePorte. From grammar saves to spotting inconsistencies in the text and noticing loose ends in the story that needed tidying up, Christine's editing is an essential part of the publishing process.

A shout-out to my daughter, Casey Kiernan, who

again agreed to serve as the cover model for a Debbie Bradley book.

Special thanks to author Gareth Davies for feedback on early drafts and for writing a review for the book. Like a pace runner on a track, having another writer push forward with their work can be a powerful motivator to finish your draft.

As a young lawyer, I'd heard stories about the St. Louis Mafia Wars from older attorneys. As a journalist, I'd bump into the lore once again. I turned to a few resources for this novel to retell the tale and check the accuracy. In particular, I'd like to recognize work written by Tim O'Neil for the *St. Louis Post Dispatch*, Scott Burnstein's account for the *Gangster Report*, and work by Ronald J. Lawrence for *Crime Magazine*.

Finally, thanks to you, the reader! So many of you read the first book in this series, *Crime Beat Girl*, and asked for more. I'm delighted to share the next installment of Debbie's adventures with you. And to those of you who wrote reviews, thank you! For the independent author, reviews are our lifeblood.

Made in the USA
Monee, IL
18 May 2024

58421000R00246